Books by T.J. Mindancer

Tales of Emoria

Jame and Tigh Saga
Book 1: Future Dreams
Book 2: Present Paths
Book 3: Past Echoes
Book 4: Fall Time

Hekolatis' Promise

Emoran Campfire Tales

Other Books

The Queen's Sister

Novellas

Bountiful Glen

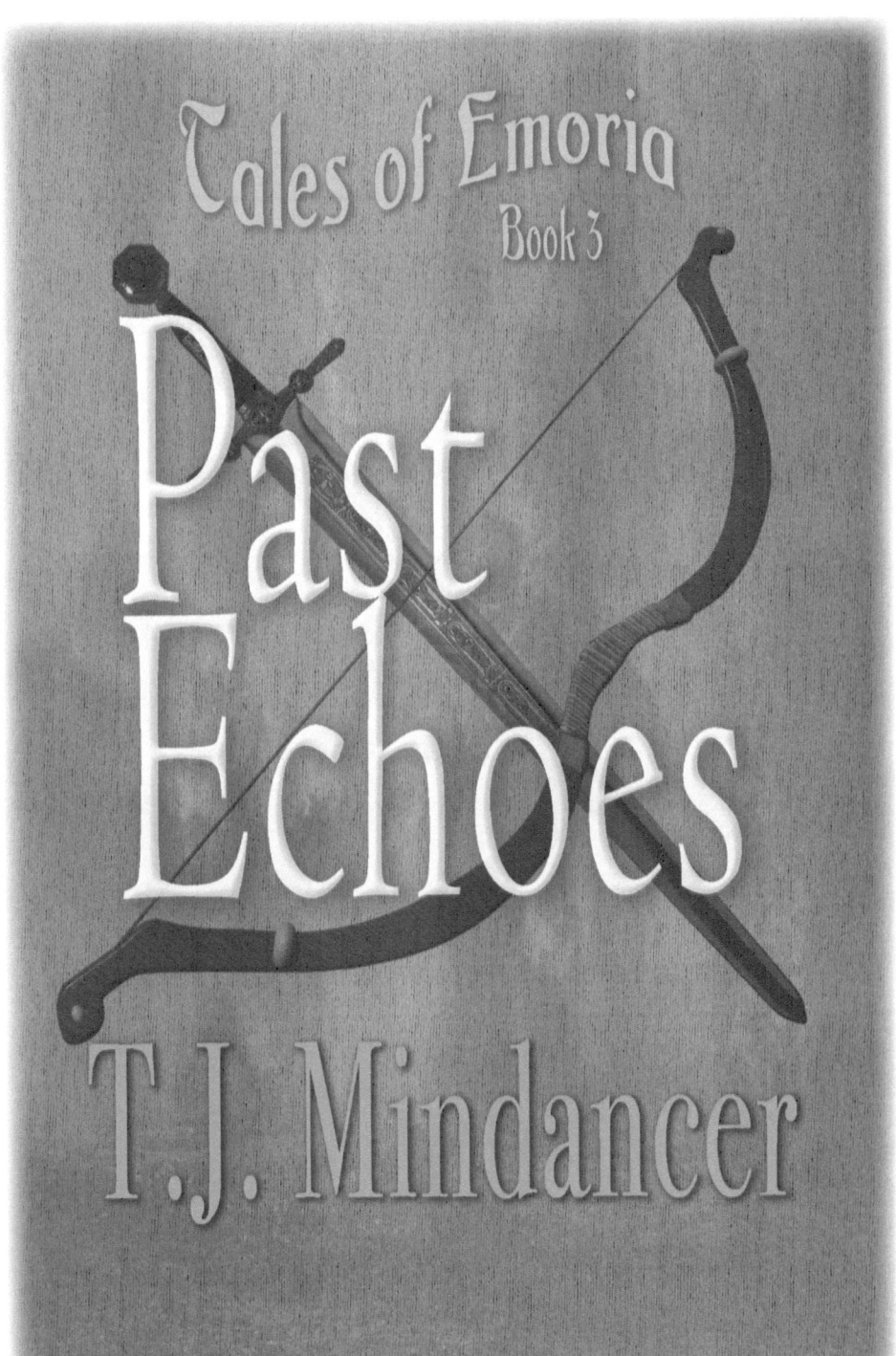

Tales of Emoria
Book 3

Past
Echoes

T.J. Mindancer

Mindancer Press
Bedazzled Ink Publishing Company • Fairfield, California

978-0-9886061-4-2 paperback

Cover Design
by

First published 2000
Renaissance Alliance Publishing
4th revised edition 2022

Mindancer Press
a division of
Bedazzled Ink Publishing, LLC
Fairfield, California
http://www.bedazzledink.com

The Saga of Jame and Tigh, Book 3

Note on Pronunciation

Jame is one syllable with a long "a." Rhymes with "fame." Tigh is pronounced "Tig." Rhymes with "twig." The spelling of her name follows the Ingoran rules of grammar where the "h" indicates the eldest daughter of the House of Tigis.

Chapter 1

THE ROAD SHOWED only traces of an earlier rain shower that had drenched Jame and Tigh and their horse. The dry heat soaked up the moisture before the plants had a chance to benefit from it. Jame had experienced weather that could make the most seasoned traveler consider giving up a journey and was barely aware that the moisture soaking her clothes was from rain rather than sweat.

"Tigh," she said. "It's been a while since we've been to Ynit."

Tigh studied the road as they walked along with easy strides that marked them as travelers. "I guess it has. We haven't promised to be back there for any reason, have we?" The soft cadences of her voice were edged with a teasing that came easily with her interactions with Jame. "Or maybe there's another reason you want to go there." She jumped in front of Jame and stood with hands on her hips, an amused twinkle in her eyes.

Jame studied Tigh. The soft black leather that encased her tall, lean body, the functional armor and the sword hilt peeking over her shoulder, said as much about Tigh as she wanted most people to know. The short black hair, kept off her face by a leather band buried under shaggy bangs, and the compelling blue eyes that gleamed over a sculpted face only enhanced her reputation as a fierce warrior. But Jame knew better, having lived with her for six years.

Jame tried to think of a cute response but knew she couldn't deceive Tigh. She sighed and did the only thing she could to get out of the box she'd put herself in. She tackled Tigh who had the good grace to topple flat on her back in the middle of the road.

"You, speechless?" Tigh tried to laugh with the extra weight on top of her.

Jame grinned and crawled off Tigh. "I was just seeing how many words I could get out of you at one time."

"You doing some kind of research?" Tigh climbed to her feet and put a hand out to Jame.

Jame laughed as Tigh pulled her to her feet and shrugged her answer.

"That's what I usually say." Tigh chuckled and gathered Gessen's reins.

"You're in a good mood," Jame said as they continued down the road.

Tigh flashed a grin.

They crested a small hill. Tigh stopped, and her grin turned grim.

Jame stayed as still as possible, always fascinated by how her playful companion could turn into an alert deadly warrior in a heartbeat.

"There's a village. Sounds like trouble." Tigh swung onto Gessen and held a hand out to Jame.

Jame grabbed Tigh's hand. Tigh pulled her up behind her and pushed Gessen to a dirt-flying gallop.

TIGH PULLED UP on Gessen and jumped to the ground, leaving Jame to settle the horse. She slipped her black-bladed sword from the scabbard on her back. The villagers fled to the safety of the rambling porch around the inn.

Jame slipped off Gessen and scanned the huddled crowd for the likely leader. A thin man wearing an imposing medallion ran toward her.

"Is this the way you show justice in this town? Where is the arbiter?" Jame asked.

The headman scowled. "We can't wait around for an arbiter to show up for every little thing."

"Arbiters aren't always far away. Sometimes they can be within calling distance." Jame pulled her arbiter's medallion, on a chain around her neck, out from beneath her tunic. "What did that person do to deserve this kind of punishment?"

"Since she came into town, all kinds of strange things have happened—"

"Did she hurt anyone or destroy property?" Jame asked.

"Well, Hemme's son tripped and fell outside the inn and—"

Jame struggled to keep down her impatience. "Did anyone see her cause injury or destroy property?"

"Not actually seen—"

"If you don't mind, we'll take her off your hands." Jame turned to Tigh who was bent over the bloody heap in the middle of the square.

"You keep strange company for an arbiter," the headman said.

"You're too quick to judge." Jame leveled a gaze at him. "Something I'd work on, if I were you."

The man snorted. "She's dangerous. Stories of her have reached even us."

"She *was* dangerous." Jame glanced at Tigh, who was still checking the woman. She prayed they weren't too late. "She's been cleansed."

"I hear that doesn't work as well as they let on," the headman said.

Jame straightened. "Are you questioning a peace arbiter's judgment in her choice of peace warrior?"

"You're a brave one," the headman muttered and retreated to the other villagers huddled around the inn.

Jame mumbled heated words about idiotic village leaders as she trotted to Tigh. She stopped a few paces away and tried to gauge the condition of the unfortunate woman. With all the blood on her face and clothing, she couldn't determine the extent of injury or much else about her for that matter.

Tigh turned to her, then glanced around. The villagers watched them with a mixture of fear and hostility. She put two fingers to her lips, let out a shrill whistle, and was rewarded a few heartbeats later by a dust cloud kicked up by Gessen. She retrieved a blanket from the saddlebag and, with Jame's help, wrapped the woman in it.

"Shock?" Jame asked.

Tigh's haunted eyes held hers for several heartbeats before she nodded.

Jame reached over the battered woman and put a comforting hand on Tigh's shoulder. During the Wars, Tigh had caused this kind of pain and worse. Now she had to live with the memory.

"I'm going to have to hold her on Gessen." Tigh signaled the horse to kneel on her front two legs, then she lifted the woman and, using an enviable combination of strength and balance, straddled the saddle. Gessen clambered back to her feet.

Jame picked up a nearby pack she suspected belonged to the woman and hung it on the saddle.

"Which way?" she asked as she took the reins.

"That way." Tigh nodded to a distant low line of bluffs.

TIGH'S INSTINCTS WERE correct about the ridge. The rocky face was pocked with shallow caves and shelter bluffs, and they found a cave large enough for them and Gessen.

Armed with their herb kit and several strips of cloth kept for emergencies, Tigh cleaned and dressed the woman's wounds—a skill she'd learned while her warrior tendencies had been cleansed from her.

Jame fetched water from the small creek that meandered along the base of the bluff and gathered wood for the fire. After the flames were hot enough to give off some needed warmth, she set a small pot of stew to simmer, then crept next to Tigh for a closer look at the woman they had saved.

Jame could tell through the matted blood and dirt the woman's hair was a pale blonde, unusual for that part of the world. She inspected what was left of the woman's clothing. High born. The fine weave and delicate cut could be found in the larger cities to the west.

Tigh picked up a bracelet and handed it to Jame.

Jame studied the intricate interlocking of metals and semi-precious stones. "Artocian?"

Tigh nodded as she rolled the woman onto her stomach and cut away the remaining material, revealing bruises, most likely from the impact of stones.

"Laur's waterfalls." Jame's indignation kicked into high gallop. "How could they do something like this without witnessing her doing anything wrong?"

Tigh dipped a rag into a bowl of water. "She looked and acted different."

"You think she's what she appears to be?"

Tigh pushed cascading hair from the woman's shoulder blade and revealed a small image of a feathered quill and ink jar etched in the skin.

Jame bent closer. "I don't think I've seen this mark before."

"She's with the University at Artocia." Tigh rummaged through her saddlebag for a clean tunic. With Jame's help, she removed the rest of the tatters from the woman's spare frame and slipped the tunic on her.

"I wonder what she was doing here." Jame went to check on the progress of the stew.

Tigh stood and stretched out her back. "Artocian scholars rarely venture to a place like this. Unless they're tracking down facts to chronicle." She stepped outside the cave.

Jame smiled as she heard Tigh splashing in the creek and ladled stew into two wooden bowls and pulled a second metal spoon from the saddlebag.

Tigh stepped back into the cave and sat next to Jame on a smooth stone— evidence they weren't the first people to use the cave.

"I'll save out some of the stew," Jame said as she handed a bowl to Tigh.

"I think we have a bit of a mystery here." Tigh scooped a spoonful into her mouth and chewed as she contemplated the injured woman. "She's not completely unworldly, for a scholar." Jame gave her a quizzical look. "She's conscious but keeps her eyes closed, determining whether we're friend or foe."

Jame stared at Tigh, then turned to the woman, then glared back at Tigh. "You can be so infuriating sometimes." She put her bowl down and went to the woman's side. "It's all right. We rescued you away from those villagers."

The woman opened her good eye and flicked it around, taking in the cave, Jame next to her, and Tigh by the fire. She swallowed with difficulty.

Tigh settled next to Jame with a water bag.

Jame tipped the bag to the woman's dry lips. "I'm Jame, peace arbiter-at-large for the Southern Districts. This is Tigh, peace warrior."

"Seeran. Historian, University of Artocia." The woman cleared her throat. "But you've already determined that."

"I've been to Artocia," Tigh said. "When I was young."

"Are you hungry?" Jame asked.

Seeran focused on her. "A little." Tigh went to the fire and rummaged through a saddlebag for their spare bowl and spoon.

"She's very efficient." Jame bit back a grin at Seeran's puzzled look.

"I'd like to hear your story sometime," Seeran said.

Tigh handed Jame the bowl of stew and spoon.

Jame gave Seeran a mouthful and grinned at her surprised expression. "Tigh's an Ingoran."

"How interesting," Seeran muttered.

Tigh laid out a fur on the opposite side of the fire and placed her sword next to it. She then checked outside the cave before she stretched out on the fur.

"'Night, Tigh." Jame gazed across the fire while Seeran worked on another spoonful of stew.

"'Night, Jame," Tigh whispered.

Jame smiled and scooped another spoonful of stew into Seeran's mouth. "She spent most of last night in search of a child who had run off in anger and had gotten lost in the woods when it got dark."

"It must be interesting—traveling the countryside," Seeran said.

"Sometimes it can be, but most of the time our jobs are pretty routine." Jame helped Seeran drink some water. "Is there anything else you need before I turn in?"

"You've done so much already. For a stranger, that is."

"We're only too happy to help." Jame settled the leather hide around Seeran's battered body. "If you need anything just give a little shout. Tigh will be awake and at your side before she even realizes she's moved. Bowstring reaction. It takes getting used to."

"I can imagine," Seeran murmured.

SEERAN OPENED HER good eye and saw dancing fingers of sunlight stretching into the cave. The aroma of sweet herbs steeping in steaming water and the crackle of flames penetrated her senses. The muffled bubbling of water and the whisper of voices outside the cave tickled her hearing.

Much better day than yesterday. Being beaten for no reason by angry villagers had not been something she wanted to experience firsthand. But it had happened, and she had to do her best to get past it and chronicle the horrible event as best she could. Firsthand reports were considered the most important sources of knowledge for scholars.

Jame popped her head around the mouth of the cave. She grinned at Seeran and disappeared. A few heartbeats later, she entered the cave, carrying a leather bundle overflowing with roots and greens.

"The morning meal will be ready in no time," Jame said as she untied the bundle, laid it out on the flat rock, and sorted through the greens.

Seeran watched with interest, having only heard of Ingoran cuisine but never witnessing its preparation. "You're not Ingoran?"

Jame chuckled. "No . . . um, actually I'm Emoran."

Seeran knew that, of course. She always wondered about how a country of fierce warrior women could produce a peace arbiter.

"I know, I know." Jame laughed. "I'm the black sheep. It happens."

Seeran frowned. "There are many old stories about Emoria, but nothing from modern times."

"We've settled down quite a bit since the Wars of Farror," Jame said.

"Settled down? As in peaceful co-existing?" Seeran asked.

"Uh, not quite," Jame said. "But enough to be peaceful most of the time. We sometimes skirmish with the Lukrians and with brigands who bother our borders. We're a country of warriors. It's in our blood."

"That's more in keeping with what I've read about Emorans." Seeran nodded, then focused on the tall, imposing shadow blocking the cave's entrance.

Tigh swept her eyes around the cave before settling them on Jame. She held up a handful of round tubers.

Jame's face lit up, and Tigh gave her an affectionate grin.

"Have I ever told you how wonderful you are?" Jame asked.

Tigh knelt beside her and deposited the tubers next to the pile of greens. "Plenty where that came from."

Jame brushed her lips on Tigh's cheek, and Tigh grinned in delight.

"Now check on our patient while I prepare this feast." Jame waved her small knife in Seeran's direction.

Tigh went to Seeran's side and, with silent but gentle efficiency, rubbed more ointment on the wounds and replaced the bandages.

Tigh finished with her work, and Seeran tried to sit. Tigh helped her scoot against the wall, and she marveled at the strength of the warrior's hands. Tigh put several furs behind her, to cushion her tender back.

"Thank you," Seeran said as she wiggled to get comfortable.

Tigh blinked at her. "You'll be fine." She looked down at her kit. "Nothing's broken. No internal bleeding."

"That's good to know," Seeran said. Tigh seemed more at ease with the art of healing than with the art of communication. "I guess I got lucky you two came along."

Tigh raised an eyebrow. Seeran almost laughed. Who needed words with a face that expressive?

"Not so lucky for being there in the first place," Jame said. She shook the flat pan full of sizzling vegetables and herbs. The aroma was Bal sent.

"I guess you're wondering why I was in Raighton." Seeran studied the wall on the far side of the cave.

"We don't mean to pry," Jame said. "If it's private . . ."

Seeran chuckled as much as her sore face muscles allowed. "No, no. Nothing like that. In fact, it's kind of embarrassing." She avoided the steady, expectant gazes of her benefactors. "I was in search of stories."

"Stories?" Jame asked.

She dished the vegetables and tubers onto three plates, handed one to Tigh, and carried the other two to Seeran.

"Yes. It's a part of our training as historians." Seeran accepted a plate from Jame. She picked up a piece of the grilled tuber and popped it into her mouth. "This is the most incredible food."

"Stories," Tigh said.

"We have to spend time witnessing history, so to speak," Seeran said between mouthfuls. "If we can't see it for ourselves, then we gather the story from eyewitnesses, visit the locations where events took place, that sort of thing."

"And this is why you were in an isolated village in the middle of the Argurian Plain?" Jame asked.

"The hard part is finding something that hasn't been chronicled yet." Seeran looked from Tigh to Jame.

"Ah." Jame nodded. "And you thought there must be a story here."

"Actually, I decided to go to the least popular place," Seeran said. "There's sometimes a problem with all of us trying to get the same story."

"There are reasons why casual visits to the Argurian Plain are not desirable," Tigh said.

"So I discovered." Seeran cleared her throat. "But I did find a story. One that has never been chronicled."

"Really?" Jame asked.

"Yes." Seeran finished chewing another mouthful. "And it happened when it was least expected." She grinned. "You."

Tigh stopped in mid-chew and stared. Jame frowned.

"The story of Tigh the Terrible and Jame the arbiter."

Tigh and Jame looked at each other, then at Seeran.

"Jame keeps a journal. So we've been chronicled." Tigh returned her attention to her plate.

"A journal is only a small part of chronicling. It represents one viewpoint out of many," Seeran said. "Don't get me wrong. Journals are wonderful because eyewitness accounts can be hard to find and are often unreliable."

"What story do you think you have here?" Jame asked. "We just travel around giving legal assistance to whoever needs it. Mostly judging disputes and criminal cases."

"You seem to do the dramatic rescue rather well." Seeran noted the blush creeping up Jame's neck. "And there are rumors. Of villages being saved from raiders, of sudden peaceful negotiations, of grateful merchants when their stolen wares are mysteriously returned." She received noncommittal expressions from Jame and Tigh. "Rumors, of course. But the only thing all these miraculous events have in common are the two of you."

"You seem to know a lot about these rumors," Tigh said as she took Seeran's empty plate.

"We historians pay a lot of attention to stories floating on the wind. It's a good way of finding some amazing tales to chronicle." Seeran didn't want to let on that she'd followed their careers close enough to pay attention when a new story about them circulated around the University. "Much of history is lost to time. We can only hope to capture the essence of what passes by every day."

"We've been at this for a few years, you can't possibly chronicle all that we've done," Jame said.

Seeran shrugged, knowing better than to argue. "What do you plan to do with me once I'm well enough to travel?"

Jame glanced at Tigh. "The choice is yours."

"Even if I choose to travel with you? At least as far as the first major city?" Seeran raised expectant eyes first to Jame, then to Tigh.

Tigh sighed. "We have no choice but to take you to the nearest city. It's too dangerous for you out here alone."

"So if you happen to do anything worth chronicling?" Seeran almost laughed at Tigh's exasperated expression.

"Most of the time our lives are uneventful. Even boring," Jame said. "We just travel from town to town offering our services."

"Then I'll have a chance to see what most historians never do." Seeran grinned.

Jame and Tigh eyed her with wary apprehension.

"A look at heroes when they're not doing something heroic."

Tigh rolled her eyes and took the dirty dishes out of the cave. To clean them in the stream, Seeran guessed.

"She doesn't like to be called a hero," Jame said. "Her past haunts her too much for her to feel she deserves it."

"I think history will see it differently," Seeran said.

"Yes. I think you're right," Jame said. "It might be interesting having you around for a while."

Chapter 2

FOUR UNEVENTFUL DAYS later, Seeran believed Jame and Tigh when they said their life was generally boring. If it weren't for the change in countryside from stark scrub to an old growth forest, there wouldn't have been anything to write about at all, except, of course, her enigmatic companions.

Seeran's wounds were almost healed, a tribute to Tigh's skill. A long cloth wound around her head and dipped down to cover her swollen eye, protecting it from the sunlight. With Jame's help, she managed to fashion the borrowed tunic and leggings into something that fit her thin frame and height. She was fortunate her boots had not been damaged during the incident in the village.

Jame had yet to tell the story of how she and Tigh met and formed their unique partnership. Seeran could only speculate they met at Ynit where the Guards were cleansed at the end of the Grappian Wars. The enhancements that had turned them into effective warriors made them unfit for society when they were no longer needed to fight. The secret to how they cleansed the Guards would be enough of a story for her, since it was a tale that had yet to be chronicled.

Tigh had wandered off again like a cat sniffing out a scent. Jame looked relaxed as usual, but Seeran noticed she was less talkative. Playing the observer, she refrained from asking if anything was amiss.

Tigh had been gone for quite a while, and Jame had stopped making an effort to converse.

"Tigh seems to have found something," Jame said as they paced along on the rugged forest trail.

Four figures dropped cat-like from the trees overhanging the path in front of them. The strangers' lithe muscular bodies and faces were encased in a patchwork of leather and armor, exposing as much skin as not. Menacing swords were strapped to their backs, and the foremost warrior grasped a fighting staff.

Seeran's knees weakened from the shock of the confrontation. She glanced at Jame, whose attention was riveted on the staff.

They stood frozen for several heartbeats then Jame let out a breath and relaxed. She nodded to the warrior holding the staff.

Seeran blinked in surprise as the foursome dropped to their knees and bowed their heads.

Jame rolled her eyes and stepped forward. "Stand up," she muttered as the strangers stood with their eyes still on the dirt path. She lifted the chin of the closest warrior. "Well met, Argis."

"Well met, my princess," Argis said and held out the staff.

Jame grasped the staff in both hands. The women pulled down the face coverings. Warriors, strong and a little scary-looking, raked their eyes over Seeran then riveted their attention on Jame.

Princess? Seeran's mind shouted, glad she didn't gasp the word out loud. *These women are Emorans.*

"I can't imagine what brings you so far from home," Jame said.

Argis glanced at the three warriors behind her, and they faded into the forest. "We will walk."

"This is Seeran, a historian," Jame said.

Argis studied Seeran and nodded. "Well met, Seeran."

"Well met, Argis," Seeran said.

Argis glanced around, then raised an eyebrow at Jame.

"She's close by," Jame said.

Argis nodded as they walked down the path.

"Now tell me, why are you here?"

"There's been trouble," Argis said. "The Lukrians have been more aggressive than usual. They've joined forces with a group of warriors from the Wars. Warriors from the Elite Guard who escaped cleansing, if the rumors can be believed." A cracking branch echoed from the trees. "I guess our friend doesn't find this to be happy news."

Jame stared into the trees. "Will the Council talk to her?"

"Given the circumstances, the Council voted to allow her to work with us . . . if she chooses," Argis said.

"Has the Council finally admitted she'd be an asset to our society?" Jame asked.

Seeran was surprised by the bitterness in Jame's voice.

"They're not ready to go that far." Argis turned to Jame. "But we can't survive this without her."

"I'll need conditions," Jame said.

"The Council anticipated as much." A glint of humor touched Argis's eyes.

"She'll be allowed to enter Emoria?" Jame asked.

"She'll have to give up her sword," Argis said. "At least until you've met with the Council and settled your terms."

Jame nodded. "I'll speak to Tigh."

"You've a duty to your people, no matter what she thinks," Argis said.

Seeran frowned at the rise of anger in Argis's voice.

"She understands and respects my duty to my people," Jame said. "But you forget, we have a duty to each other."

"Your joining has not been recognized by the Council," Argis said.

Jame stared off into the trees. "That doesn't make it any less real in our hearts."

Argis shrugged. "You'll have to work out with the Council."

THEY CAME TO A clearing dominated by a small lake, and Jame was not surprised to find a neat fire nestled in a close circle of stones. A familiar leather pouch hung from a trio of sticks tied together with a vine.

The three scouts materialized in front of Jame, Argis, and Seeran and approached the camp to make a quick investigation.

Jame grinned. "I guess we stay here tonight." Tigh had a knack for finding the best places to camp.

"Why hasn't she shown herself?" Argis asked as they settled their belongings around the fire.

Jame looked up from rummaging through one of Gessen's saddlebags. "She will. She's probably gathering food for the evening meal. If you want me to cook, you'll be eating Ingoran. If not, that lake has fish in it."

The Emorans exchanged glances.

"We'll try Ingoran food," Argis said.

"Very well." Jame winked at Seeran. She pulled her cooking pans and utensils from the saddlebags.

The sun was almost gone, and Jame settled into the task of preparing the evening meal, separating out the herbs and greens for whatever delicacy Tigh found. She smiled as the Emorans, with hands on their belt knives, jumped to their feet and peered into the darkened edge of trees.

Tigh, carrying a large bundle, stepped into the clearing.

"Argis." She entered the circle of firelight, then cast her eyes over the scouts. "More mouths to feed than usual." She held up the bundle and knelt next to Jame.

Jame captured Tigh's eyes, sparkling in the dancing firelight, with her own. They gazed at each other for several heartbeats until Tigh shrugged, placed the bundle on the ground, and opened it.

Jame sucked in a breath of relief and inspected what Tigh had foraged. She squeaked with delight, and the skittish Emorans jumped to their feet. She flung her arms around Tigh's neck and gave her a happy hug.

The Emorans, eyeing this display of affection, sank onto the ground and continued cleaning their weapons.

Jame separated several plump apples from the usual assortment of roots and greens. "A special treat for after our meal." She grinned as Tigh ruffled her bangs.

"You live such a life that apples are a treat?" Argis leveled her gaze at Tigh, the flames casting dappled shadows over her strong features.

Tigh stood and stepped into the firelight, her expression set as she met Argis's eyes. "We travel to places where apples are not common."

Argis nodded, not looking at all satisfied with the answer.

"Tigh has a knack for finding them in the most unlikely places," Jame said.

Argis gave Jame a long look. She sighed and continued to hone her sword with slow, long swipes of the whetstone.

"I'M GOING TO check the area," Tigh said as Jame crawled into their blankets. "Get some rest. I have a feeling tomorrow's going to be a long day."

"Master of understatement." Jame sighed and leaned closer to Tigh's ear. "Don't let Argis get to you."

Tigh squeezed Jame's hand. "Only for you."

Jame gazed into her eyes and gave her a good night kiss.

Tigh slipped out of the circle of firelight and paused just inside the line of trees to focus her senses on the restless forest. The scuttle of a nocturnal rodent, the creak of branches overhead, and the slow flap of an owl's expansive wings touched her keen hearing. Not a sound out of place . . . except, of course, the Emoran over to her left, close enough to see her, and something else . . . further into the trees.

Tigh sighed. Life with Jame was complicated enough, but it would be a lot less complicated if she weren't an Emoran princess.

Tigh almost smiled at the faint rustle behind her. She turned her head and gazed into the dark woods.

After a few heartbeats, Argis stepped out from behind a tree. "Did they teach you to see through things?" She crossed her arms.

"They taught us to listen." Tigh whipped her head around, threw up her hand, and caught a streak of darkness. A heartbeat later, the undergrowth, maybe fifty paces into the forest, rustled—the sound rushing away from them. "Sometimes it can save your life."

Argis stepped forward and held out her hand. Tigh gave her the arrow. "Why were they shooting at me?" She examined the shaft—all black except for a single yellow feather.

"You don't know who they are?" Tigh picked through the forest to the place where her senses told her the assailant had been.

Argis stumbled after her.

She flicked a curious glance at Argis. "They've been stalking you all day."

"What?" Argis grabbed Tigh's arm and turned her around.

Tigh flinched at the contact and reined in her battle-sharpened reaction.

"You were looking for us, they were following you." Tigh lifted an eyebrow and went back to studying the recently disturbed underbrush.

"Why didn't you say anything?" Argis asked.

"I didn't know who they were after." Tigh studied the shreds of reddish leather on the rough tree bark. "There are three of them. Dressed in this leather. Their only weapons are bow and arrow. Faces partially covered—like Emorans." She flicked another glance at Argis. "Lean and muscular—like women." Tigh gazed at Argis.

"We're at war with Lukria," Argis said. "That's why we're here."

"Why would they be stalking you, though?" Tigh turned to go back to the camp. "Perhaps they know you were looking for your princess. Someone who could be used as a valuable hostage."

"Which is more the reason we need to get her safely home," Argis said.

Tigh straightened. "She was safe until you brought attention to her."

DAWN FOUND TIGH wrapped around Jame beneath their furs to fight off the cold night. Before sleep overtook her, she had spent much of the night pushing down her anger at the Emorans for endangering Jame's life. She finally let the warm comfort of the woman she felt she didn't deserve to share her life with, placate her. Nothing else mattered to her. Only Jame.

She hitched up on her elbow at the snap of a twig. Only Argis, wrapped in a cloak of fur, on last watch in the mist that drifted off the lake.

Argis was twisting bits of the twig and watching them. She stood and glared at Tigh for several heartbeats then stomped off to the lake.

Tigh gazed down at the tangle of blonde hair and brushed a few strands away from Jame's face. She hated to wake her, but the sooner they were on their way, the sooner they could get her to a safe place.

She kissed Jame's cheek and was rewarded with an annoyed twitch. She kissed her ear and lingered a little longer, then moved out of the way to avoid Jame's rolling body—she was still asleep but not as deeply. She brushed her lips against Jame's, who responded with a tiny moan. Almost there. She pressed her lips against Jame's, and after a heartbeat received a return morning kiss.

Jame's eyes fluttered opened as Tigh pulled away a little. "It must be really early."

"It is," Tigh said. "There have been developments. We must travel quickly."

"Developments?"

"I'll explain when we're on the road," Tigh said.

"You won't be playing cat and mouse with the scouts again?" Jame asked.

"I'm not leaving your side," Tigh breathed in her ear.

"That bad?"

"Not good," Tigh said. "But not anything I can't handle."

"WE'RE NOT GOING to be able to drop you off at the nearest city." Jame handed Seeran a plate of cold odds and ends that was the morning meal.

"That's all right." Seeran tried to keep down her excitement.

"This isn't some adventure with a guaranteed happy ending," Jame said.

"I know," Seeran said. "I honestly do understand. But I can't let this opportunity pass simply because it may be dangerous."

"Not may be. Will be dangerous." Jame knelt in front of her.

"I know it's dangerous," Seeran said. "I'll probably be in terror most of the time and wish I were in my safe little room back in Artocia. But if I don't go with you, I'll spend the rest of my life regretting this chance."

Jame glanced over Seeran's shoulder at Tigh, who stood a few paces away. Seeran glanced back. Tigh gave a small nod.

"All right," Jame said. "You can stay as long as you can stand it. But remember, we may not be able to get you to safety if you change your mind."

"I understand." Seeran knew she didn't understand the true depth of the danger of joining this adventure, but she couldn't stay away even if they sent her on her way.

"IF I'D KNOWN we were being stalked . . ." Jame said.

Tigh rolled her eyes. "I didn't know who they were stalking."

"It doesn't matter. You were playing cat and mouse with them," Jame said.

"I was keeping track of their movements," Tigh said.

"You were playing with them." Jame leveled heated eyes at Tigh. "Tell me you weren't."

Tigh's mouth went dry as she gazed at Jame. Facing a hostile army was easier than facing her sometimes. "I was sharpening my tracking skills. I don't get much chance anymore." She raised a sheepish eyebrow for good measure.

Jame sighed. "I'm sorry. It's only natural to worry."

"You know I'm always careful," Tigh whispered then glanced back at Argis trailing close behind and at Seeran who swayed on Gessen ahead of them. She met Jame's eyes, and they exchanged their wordless promise to each other. Despite the dangers and rigors of their life, they were determined to live long enough to retire from the road—even if it was as Queen of Emoria and her consort.

Jame grinned and nodded.

The path curved, and the massive roots of ancient trees snaked close to their feet. Tigh hid her amusement as Seeran twisted and gaped at the rough-barked wonders. Even the forest sounds seemed to change as the domineering spirit of the trees saturated the air. Seeran turned back and opened her mouth. Tigh stopped and threw her hand up.

Everyone stopped. Gessen, trained for this kind of stillness, flicked her ears to pick up anything out of the ordinary.

Tigh looked around before settling her eyes on the massive root system of an uprooted tree. The area under the roots could easily shelter all of them, with another tree close by to protect Gessen, if necessary. She led them to the sheltered roots.

"What's going on?" Argis vented some of her anger toward Tigh that clung to her like well-worn leathers.

Tigh flashed an impatient glance at her. "Your scouts."

"What about my scouts?" Argis crossed her arms.

"They are no longer with us," Tigh said.

Argis lunged with her knife. Tigh caught her wrist. They pushed against each other with straining muscles. Tigh drew her sword with her free hand and pressed the tip against Argis's throat.

"Warriors." Jame put her hands on her hips. "Argis, drop the knife. It's not Tigh's fault the scouts are missing."

"I don't like her attitude." Argis winced from the grip on her wrist.

"You just don't like her," Jame said. "Drop the knife. We have to find the scouts."

Argis raked cold eyes over Tigh, then dropped the blade. She stepped back as soon as Tigh let go of her wrist and rubbed the feeling back into her arm.

Jame picked up the knife and handed it to Argis. "This can't go on. Not when we have to work together to get safely to Emoria. I know I can't make you like Tigh but at least accept her as an ally. You *do* owe her your life."

Argis struggled to bring her rage under control.

"Please. Do it for me?"

Tigh found a lump of dirt to study as the unfamiliar sensation of jealousy rippled through her. She knew Jame wouldn't have pulled that tactic if this weren't such a desperate circumstance. The fact that she wasn't the first warrior to cave in to Jame's persuasive spell bothered her more than she wanted to admit. But a charming and persuasive personality was Jame's gift, and she had to use it at full power sometimes.

Argis took a deep breath and stared into Jame's unwavering eyes. "Only for you."

Tigh winced at her words.

Jame put strong fingers under Tigh's bowed chin.

Tigh raised her head and soaked up the aching apology in Jame's eyes. She nodded and pulled Jame into a gentle hug. "Time to see what kind of trouble your scouts have gotten themselves into."

Chapter 3

TIGH LET OUT a slow breath as she peeked through the branches of a massive tree overlooking the path. The scouts appeared unharmed, other than their bound hands and the dirty rags wrapped around their mouths. They were roped together and led like a string of oxen by a red leather-clad Lukrian. The other two Lukrians followed behind the captives.

Tigh realized the Lukrians' instructions had been to capture hostages—any hostages—and that was the reason they'd been stalking the Emorans. Tears stung her eyes with the knowledge they weren't after Jame. They didn't know why Argis and company were away from Emoria and never got close enough to learn Jame's identity. Jame, after all, was not dressed as an Emoran, even with her old fighting staff—the only weapon she agreed to learn in warrior training.

The Lukrians' skills at stalking were formidable to have captured the forest-trained Emorans. Tigh knew of no one who could sneak up on Emorans in the woods, especially those trained to be scouts. They knew forests as well, if not better, than the wild creatures that inhabited them. Yet these scouts had been taken, unharmed.

"Stop talking." The leader turned to the prisoners and shot a warning glare at the rear guard.

"We're far enough away," another Lukrian said. "They won't know these clumsy scouts are missing until they make camp tonight."

"You don't lower your guard until I say so," the leader said.

Tigh studied the accessories attached to the Lukrians' belts as they passed below. She focused on a pair of small stained leather bags dangling from the leader's belt and just stopped from cursing out loud.

JAME WAS SURPRISED at how uncomfortable she felt around her closest friend from childhood. The few heartbeats after Tigh left seemed much longer as she realized she and Argis had too much and really nothing to say to each other. She couldn't think of a middle ground.

Jame had drifted too far away from the world she grew up in. It didn't help that their last meetings had been serious confrontations. The first one had been that strange, wonderful, agonizing time when she made the decision to leave her family and friends to become an arbiter when her schooling was complete. The last one had been when Argis had come to Ynit to confront her with the reports that she had cultivated a dangerous relationship with the notorious Tigh the Terrible. That meeting had been . . . difficult. Jame almost laughed at the understatement.

She had hoped Argis had forgotten about her and found someone else to share her life with. She glanced at Argis, who sat with her knees pulled to her chin, and knew this mission was a miserable ordeal for her. But she also knew whatever Argis felt was her own fault. She mustn't feel guilty about it.

Jame saw that Seeran had dozed off in a tangle of roots against the upturned base of the tree. She crept to Argis and nestled into a mess of wiry roots.

Argis darted glances at her but focused on the surrounding forest. "You should stay back. We don't know what's out there."

"I'll keep alert." Jame caught the look Argis flashed her. "I'm not the same person who left Emoria ten years ago. I've grasped enough of the warrior within me to keep up my self-defense skills."

Argis pulled her knees closer to her chin. "I'm not the same person I was ten years ago either. But you never gave me a chance to grow with you."

"I know," Jame said. "But I'd already grown apart from you after my first season in school." She sighed and decided to bite the arrowhead. "I should have told you then. But I was young and wasn't sure what I was really feeling. I was struggling with the idea of leaving home to pursue something I wanted to do more than anything else. I truly thought you'd realize we weren't meant to be together and find someone else. It's not like we had made any kind of formal commitment to each other."

"You were going to be Queen and I was to be the great warrior at your side," Argis said.

"Those were the daydreams of children." Jame sighed. "You can still be a great warrior at my side." Argis gazed at her with intense eyes. "You just won't be my consort." Argis stared into the forest. "I'd already grown apart from you before I met Tigh. You have to know it in your heart. Please don't hate her for it. It's not her fault."

A silence settled over them. The squeaking of treetops rubbing together in the breeze and the scuttling of tiny creatures in the undergrowth occupied Jame's senses for several heartbeats.

Argis took a deep breath and addressed the trees. "I knew in my heart you no longer felt the same way for me. That you'd outgrown our childhood dreams." She turned sad eyes to Jame. "A part of me tried to outgrow them, too. But that was too powerful a dream to let go of. I wouldn't have been just a warrior. I would've been your warrior. Being your friend distinguished me from the others. It gave me the incentive to excel, and to live up to the title of Queen's Warrior."

"But you have excelled. You're the best warrior in Emoria." Jame nodded at the Master Warrior braid wrapped around Argis's belt.

"I did it for you." Argis captured Jame's eyes with her own. "I did it because I knew you'd come back someday. After you'd seen the world and were ready to settle down, I'd be there."

"I told you not to wait for me if I decided to pursue being an arbiter after I finished my studies," Jame whispered as the guilt washed over her. She mustn't feel guilty. Argis made her own choice. "The last time I visited Emor."

"Had you met Tigh by that time?" Argis asked.

Jame studied her hands. "I'd seen her when they brought her to Ynit to be cleansed. She was as fierce as a wild animal, as they all were when they were captured and caged." She stared into the forest, seeing not trees but a stone courtyard drenched in the orange glow of the late evening sun. "I was on my way to a lecture when a wagon with a cage on it came through the gate. It wasn't an uncommon sight at the time. Many of the uncleansed Guards hadn't yet been found. The wagon headed my way, and I got a good look at the woman inside the cage." Vivid images filled her mind. "She looked as if she'd been chased for thousands of paces. Covered with mud and blood, she was wild and feral and frightening. She was also alert to everything around her, like an animal. She clung to the bars of the cage and captured my eyes with the most compelling, icy blue I'd ever seen. They made her even less human than the mud and blood. Those eyes enveloped me with her personality until I was frozen and couldn't look away. As the wagon passed by, she laughed, intentionally breaking the spell. It was then I saw a hint of sadness and humanity touching her eyes and echoing in that laugh. In that tiny breath of time, the woman beneath the warrior peeked through and captured my interest."

Argis stared at her. "You've always been a good weaver of tales."

Jame picked up a twig and bent it without breaking it. "I hadn't actually met her face to face when I visited Emoria a few weeks later, but I unconsciously knew I had witnessed my destiny."

"How did they capture them?" Argis asked.

"They used a special mixture of herbs developed as a weapon for the Elite Guard," Jame said. "It can be put on the end of a dart or arrow. Its effects are almost immediate and can knock a person out for many sandmarks. It was ironic they used one of the Guards' own weapons against them."

"I've never heard of such a thing," Argis said.

"The formula is known only to the Elite Guard, and those who trained and subsequently cleansed them," Jame said.

"So how did you actually meet her?" Argis asked.

"I met her two moons later." Jame looked into her mind at the memory of that first meeting—if it could be called a meeting. "When a person completes the training to become an Elite Guard, they exhibit personality traits that are near opposite of those they possessed before the training. That's one of the reasons why they stopped recruiting career soldiers and convicts. They actually lost their ruthlessness and willingness to kill when trained. Most Guards had a mix of good and bad traits, just as we all do, and they made up the bulk of the regiment. But the recruiters set out to find young law-abiding, peaceful citizens with the necessary physical characteristics and trained them to be the Elite Guard to lead these regiments."

"Laur's waterfalls," Argis whispered.

"It was a terrible crime against those people," Jame said. "The most difficult part of the rehabilitation was mentally restoring them to who they'd been before their recruitment."

"Are you saying Tigh the Terrible was one of these law-abiding, peaceful citizens before she became a Guard?" Argis asked.

"Yes," Jame said. "She won't talk about it, but she was going to go to Artocia and study to become a scholar." She pulled the stopper from her water sack and gulped several mouthfuls of warm water. "She was ready to undergo the next part of her rehabilitation—learning to be around people—but her reputation kept the assistant arbiters from stepping forward to present her case. Her Guard training had changed her so much that no one was sure if the cleansing had really worked on her. A part of our internship was to argue on behalf of the Guards as they progressed through the levels of rehabilitation. No one wanted to argue Tigh's case. No one even wanted to be in the same room with her. Some argued for leaving her in that tiny cell forever. What was worse, she thought this was the proper punishment for what she had done."

"Tigh the Terrible felt remorse for her ruthless behavior during the Wars?" Argis looked as if the certainties in her world had shattered, then she gazed at Jame with knowing eyes. "You couldn't let her be locked away forever. You've always been able to see the good in people."

Jame nodded. "I remembered that brief glimpse of humanity and I knew I had to try."

"So you argued her case."

"Not quite yet." Jame chuckled. "The moment I said I wanted to defend Tigh, several others stepped forward and volunteered. Being a princess really gets in the way sometimes. They insisted it was too much of a risk for me, but if I felt that strongly about it they would give it a try. A dozen tried, one after another. Tigh wouldn't have anything to do with them. Although she'd been cleansed, she still had that compelling personality, and she frightened the other arbiters away. I finally convinced them to let me visit her once. If she frightened or threatened me I promised I wouldn't pursue it. Not wanting to hold her captive forever, they agreed."

Argis smiled. "She's not the only one with the persuasive personality."

Jame cleared her throat. "I have to admit I was nervous when I went to see her that first time." She stared out at the trees as she recounted her first meeting with Tigh. How Tigh wouldn't even look at her.

Argis cocked her head. "I presume you finally got through to her."

"She let me visit and listened to the argument as I wrote it," Jame said. "But she didn't really let me into her thoughts until my fourth visit. By that time she was up to grunts and nods in response to what I said to her. Little did I know this was her normal method of communication."

"It was easier to think she forced herself on you," Argis said.

"So you could have a reason to hate her." Jame nodded. "She's a human being—and a vulnerable one at that, because of what she has to live with every day."

Seeran rustled the roots. Jame glanced back and saw she was awake.

A half sandmark later, Jame and Argis jumped to their feet and froze. They listened to a rustling in the undergrowth just beyond the trees. Argis unsheathed her sword and motioned Jame to get back against the upturned tree. For once, Jame didn't argue and crept back to Seeran, who watched the forest with wide-eyed fright.

The noise stopped. Tigh stepped from behind a tree.

Argis lowered her sword. "Where are the scouts?"

Tigh brushed her eyes past Argis to Jame, who approached her. "Your scouts are unharmed." Jame closed her eyes in relief. "It seems our stalkers were looking for any hostages they could get. Fortunately, they didn't get close enough to find out your identity."

"How were they captured without being injured?" Argis asked.

Tigh flicked her eyes at Argis before capturing Jame's again. "The same way they captured me."

Jame gasped.

"That confirms who we're up against."

"They drugged them?" Argis asked.

Tigh gave Jame a questioning look.

"We've been trying to make peace," Jame said.

Tigh nodded. "I think they drugged them just enough to capture them. They're moving quickly back to their territory."

"We can't just let them be taken—"

Tigh flashed a sharp look at her and raised her hand. "I want you three to take the quickest, straightest route to Emoria." Tigh turned to Jame. "I'll catch up to you."

"If they caught the scouts, they can capture you," Jame said.

Tigh shrugged. "They have what they came for. They think we won't notice the scouts are missing until this evening, and by that time they'll be too far away—even if we figured out what had happened to them. They don't know we know who they are, and they're certainly not expecting an attack." She turned to Argis. "Capturing three Emorans is too ambitious for only three of them this far from their territory. I suspect they're part of a larger party. I'm going to follow them a bit. The more knowledge we have going into this conflict, the better our chances of defeating them. Don't worry. I'll rescue the scouts."

Jame gestured for Argis to stay back, then trotted to Tigh as she strode to Gessen. They separated the supplies in silence, adding most of the foodstuff and some of the bedding to the packs that Jame, Seeran, and Argis carried. The chore was done, she stood with arms crossed and waited for Tigh to stop adjusting Gessen's tack.

"I'll be careful," Tigh said.

"Be extra careful." Jame stood her ground.

Tigh turned with a lopsided grin.

Jame wrapped her arms around Tigh and pressed her face against the soft, black leather between the plates of armor. She raised her head and found gentle, affectionate eyes gazing down at her, and met Tigh's tender kiss.

"After I rescue the scouts, I'll have to rescue you from Argis," Tigh breathed into Jame's ear.

Jame chuckled. "My protector."

They grinned as they separated.

Tigh shot one last glance at Argis and Seeran then climbed onto Gessen's back. "I'll find you as soon as I can." She nudged Gessen through the underbrush and onto the trail.

Chapter 4

Tigh was surprised at the Lukrians' cockiness as they led their prisoners along the road as if it was an everyday activity. The other travelers passed quickly or hung behind the strange little group. Their fear didn't stop them from staring. She heard whispers of "Emorans" from the people around her. She grinned at what Argis's reaction would be to that. But no matter what they chose to call themselves, the Lukrians *did* look like Emorans.

Tigh had taken the time to exchange her black leather tunic for a finely cut fawn-colored leather that reflected her Ingoran merchant heritage. She could pass without recognition, unless she somehow attracted the wrong kind of attention. Even the sword on her back brought little notice since it wasn't unusual for a merchant traveling alone to carry a weapon.

The road was crowded even for a land as populated as the Balderon valley. She guided Gessen past a small group of travelers and learned that the Festival of Bal was to begin that evening in the city of Balderon.

Tigh kept the Lukrians in sight as she trotted Gessen behind a pair of wagons heaped high with pumpkins and other colorful squashes for the festival—a reminder that the cold season was fast approaching.

"Good day to you." A rather portly man on a stout gray horse trotted up next to her. He had the friendly air of a merchant who enjoyed talking to people but was always on alert for a potential sale.

Tigh nodded. "Good day, good merchant."

The merchant studied Tigh and glanced at the sword hilt peeking over her shoulder. He grinned. "Salonis Grender, recruitment consultant."

Recruitment consultant. Tigh kept her expression passive as she bit back her disgust and anger at the benign sounding title. She'd been recruited to the Guards by one such as Salonis.

"Paldar Tigis, arms merchant."

"I thought so, the moment I saw you," Salonis said in delight. He glanced around and lowered his voice. "So you've heard the rumors?"

Tigh shrugged. "I'm always hearing rumors."

"I thought I'd be the first on the scene, so to speak," Salonis said. "I should have known an Ingoran, from the House of Tigis no less, would get a whiff of what was going on—even this far from your part of the world."

"We enjoy the fresh air," Tigh said. "Sometimes there's more in it than the scent of flowers and flowing water." The traditional Ingoran response put others at ease. Ritual was an important part of merchant interaction.

Salonis glanced around again and leaned in closer. "What do you make of them?" He nodded at the Lukrians.

Tigh shrugged. "Emorans."

Salonis chuckled. "That's what they want everyone to think."

"Why do you think that is?" Tigh asked.

Salonis blinked at her, then grinned. "You mean, why all of a sudden is there a group of Emoran imitators for this little rise to arms and not for the Grappian Wars?"

"It's something to ponder." Tigh wondered how small the little rise to arms really was if recruitment consultants, like Salonis, believed there was a profit to be made from it.

"Rumor has it they're already fighting amongst themselves," Salonis said. "This group seems to confirm it with those prisoners."

"Warriors are warriors, no matter what they choose to call themselves," Tigh said.

"At least they're not so stupid to call themselves Emoran." Salonis winced as a Lukrian bringing up the rear of the group slapped a prisoner who appeared to have made a comment.

Tigh hoped that was the extent of the abuse toward the scouts.

"They call themselves Lukrians."

"Interesting," Tigh said. "Lukrians splintered away from the Emorans ages ago. Or so the legends go."

"It doesn't matter what they call themselves. They just need to be good fighters. This new faction. I hear they're based in those mountains somewhere." Salonis nodded at the distant peaks rising above the valley. "They're looking for the best fighters they can find." He leaned toward Tigh. "Rumor has it the leaders are uncleansed Guards."

Tigh raised an eyebrow. "I thought they'd all been caught."

Salonis shrugged. "That's what they say. But we know how that is."

All too well, Tigh mused.

"But merchants in our line of work go where the business is." Salonis gave Tigh a conspiratorial wink. "Silver is silver."

"You're so right." Tigh managed a grin and then settled her gaze on the Lukrians. *Silver is silver, but where would a handful of uncleansed Guards find enough silver to start another war?* She looked beyond the walled city in the distance to the peaks dancing in the clouds much farther away.

SEERAN'S TIGHT CALF muscles and burning lungs reminded her, too late, that adventuring required a physical conditioning that wasn't a part of the curriculum at the University of Artocia. The forest gave way to a rocky terrain, and she was forced to keep her eyes on where she placed her feet. She tried not to wince at the impatient, searing looks a grumpy Argis threw over her shoulder at her. She expected to be abandoned after each step because she held them back from getting Jame safely to Emoria. Historians were supposed to be unobtrusive observers, not the recipients of hostile glares.

She decided complaining or asking for a brief rest would only make things worse with Argis. To push away the discomfort, she recited long epics to herself, concentrating on remembering every word. Lost in the world of word images, she kept walking—almost matching the pace of her companions. She concentrated on a difficult passage filled with alliterations and mythical allusion and walked for several heartbeats before she noticed the others had stopped. She looked up from her careful scrutiny of the broken ground and was surprised to see a low hill blocking their way.

"Stay here while I have a look around," Argis muttered as she started up the rocky.

Jame stared at Argis's receding back for a few heartbeats and took a deep breath. She went to several small boulders, pulled the pack off her back, and plopped it onto a sizable rock.

"May as well have something to eat while Argis is in a protective mood," she mumbled as she rummaged through the pack.

Seeran stood where she had stopped. The feeling of being a burden crashed down on her now that she wasn't concentrating on the simple act of walking.

Jame flashed her a puzzled look. "Come, sit down and have something to eat. Keep your strength up."

Seeran walked against her stiffening muscles and eased down on the boulder next to Jame. "I'm sorry. It's just, if I'm holding you back . . ."

Jame gave her an alarmed look. "Wait. What are you talking about?"

"I'm holding you back," Seeran said. "I can't walk as fast as you."

Jame grinned. "You think you've been holding us back? You should have seen me when I started traveling with Tigh. I thought I was in pretty good shape after growing up in Emoria and keeping up an exercise regime when I was a student." She laughed and motioned Seeran to an assortment of berries, hunks of white cheese, and dark bread. "She has the stamina of a horse and extremely long legs. It was a half season before we found a compromise."

"But Argis—"

"Argis has lived in Emoria her whole life. She doesn't understand a woman who hasn't spent her life walking, running, and climbing," Jame said. "The only opinion you have to worry about is mine. If that weren't true, Argis would have been barking at you all day as if you were a first season warrior. I think you're doing great for not being used to walking on anything but well-maintained paths and roads."

Seeran nibbled a piece of cheese as she pondered Jame's words. "She must be an excellent teacher because she certainly put the fear of Hador into me."

"You're stronger than you think," Jame said. "Emorans respect strength more than they respect the ability to whack someone into the next moon. Believe me, after this trek today, Argis has more respect for you than she did this morning. The harder she glares at you the more she wants to push you to develop that strength. The teacher in her sees potential, and it's difficult for her not to want to develop it."

Seeran bowed her head in shame. "I think you're just trying to be kind."

"You want to learn about Emorans?" Jame asked. "The best place to start is with how we think. Talk to Argis. Ask her why she glared at you all day." Seeran scrunched her face. "She may scowl and complain, but she'll be secretly pleased that you want to know these things from her. In our society the most successful are those who speak up and ask questions. It shows courage, curiosity, and persistence—the qualities that make a leader."

"I'm no leader," Seeran said. "I'm too content being a slave to my work."

Jame grinned. "You showed all three traits by seeking out your stories in a place where no other scholar would venture."

Seeran laughed. "That wasn't courage, that was foolhardiness."

"There's a fine line between the two." Jame popped a berry into her mouth. "Talk to Argis. She's spent a good deal of time instructing her warriors in the difference between foolhardiness and courage."

They looked up as Argis scampered down the hill. She took the hunk of cheese and bread that Jame held out to her.

"See anything interesting?" Jame asked after Argis finished her food and washed it down with a long swig of water.

"There's a large valley just over these hills." Argis pulled herself up onto the boulder next to Jame and Seeran. "To the east is Balderon and beyond that are the Phytians. We're making good time."

Jame flashed an amused glance at Seeran, who let out a breath in relief.

"The road into the city winds close to the base of the hill just beyond this one. The quickest way is to follow it to the mountains. It's heavy with travelers headed for Balderon."

"Then that'll make it easier for us to be on the road without drawing attention," Jame said. "I have a set of Tigh's clothes that should fit you well enough. If it's a festival or celebration of some sort, we can camp outside the city with the people who can't find accommodations."

"I'll only agree to it because I won't rest until we have you safely home." Argis captured Jame's eyes with her own. "I'm considering your . . . offer . . .

to be your warrior and nothing more, when you are queen." She jumped off the boulder and looked up at her surprised companions. "I'll try to do justice to Tigh's clothing."

THE AIRY BALLS of multicolored light hissed as they shot upward. They remained suspended longer than possible, threw off sparks in all directions, and then winked out into darkness. Before Seeran had time to adjust her eyes, a fiery dragonfly flashed and melted in a cascade of tumbling sparks . . .

"Seeran?"

She blinked and spun around to face her companions. "Sorry," she mumbled, surprised to see amusement rather than impatience in their eyes.

The laughing crowds shifted and pressed around them as they continued their search for a door with a crossed sword and bow etched on it. They had abandoned the decision to camp outside when Argis saw the campfires spiraling away from the city walls as far as they could see. She gave in to her unease and thought it wiser to find the Emoran safe house.

"They're usually just off the central plaza," Jame said.

Argis looked around. "How can we find it in all this chaos?"

Seeran stood on her tiptoes and peered in all directions over the heads of the surging people. "This way."

Jame and Argis blinked at each other, shrugged, and pushed after Seeran.

They managed to go several blocks with Seeran leading the way. She glanced back and hid a grin at how the Emorans were less than successful in the art of plowing around inattentive people. Both struggled to keep her in sight and not cause injury to anyone. Argis nearly crashed into a tipsy group of loudly dressed women when she was distracted by Jame's colorful language.

They finally entered the central plaza, a formidable expanse of smooth stone, quiet and almost empty in spite of the festivities in the surrounding streets. An imposing granite statue in an octagon-shaped shallow pool at the center of the plaza drew their attention.

They stared across the dark water at the brilliant military leader who had liberated the city from the Kuntics, the legendary barbarians of the east. The larger-than-life warrior with tousled short hair peeking from beneath a half helmet stared out at them, victorious eyes sparkling in the light from torches placed to highlight the face. In full armor atop a magnificent warhorse, the statue looked ready to come to life at the sound of a battle cry and splash through the water to lead a charge to another victory.

"She was the greatest of them all," Argis whispered.

Seeran read the dedication plate on the lip of the pool. "That's Hekolatis. An Emoran."

"Yes," Jame said. "She led the army that liberated this whole region from the Kuntics. I'm glad the people of Balderon didn't let her memory die."

"This is interesting," Seeran said. "It says that Hekolatis promised the people of Balderon that an Emoran warrior would come and ensure victory for Balderon if they were ever threatened by an army of conquerors."

Jame and Argis exchanged puzzled glances. They shuffled next to Seeran and read the inscription.

"It must be something the people here made up," Jame said. "Probably to give them hope after rebuilding the city."

"Ah, but it could be true," a voice behind them said.

They spun around. Argis had her hand over her belt knife as she studied the benign-looking portly man of middle age, dressed in the flamboyant robes of a merchant from the eastern territories.

The merchant shrugged. "Of course, since Emorans only exist in legends, any woman warrior could do the job just as well."

Argis raised an eyebrow and lowered her hand from her knife.

"Made up or not, it's a nice sentiment," Jame said.

"Very nice," the merchant said. "I'm Salonis, by the way, recruitment consultant." He gazed at Argis.

"Here for the festival?" Jame asked.

Salonis glanced around, then lowered his voice. "Actually I heard there might be some business for me here. I'm only telling you this because your tall friend there might be able to find gainful employment, if you know what I mean."

Argis swaggered forward and looked down at the man. "Gainful employment sounds good. Tell me more, little man."

Salonis took a step back, cleared his throat and, with a shaky hand, rubbed the sunburn on the top of his head. "It's obvious you're a warrior, probably fought in the Grappian Wars. I know, better than anyone, how difficult it's been for you warriors to adjust to peacetime."

He paused to gauge Argis's expression, but she stood, arms folded, waiting for him to continue.

"I just happen to know we may be on the verge of another war."

"Who'd dare go against the Southern Territories after what happened in the last war?" Argis pulled herself up a little taller.

"Ah, that's the question, isn't it?" Salonis leaned forward. "I hear there are a few disgruntled, uncleansed Guards forming an army up in those mountains, even as we speak." He dramatically pointed west.

"If you mean those mountains," Jame pointed east, "it'd be difficult to hide something as large as an army up there. People live and work in all the habitable places."

"If rumors are to be believed, they live in a warren of caves deep in the belly of one of those great peaks," Salonis said.

"And if this is true, which side are you the recruitment consultant for?" Argis asked.

Salonis pulled a blue silk rag from his sleeve and patted his forehead with it. "I never offer my services to aggressors who are mentally unstable."

Argis grinned. "Harder to get your fee from them, huh?"

Salonis chuckled and cleared his throat. "I like a warrior with a sense of humor. If you're interested, I'll be at The Tiger and Bear. An experienced warrior such as yourself will be needed when that army in the mountains starts to move."

Argis nodded. "I'll think about it."

"Good evening to all of you." Salonis bowed his head.

"Have a good night, merchant," Jame said as Salonis disappeared into the crowd that started to spill onto the plaza from the surrounding streets.

"Things are more serious than we thought." Argis jumped up on the lip of the pool and scanned the buildings facing the plaza. "There." She dropped to the ground. "Come on."

A few heartbeats later, they stood before an ancient wooden door covered with faded sea green paint and an etching of a crossed sword and bow. Argis pulled the heavy brass knocker and let it drop against the thick wood. A little panel slid open and eyes looked them over before the panel clicked shut. The muffled sounds of several bolts being pulled was followed by the door easing open and a low voice telling them to enter.

A TALL WOMAN with gray-streaked auburn hair and a lean body softened by age and indoor work led them down a narrow darkened corridor that opened onto a cavernous common room.

"We're a little tight for rooms right now—the festival and all," the woman said. "The best we can do is one room for all of you."

"That'd be more than fine," Jame said. "I'm Jame, peace arbiter-at-large for the Southern Districts. This is Seeran, a historian from the University in Artocia, and Argis, Master Warrior and weapons instructor from Emoria."

"Well met," the woman said. "It's an honor to be visited by a member of the royal family. I'm Wence, proprietor of The Sword and Bow."

"Thank you." Jame smiled as they walked down several steps into the spacious room, banked on three sides by fireplaces tall enough for Argis to walk into.

As always, Jame felt pangs of . . . she couldn't even find words for it. Just an ache as she gazed at the tapestries depicting Emoran victories that hung on the walls next to heroic displays of swords, bows, and spears. She wasn't surprised to see nearly every table occupied. Some women already looked as if they had too much of the celebrated Emoran ale, while others traded soft words over steaming cups of spiced tea.

The smell of stew and fresh-baked bread hit her senses, reminding her that they'd been on meager rations all day.

"There's a table over there," Argis said.

"Looks good." Jame looked back at a gaping Seeran and smiled. "Seeran."

Seeran blinked and gave Jame a sheepish look. "I never imagined a place like this existed in our cities. Hidden in plain sight."

"No one expects them to be here so they're overlooked," Jame said.

They went to the table where Argis was seated and already talking to a server.

"Do you have any Ingoran dishes?" Jame sat down, relieved to be off her feet.

"Our cook always has a pot of Ingoran stew on the fire. You'd be surprised how many Ingoran merchants pass through," the girl said. "We even had one earlier today."

"I'll have a bowl then," Jame said.

The fine Ingoran stew and Emoran bread, topped off with spiced tea helped Jame relax enough to sit back and let the friendly atmosphere of the common room occupy her senses for a while. When Wence told them their room was available, she was more than ready to call it a day.

Wence led them up a back flight of stairs to a more intimate version of the common room downstairs. A few women were gathered, talking or playing sticks and strings. Each wall, except the one with the fireplace, had two doors. Small brass renderings of animals distinguished the rooms from each other, and Wence took them to the door boasting an artfully cast wolf.

The room, even with three narrow beds, was larger than what Jame and Tigh were accustomed to. A welcoming fire flickered in a small fireplace and an even more welcoming tub of steaming water sat behind a curtain in one corner.

"A bath. Thank you, thank you," Jame said.

"It's an Emoran tradition, as you well know," Wence said with a wink.

"I've spent too much time away from Emoria," Jame said. "I've learned not to expect those things that are traditional to us."

"Enjoy then. Put that statue outside the door if you need anything." She pointed to a stone rendering of a wolf next to the door, then slipped out of the room.

"You should go first, my princess," Argis said.

"That's not fair to Seeran. I'm not her princess," Jame said. "We'll go in alphabetical order."

Argis's expression was almost comical. "It's not proper for me to go before a princess."

"The water's getting cold, Argis," Jame said.

The argument seemed to drain out of Argis, and she pulled off her gear.

"I think I'll jot down a few notes while I'm waiting." Seeran put her pack on a small table in the corner opposite the tub.

"Good. I'm going to get us a pitcher of tea," Jame said.

Argis stiffened and then relaxed in resignation.

Jame slipped out the door. The sticks and string game had become the most engaging activity in the common room and everyone, except a woman reading near the window, was gathered around the four players. She trotted down the stairs, following her nose to the kitchen. Most Balderon kitchens opened onto the alley, and this one was no exception. The back of the building was of older, more eccentric construction, and she took a few too many corridors before her nose told her she was on the right track again.

"Really wasn't planning on all this exercise," she muttered as she rounded a sharp corner.

Hands grabbed her from behind, and she struggled to get free.

Chapter 5

"HAVE YOU FORGOTTEN what you were taught about blind corners?" a low voice said in Jame's ear.

"This is a safe house. Now let go." Jame turned around and glared at an unrepentant Argis. "Why aren't you taking a bath?"

"I took one." Argis straightened. "You were gone too long. I decided to make sure my princess was all right."

"I've been gone only a few heartbeats and I'm fine. I just got a little turned around." Jame continued down the corridor with Argis trailing behind her. She heard the door she just passed open. She spun around as a figure popped out and put a large hand over Argis's mouth while the other hand grabbed an arm and pulled it behind her back.

Jame crossed her arms. "I seem to remember a lesson about doors, too."

"You're giving away my clothing. Should I be worried?" Tigh asked.

Argis struggled and spewed muffled curses. Tigh released her.

"You ungrateful offspring of a Yitsian snow monster." Argis backed away then pounced on Tigh, sending them through the opened door and thudding to the floor. "Where are my scouts?" She looked up at three sets of astonished eyes staring down at her.

"They're looking after their prisoners," Tigh said.

Argis gave her head a shake, then climbed to her feet.

Jame helped Tigh up and then took in the latest handiwork of her resourceful partner. "Good job." She wound an arm around Tigh's waist.

The scouts were not only free, but bathed, and from the looks of the remnants of a meal on a side table, well fed. Aside from an assortment of scrapes and bruises, they appeared to be in good shape. The Lukrians, on the other hand, didn't look like they were having a good day at all. They were seated against the far wall with feet and hands tied together in front and gagged with rags.

"Are you all right?" Argis studied the scouts, who grinned and seemed to be in good spirits.

"We're fine." Poylin chuckled as the other two covered their mouths to stop from laughing.

Tigh met Argis's narrowed eyes with an innocent expression.

Argis sighed. "We'll have to figure out a way to get them out of here."

"How did you get them in here in the first place?" Jame asked.

"They were the ones who brought the scouts in," Tigh said. "They gave them a small dose of the potion to make them appear drunk, and just before they approached the door, they removed their bindings and made the excuse to the proprietor that the scouts had engaged in some early celebrations to Bal."

"Clever," Jame said. "You mean they just walked into the city with bound and gagged prisoners?"

"They traveled the great road as if it were the most natural sight in the world." Tigh gave Jame a squeeze, then went to the jumble of packs on one of the beds. She pulled a scrap of paper from a belt pouch and handed it to Jame.

Jame scanned the note and then handed it to Argis. "So the little merchant was right."

"You met Salonis?" Tigh asked.

"He spotted Argis as a potential recruit," Jame said. "How did you meet him?"

Tigh shrugged. "He mistook me for an Ingoran arms merchant."

Argis scowled. "I'm wearing your civilian clothes, why didn't he mistake me for a merchant?"

"Once an Ingoran, always an Ingoran. It's the attitude, not the clothes." Tigh grinned. "I know the one who signed that order. She was an Elite Guard, but not one of the more . . . zealous ones. Just a good fighter, and solid in her loyalty to the Guard."

"In other words, not the one we should be worrying about," Jame said.

"No." Tigh sighed and stared into the dying flame in the fireplace. She put a log on the fire and turned to find the others watching her. "The Guard we have to worry about is someone as bad as I was, or worse."

"No one was as bad as you," Argis said.

"That's not entirely true." Tigh's eyes reflected some bleak memory from her past.

Jame went to Tigh and wrapped her arms around her.

Tigh drew a proper breath and relaxed. She put a hand on Jame's shoulder and gave it an affectionate, reassuring squeeze. "There were two. An acolyte of the Shrouded One and an archivist at the Maridee Institute. They became such monsters that they were immediately locked away."

Jame frowned. "I don't remember them at Ynit. Whatever became of them?"

"I don't know," Tigh said. "No one ever spoke of them from the moment they were confined."

"We're safe for now, at least," Jame said. "I suggest we get a good night's sleep in real beds for a change. We can work out our strategy tomorrow."

Tigh gave Jame an endearing puppy dog look. "Got room for one more?"

Jame laughed and pulled away. "Always, for you." She held out a hand to her warrior.

JAME GRINNED AS the serving girl put plates of Ingoran style potatoes and greens in front of herself and Tigh without even asking for them.

Argis eyed the Ingoran food and just shook her head. "You have a plan?" She glanced at Tigh.

"Yes." Tigh broke off a piece of the coarse-grained bread and dipped it into a green sauce.

Argis stopped chewing and watched Tigh.

"You might as well tell us what you have in mind." Jame sighed.

Tigh and Argis were like mismatched bolts and screws—they grated even when trying to work together.

"I'm supposed to be an arms merchant." Tigh shrugged. "It wouldn't be out of the ordinary if I sold a load of weapons to that army up in the mountains. We hire a wagon, purchase a few weapons for show and keep our Lukrian friends under some hides until we are clear of the city."

"Nice, simple plan. Hekolatis did something like that to rescue Zander from Artocia. I see only one problem." Argis put down a chop. "We barely have enough silver as a donation for the meals and lodging for ten people— if we include our Lukrian friends. What can we use for the wagon and weapons?"

Tigh opened her belt pouch, pulled out a small, bulging leather bag, and handed it to Jame.

Jame opened the bag and peered inside. A pile of silver sparkled back at her. "Where did you get this?"

"I decided to see what kinds of arms were passing through this territory. A lot can be determined by what people are interested in buying and trading. So I visited several arms shops. A noble with too much money and too little sense insisted the sword the merchant had sold to her had not been forged where she said it had been. Being an arms merchant, I settled the dispute which was in favor of the shopkeeper." Tigh nodded at the bag. "That's the usual commission for an appraisal of such a fine sword."

Argis whistled. "That must have been some sword."

Tigh lifted her mug and took a sip. "It was Emoran."

Argis shrugged. "So is almost every sword in the Southern Territories. Even that black thing you carry around."

Tigh put down her mug. "This one was a ceremonial sword."

"What?" Jame and Argis said.

"Those swords are sacred family relics." Argis looked as if she'd been slapped. "No Emoran would give one away, much less sell it."

"There seems to be a market for them," Tigh said.

"No one should even know they exist," Argis muttered.

"Just another piece in the puzzle," Jame said.

EVERY PARTICLE OF air in the room turned to ice. Tigh looked up from her customary place against the wall and stared into a pair of granite-hard nut-brown eyes of a woman on the back stairs. Shocked, she stumbled to her feet, trying to keep fear from closing around her dry throat.

The others twisted to see what had captured her attention. She was riveted on the tall, somberly dressed woman with flaxen hair, walking toward them. The woman's face was hardened into an arrogant smirk as she rested indolent eyes on Tigh. The women at the other tables cringed away as evil radiated in her wake.

"Well, well. If it isn't Tigh the Terrible," the woman said as she stopped in front of the back table. "It's been a long time, old friend."

Tigh tried to pull air into her lungs. "Meah. I don't understand."

An airy laugh escaped Meah's throat. "Oh, you mean this?" She held out her arms and looked down at herself like a girl showing off a new set of leathers. "Did you think they could really keep us cleansed?"

Sparkles of light danced in front of Tigh's eyes as she faced her worst nightmare. "You were cleansed. The cleansing doesn't just rub off."

"That's true." Meah nodded. "But it only masks the true warrior. It doesn't wash her away. A small dose of this," she held up a stone vial hanging on a chain around her neck, "makes a very effective soap."

Tigh focused on the vial. "You're uncleansing Guards that have been cleansed?"

"We're only setting things back to the way they should be." Meah's eyes flashed. "They rounded us up like animals and forced the cleansing on us."

"They were just fixing the damage they had made in the first place," Tigh said.

"They didn't damage us, they allowed us to find our true selves," Meah said. "I could have dosed you any time. Your food, your drink, even the water you bathed in. It only needs to touch your skin, you see. The really interesting thing is, it's harmless to anyone else. I didn't dose you because it's more fun for you to know that a sip of water, or a casual brush against a chair or table can bring back Tigh the Terrible in an instant."

The tension flowed out of Tigh, and she straightened to her full height. "You were never this cruel."

"Ah, now that's the really good part." Meah's face creased in a wicked grin. "We've discovered how to delve deeper into our true selves."

"True selves. You're either being deceived or are deceiving yourselves." Tigh put a low menacing edge to her voice. "Now that I know what's going on, the next time we meet, we'll dance to the old tunes."

Meah straightened and gazed at Tigh. "We'll be leading the dance together. It's a destiny that you won't be able to fight against."

She glanced at Tigh's tablemates, mock-bowed, and turned to leave the establishment. She flipped a coin to Wence, who stared at it for a heartbeat before pitching it into the fire.

JAME STUDIED HER companions as they worked on their reactions to Meah in their own ways. Argis sat in a bed with her head in her hands, as if trying to deal with facing pure evil for the first time in her life.

Seeran didn't hide that she was frightened beyond imagination, and her writing was shaky and blotched as she scraped her quill in a small journal.

Jame should have been as frightened as her companions, but all she could muster was confusion as she watched Tigh count out the silver on the wide stone windowsill, check through their supplies, jot down a few words on a scrap of paper . . . acting as if nothing out of the ordinary had just happened. She knew Tigh had been terrified of Meah. That woman was a walking nightmare that penetrated Tigh's deepest, darkest sleep, and she had trembled during the confrontation. Then the fear was gone. She felt the change in Tigh and had been momentarily panicked that the food she had just eaten contained the stuff in that vial.

"How could they have let such monsters fight for us?" Argis muttered to the floor.

"She was an archivist from the Maymi Peninsula," Tigh said while she repacked a saddlebag.

Argis lifted her head from her hands and stared at her. "You mean you were just threatened by a lunatic librarian?"

"No," Tigh said. "I was just threatened by a former member of the Elite Guard who seemed to resent the fact that society wanted her to go back to being a librarian."

"Exactly what did she mean by delving deeper into their true selves?" Jame asked.

"I think they're enhancing the enhancements that turned us into Guards," Tigh said in a steady voice, but Jame caught a flash of the haunted expression that had been common during their early days in Ynit. "You thought Tigh the Terrible was bad . . ." She walked to the window and stared out.

The other three exchanged uncertain glances.

Jame turned at a gentle knock sounded on the door. Tigh still looked out the window. Argis held her sword ready.

Wence slipped in as Jame opened the door. She swept a glance at Argis, who sheathed her sword, then rested her eyes on Tigh's back. "Pardon the intrusion. I just want to apologize for allowing that . . . person into this establishment. My initial instinct was to not let her in."

"You don't need to apologize," Jame said. "You had no way of knowing who she was or what she represented."

"I felt the evil from her," Wence said. "The times have been getting too strange for me not to be paying more attention to my instincts. That's why I need to tell you about the Lukrians. Three of them came here with three Emorans. They said the Emorans had started celebrating the festival a little early. I couldn't turn them away, but I fear they're up to no good."

Jame and Argis exchanged glances and chuckled.

"Forgive us, Wence," Jame said. "Our friend over there made sure the Lukrians received what was coming to them for helping our Emoran scouts. They'll be visiting Emoria as our special guests."

"How are you planning to get them out of the city?" Wence asked. "Lukrians have been a common sight in these parts of late. Rumor has it they come into the city for many more supplies than needed by their people."

Argis narrowed her eyes. "I've never known Lukrians to play fetch it for anyone."

"We're not talking about just anyone," Tigh said to the window.

"There have been whispers." Wence eyed Tigh.

"We've heard them," Jame said. "That's why we're here."

"Fighting fire with fire?" Wence nodded. "What about what that evil woman said? Your fire could become a part of their flame."

"That's not going to happen." Tigh turned from the window. "I've no doubt whatever is in that vial can do what she says it can, but everything she said about contact with it isn't true."

"How do you know?" Argis asked.

"We retained some residual skills from our enhancements. We know when someone is lying," Tigh said. "Only a part of what she said was true. The more troubling things were lies."

Jame relaxed a bit. "Such as being dosed by brushing against furniture."

"Yes," Tigh said. "What I don't understand is, she knew I knew she was lying."

"So the truth could be worse than the lie." A chill traveled up Jame's spine.

"Or she's just playing with my mind. It's something the Elite Guards took delight in." Tigh turned to Wence. "We're planning to hire a wagon to smuggle the Lukrians out of the city."

"Then let me offer my apology in the form of a wagon," Wence said. "My niece can help you drive it. It's time for her to see the home country."

"This may not be the best time for your niece to visit Emoria," Jame said. "We're on the verge of war with the Lukrians. There's also the rumored trouble in the mountains to worry about."

"My niece is sixteen. She's spent her life living and working in this establishment, longing to get out and see the world." Wence's gaze grew distant. "She's been talking about setting out on her own, and I can't keep her from doing that. Even with all the danger surrounding you and Emoria right now, she'd be safer with you than out on her own."

Jame exchanged a long look with Tigh and put a comforting hand on Wence's arm. "We'd be honored to have your niece accompany us."

Argis sighed. "I guess there are worse things than being pestered the whole trip by a warrior-worshipping adolescent."

JAME ALMOST LAUGHED at Argis's inscrutable expression. Emoran warriors were trained to endure the greatest discomforts, but the sight of a tall, healthy, young girl hanging on every word that Seeran muttered seemed to be more torture than Argis could stand.

From the moment the little band had set off early in the morning, Gelder, Wence's niece, had never moved from Seeran's side on the wagon seat. The girl couldn't stop asking questions about the University at Artocia and about the interesting life of a historian.

As they cleared the city gates and the endless camps of festival celebrants, Argis signaled the scouts to go out into the countryside.

"Try not to get caught this time," Tigh said, and was gifted with three hostile glares before the scouts slipped away from the road and vanished in a field of boulders and scrubby plants.

Argis almost smiled at the remark, Jame noted as she strode alongside Tigh who led Gessen by the reins behind the wagon.

A fur-hide tent over the wagon bed allowed the Lukrians to be tied to the wagon in a fairly comfortable sitting position. Argis was not happy with this arrangement, but Jame reminded her that she traveled with a peace arbiter, and the Lukrians were in her care until they were brought to justice.

"Oh, please, please. Describe the bards' competition." Gelder's excited voice cut through the soft grinding of the wagon wheels on the packed road.

Argis's scowl was matched by a muffled chorus of groans from the wagon bed. Tigh grinned, and Jame shook her head.

"We may have to take some time off their confinement for enduring this," Tigh breathed in Jame's ear. "They might even bring charges against Seeran for cruel torture."

"Argis is ready to beat up a roomful of historians," Jame whispered.

Tigh chuckled. "She's not used to unarmed competition."

Jame studied the wisps of dust that shot out from beneath each turn of the wagon wheels. "Lucky for you because they're going to make you give up your sword before entering Emoria."

"I figured as much." Tigh gazed at a mountain peak dancing above wispy layers of clouds.

"Only until I have a little chat with the Council." Jame laid a hand on Tigh's arm. "If they don't agree to everything I ask, we'll help with this problem—because it's a threat that goes far beyond Emoria—but we'll never set foot in Emoria again."

Tigh stopped walking. Jame waited for her response as inexpressible emotions flash across Tigh's face.

Tigh closed her eyes for a few heartbeats then opened them. "We'll talk more about this."

"I just wanted to make sure you understood how I feel." Jame searched Tigh's eyes. "We'll talk more—until you *do* understand."

The wagon stopped, and three sets of eyes looked back at them.

"I guess we're more interesting than the bards' competition," Tigh said.

"That's not saying much." Jame relaxed a bit.

Tigh draped an arm over Jame's shoulders, and they caught up to the wagon. She raised an eyebrow at Argis. "Taking a break?"

Argis rolled her eyes and lead the procession.

BY MID-AFTERNOON THE road started to follow the outer bank of foothills to the Phytian Mountains. The cooler air, despite the position of the sun, told Tigh they'd been climbing since midday. The arid land, painted with shades of scruffy browns relieved by rocky grays and whites, cast a somber mood over the little band. Even Gelder stopped talking.

Around the next curve, the scouts lounged on a boulder to the side of the road.

Poylin slid off the rock and strode to Argis. "There's a settlement in the next valley."

Argis stiffened. "An army? Raiders?"

"Farmers mostly, I think," Poylin said. "Families. Just moved here, by the looks of it."

"Why would anyone settle in a place like this?" Jame asked.

"The question is, what could be bad enough to force them to abandon their homes?" Tigh felt a chill that had little to do with the wind that whipped through the hills.

"They may be able to tell us more than rumors," Jame said. "The more we know, the better chance we'll have to defeat whoever it is in those mountains."

"I just want to go up there and fight until we're rid of them." Argis stomped the hardened road in frustration.

"If rogue Guards are behind this," Tigh pinned Argis with a stare, "there's one small factor to keep in mind. The secret behind the Elite Guards' victories had less to do with fighting skills than with out-thinking the opponent. We were masters of mental manipulation."

"So you think they're starting these rumors?" Jame pulled Tigh's attention away from Argis.

"Yes. The strongest weapon is fear."

Argis kept her tense demeanor for a bit longer before she relaxed. "I'll concede to your greater knowledge." She turned and continued down the road, not observing a puzzled Tigh and a smiling Jame.

Chapter 6

TIGH HAD ENCOUNTERED much in her travels but never had she felt such exhaustion and grief, hanging in the air so thick it seemed to drape the dismal jumble of rocks and animal hides that barely passed as shelters.

The five score inhabitants looked as if their souls had been ripped away along with any kind of hope. They were so encrusted with grime, the only way to tell man, woman, or child was by size and bearing.

Tigh peered into a stone well already going dry. Unless these people found other pockets of water, they'd have to move on.

"You never actually saw anything?" Jame asked Matlo, a tall man with thick shoulders.

"Only the fear and distrust growing in the eyes of our people." Matlo's expressive way with language was common to mountain folk—developed from the tradition of weaving imaginative tales far into the frozen winter nights.

"This cold feeling," Jame said. "It comes up from the ground?"

"In certain places it was so strong a step away from it was noticeably warmer. The evil was worse than the cold." Matlo shivered. "It felt as if Bal was punishing us for being too happy and satisfied with our lives. It was bad enough that it clung to these cold spots, but it began to affect how we looked at each other. Friends and families whose hearts were always open were suddenly closed with mistrust and unfounded anger. The only explanation we had were these sudden cold spots. As they spread and grew stronger, so did our anger and mistrust. When we were away from our valley, all those feelings simply vanished."

"You took water and food with you?" Tigh asked.

"Yes. All that we could carry." Matlo gazed at the men, who were slicing bits of whatever they could scrounge and putting them into three huge iron pots simmering over fires. "Wish we had some of that now."

"So it was just the cold spots that were causing your feelings of ill will." Tigh frowned and looked within herself, allowing the uneasy thought that something beyond rogue Guards was behind this mystery.

"It seemed that way, yes." Matlo turned at a shout from a small huddle of people further up the streambed. "I hope they found more water." He nodded to Tigh and Jame and trotted to his friends.

"What do you think?" Jame asked as she and Tigh sauntered back to their camp on the edge of the settlement.

"I think there's a missing piece to this puzzle." Something teased the outer tendrils of Tigh's mind. She forced her thoughts to a high class tavern in the city of Operal, which they had just taken at the point of her strategy and sword. They were long into their celebration of victory when one of the newer Guards spoke of improvements to their training—new ways of making them even more powerful and invincible. Even as Tigh walked in that wind-swept, barren valley, she could hear Patch Llachlan's ale-roughened voice echo through the tavern, demanding to know why they hadn't received these enhancements. The new recruit explained that there was a problem that hindered the Guards' legendary skills at stealth. Maybe the cold evil that flowed from Meah was more than just another trick the Guards used to spread fear before they conquered. It could be an unwanted aftereffect of the enhancements.

"Do you think these people are safe here?" Jame asked.

"They're as safe as any when this kind of evil is out and about," Tigh said as they entered their camp.

A fire ringed with rocks crackled in the cooling air. A cross-legged Seeran was showing an attentive Gelder how she devised her notes for her journal. The Emorans were sprawled out on the scrubby ground.

"Find anything?" Argis was stretched out with her hands behind her head and her ankles crossed.

Jame waggled her hand. "A little."

"I think the rumor that something is going on in the caverns below the mountains is correct." Tigh heard a soft impact on rock. She spun around. A Lukrian stood on a boulder some forty paces away. Something stung her shoulder. "What the . . . ?" She stared, stunned, at the thin reed protruding from her leathers.

Argis and the scouts sprang to their feet, ready to go after the Lukrian. Wild laughter wafted to them from the opposite direction. Meah stood close enough to be heard but far enough away to bolt if need be.

Tigh, feeling warmth—both familiar and awful—fill her veins, pulled the dart from her shoulder and threw it to the ground.

Meah just grinned and waited.

Jame let out a gasp. "Tigh!"

Tigh glanced back as Jame almost grabbed her arm.

Argis leapt forward and landed Jame hard on the stone-littered ground. She held onto a struggling Jame.

Tigh glared at Meah. "You're dead." She emitted an inhuman growl from deep within her psyche as the remnants of her cleansing was in tatters within her confused mind. She couldn't remember why she was angry with

Meah. How could she be angry with the person who freed the power within her soul?

Taunting laughter met her words, and Tigh hardened into granite resolve. This laughter alone was enough for her anger—for Tigh the Terrible's anger. Meah was a dead woman.

She couldn't help the malicious grin as she unsheathed her sword. She took a determined step forward. An anguished sob from behind compelled her to turn around.

Her companions gasped, and she swept her eyes over them with a sneer of contempt. The potion jolting through her blinded her to everything but the sweet surge of power.

"Tigh."

Jame's tear-strained voice stung her ears. She glared in the direction of the whimper and found pleading, heart-breaking emerald eyes, and she softened for a heartbeat.

She turned back to Meah, possessed with an irrational need to torture the laughing woman before striking the death blow. She tore after Meah, who never stopped laughing as she ran toward the hills.

TIGH CAUGHT UP with Meah in the deepest part of the second night of chase. To her befuddled mind she was sure Meah allowed herself to be approached. She stood in the middle of a high meadow, smirking at Tigh who stumbled toward her. The moonlight painted a chalky tint across the still grasses and sent ghostly flashes off Meah's armor and sword.

Tigh's mind spun, as it had for a full day, sending her body reeling to the ground. She growled in frustration at her unruly balance and sat clutching her head with both hands, willing the landscape to stop spinning. Someone was after her. No. She was after someone. That was it. She was angry at this person for some reason. Why was she angry?

She used her sword as a crutch and struggled to her feet. She was Tigh the Terrible. This person she chased was of no consequence or else she'd remember what had made her so angry. She straightened and took several steps before she saw the pale figure across the meadow.

"You'd better get out of my way," Tigh said, startled by the raspiness in her voice. "I'm not in a very good mood."

Meah's harsh laugh fell sour on Tigh's ears, and her elusive anger was renewed with startling vigor.

She lifted her sword and rushed toward the moonlit woman, but her only battle was with the world as it tumbled against her, and she landed on her back.

A cold shadow draped over her and a face she had once known in friendship leaned in close. "It's really too bad we voted not to invite you back into our fellowship." Meah's voice was thoughtful as she studied Tigh. "You were the best looking of the lot, I'll give you that." She placed long fingers on Tigh's chin, then jerked her head from side to side.

Tigh rolled onto her elbow as she tried to fight the dizziness and nausea.

Meah sat back and waited for Tigh's dry heaves to ease. "You know, you used to be a lot more fun in the middle of the night."

A sweat-soaked Tigh thumped onto her back. Her labored breathing caught in her dry throat. "What . . . voted."

"It's a simple thing." Meah ran a long blade of grass down the side of Tigh's face. "If you joined us, you'd insist on being in charge. Unfortunately, you've not been setting the right example lately. You've been playing at peace warrior like you believe it. If we enhanced you, you'd be more of a monster than we could ever handle."

"Peace warrior." Tigh scowled at the idea then realized that's what she was. *How had that happened?* A fair-haired young woman with sparkling green eyes stared down at her. Startled, she blinked. Meah, chewing on the blade of grass, studied her.

"They always said love ruined a Guard." Meah stood up. "If I see her, I'll be sure to tell her how you died." She stayed there a few heartbeats longer. "Goodbye, old friend."

THE LEATHER THONG Argis had tied to her belt three days earlier when Tigh had run off, whipped around the hilt of her knife in the capricious winds that plagued Atler Pass. She was prepared to hog-tie Jame if she tried to bolt or cause injury to herself. Her primary duty, now more than ever, was to get Jame safely to Emoria.

She stopped at a rough patch of stone and partly frozen mud and choked up on Gessen's reins. She guided the horse and her precious passenger around the treacherous area.

"Careful here," she called back to Poylin who led the gray and white mare and wagon through the pass. Seeran and Gelder clung to the wagon seat as it rocked and pitched over the rough ground.

Jame swayed with the motion of the horse.

Argis held the reins close to Gessen's muzzle and gazed at the mumbling Jame lost in her own world. She wanted to say something, do something. It took this terrible joke of Laur for her to face the truth that the Jame she once knew had fled with Tigh. And the Jame Argis always wanted her to be was gone as well.

To pass the time, Seeran taught Gelder some of the memorization techniques used by historians. The girl's earnest practice gave the others something to focus on.

The sun was low in the sky by the time the pass opened onto a high valley bordered on one side by a stand of trees. An overgrown track arched away from the road toward the woods. Argis paused at the branch and allowed some relief to wash over her. Home was just a day's walk from that spot.

They eased the wagon along the ragged track until they reached the small, diamond-clear lake just outside the edge of the trees, and a camp used by generations of Emorans.

The scouts built a fire and fetched water for the pot. Seeran, with Gelder's willing assistance, had taken over the cooking and prepared, as best she could, Ingoran-like dishes. Jame had tried to eat a few mouthfuls at each meal but she had no appetite. Argis knew better than to make her eat any more than she could. Jame had to work through her grief in her own way.

Argis cast a net into the clear waters of the lake and watched it sink beneath the surface. The crunch of boots on the fine-shelled shore dragged her black musings back to the task at hand.

"Jyac isn't going to be pleased." Poylin crouched next to her. "About any of this."

Argis nodded and pulled in the net. Two small fish wiggled in the thin ropes. She shook them onto a leather scrap. "This whole thing. It's much bigger than we thought. She won't be pleased, but she'll understand."

"But we don't have what we set out to get." Poylin ran a hand through unruly, sand-colored hair. "Not only don't we have the woman who could help us win, she's been turned to the other side."

Argis flung the net into the waters. "We still have Jame. She's lived and worked around the Guards, argued their cases for them, and witnessed the cleansing process."

"Helping us would be fighting Tigh." Poylin shook her head. "I don't think she can do that."

"She'll do it . . . for Emoria," Argis said.

"Maybe," Poylin said, "if she hadn't gotten a glimpse of Tigh the Terrible."

Argis stopped pulling on the net and turned to Poylin, who rose out of her crouched position. "Why would that make a difference?"

"From our point of view, we see an injured, tamed animal returning to the wild," Poylin said. "She sees an animal that she's tamed and can be tamed again."

Argis hauled in the forgotten net and liberated several more fish. "Jyac will get through to her," she said without much conviction.

The water lapping against the shore grew louder as the forest sounds around them died away. They turned to the camp, where all eyes were riveted on the darkened trees.

A woman stepped into the clearing, clad in ripped black leather, face streaked with dirt and sweat, hair scattered and wild.

Argis dropped the net, pulled her sword, and rushed toward Tigh. Jame swung her staff and knocked the sword out of her hand. She landed hard on the ground.

"Jame . . . no," Argis cried in frustration as she scrambled to her feet, but Jame was already within a few paces of Tigh who dropped to her knees.

JAME STOPPED RUNNING and stood as still as possible to let reality catch up with her. She studied the kneeling and passive Tigh and captured her eyes with her own. She had to push down her feelings and judge what was before her.

The grass crunched behind her from several pairs of running boots.

"Stay back."

"I beg you, Jame." Argis's voice cracked with frustration.

"If she was Tigh the Terrible," Jame gazed into the heart-breaking eyes staring back at her, "we'd all be dead by now."

The impact of the words dropped a hush over them.

Jame stepped forward until she gazed down at Tigh. She saw pain, agony, exhaustion, pleading, fear, trust . . . love. She saw Tigh in those eyes. She lifted her head in thanks to whatever deity heard her prayers.

TIGH STRIPPED OFF her dirty and torn leathers and plunged into the chilled waters of the lake. Her world felt right side up again as she pulled back onto the bank. Jame rubbed her damp skin with their drying rag and helped her into her spare set of black leathers. As Jame worked on the lace of the tunic, Tigh caught her attention by lifting her chin with a finger. She studied Jame's sallow cheeks and bloodshot eyes and realized they would suffer the same way—no matter the ordeal, together or apart.

"I'm sorry." Tigh choked as she was socked with a wave of grief. She had nearly lost this precious gift.

"I was going to save you." Jame's voice was raw but determined. "Whatever it took, I'd have done it."

Tigh tried to swallow but her throat was too dry. Anyone else would have done everything in her power to destroy her. She pictured Jame standing up for her and convincing the most unlikely allies to join her in a mad quest to redeem Tigh the Terrible again. She kissed Jame, letting action say those things that words could never touch. Jame's devotion was a balm for her battered psyche.

The smell of food simmering on the fire reminded Tigh that she hadn't consumed anything of substance in three days.

"Hungry?" She raised an eyebrow.

Overwhelming affection radiated from Jame's grin.

Jame filled a plate for herself and Tigh as the others helped themselves to the fish Seeran had prepared.

Tigh plowed through her food and felt much better once her stomach was full. She was surprised at how swiftly she recovered once the potion wore off.

She looked up at her expectant audience gathered around the fire with their plates of fish and flat bread. They had too many questions and concerns to put off until morning.

Argis watched her with unconcealed wariness.

"How did you find us?" Jame took Tigh's empty plate and put it on the ground.

"I chased her all the way to the meadow over there." Tigh nodded in the direction of the distant road.

"You mean we went right by you?" Jame asked.

"You'd have seen me if I hadn't moved into the trees," Tigh said. "Meah said she left me to die. I know now she wanted you to find me."

"Why didn't you die?" Argis arched an eyebrow.

Tigh gave her a long look, seeing a bit of compassion beneath the wariness. "I don't know. The answer probably lies with that dart."

Argis removed a soft cloth scrap from her belt pouch. The dart was tucked in the folds. "I thought the healers might be able to detect what's on it." She re-wrapped the thin reed and returned it to her pouch.

"Thank you for saving it," Tigh said.

Argis shot her a look, then nodded.

"So what exactly happened?" Jame asked.

"I chased after Meah for I don't know how long." Tigh tried to fit together the nightmarish images that flickered through her mind. "At least a day, I think. It was night when she finally stopped. Whatever is on that dart *did* turn me into Tigh the Terrible. It also made me dizzy and intoxicated. I kept forgetting what I was angry about, but she always reminded me with that laugh."

Jame frowned. "You were angry about being changed?"

Tigh glanced at Jame, then gazed at her restless hands. "I was angry because she dared laugh at me. The change was complete. It was as if I'd never been cleansed."

"But you're all right now." Jame tightened her grasp on Tigh's arm.

"I knew Meah was holding back on something in the safe house. I think the effects of this potion are short-lived."

Argis scratched her head. "They haven't found a way to change back permanently?"

Tigh sighed and wrapped an arm around Jame. "You have to understand this is all about mind games. Meah said she was leaving me to die but it could have been just a part of the game. Maybe she didn't give me the full potency, letting us think it isn't permanent. Maybe I really was meant to die, and my body was able to fight off the poison."

"Why play all these games?" Argis asked. "Why not come out of hiding and fight like true warriors?"

"Because the Elite Guards weren't true warriors," Tigh said. "We were scholars and archivists and librarians and lawyers and merchants . . . It's true we were trained to be warriors once we were recruited, but what made the Elite Guard all-powerful was what we brought to it from our lives before. Our ability to use our minds."

"How can we be sure the potion has worn off? Or that it won't cause flashbacks?" Argis asked.

"We can't be sure, but I don't think that would suit their purposes." Tigh studied her hands. "They don't want Tigh the Terrible. What I've done for the last few years would make me too powerful for them."

A wolf's howl sounded from the trees. Argis narrowed her eyes, then sounded a blue jay cry. A few heartbeats later, a pair of Emorans with mask-covered faces stepped into the clearing. They pulled away the masks, revealing relieved and smiling faces.

"Tas, Olet, what are you doing out here?" Argis stood and crossed her arms.

The young warriors approached the fire.

"We've been on the lookout for several days now," Tas said. She was small, bright-eyed with shaggy blonde hair. "My princess." She and Olet unsheathed their swords and touched the blades to their foreheads.

"Give me a proper welcome, you two." Jame laughed.

Tas and Olet sheathed their swords and embraced their old friend.

"This is Tigh."

"Well met, Tigh," Olet said.

"I'm still a bit sore from the last time we met." Tas rubbed her backside.

"Well met, Olet." Tigh grinned at Tas. "Your backside has a long memory."

"Is this just your usual impatience, Tas, or are you on the lookout for a reason?" Argis gave Tas a knowing look.

Tas shifted. "Well . . . uh . . . I mean, it's important to know when our princess is close to Emoria."

"Don't give her a hard time, Argis." Jame laughed.

Tas grinned. "Just like old times, eh?"

Chapter 7

JAME HELD THE soaked cloth to her face, hoping the cold water would shock away the apprehension she felt at returning to Emoria for the first time in six years.

"I'm the one who should be nervous," Tigh said.

Jame shrugged and pulled the cloth from her face. "I guess I just don't know when to stop sharing."

"It's all right for both of us to be nervous." Tigh gazed at the rippling lake. "As long as we deal with it together."

"It's not going to be easy for either of us," Jame said. "What's happened the last few days isn't going to help."

"It may have helped." Tigh rubbed her chin. "The worst has happened. I became Tigh the Terrible again and overcame it."

"That's only because the potion wore off," Jame said.

"We don't know that for sure," Tigh said.

"You mean you could have fought off the effects?" Jame asked.

"Meah *did* give me a powerful incentive to fight against it." Tigh picked up a smooth, flat stone and studied the quartz layers running through it.

"What kind of incentive?"

"She reminded me of the old warning that love ruined a Guard." Tigh cast an affectionate look at Jame. "As I lay there trying to work through my confusion, something kept pressing against my thoughts. I was Tigh the Terrible, but I couldn't completely give in to it. My feelings were tempered by something that hadn't been there before."

Jame placed a hand against Tigh's cheek. "Love."

Tigh nodded. "Yes. I guess that warning had some truth to it."

"But we don't know if that's the reason you're back to normal," Jame said.

"That's true," Tigh said. "But the way Meah said it makes me think there's something to it. She was never the same after her lover was killed."

Jame squeezed the excess water out of the cloth into the lake and watched the droplets form independent ripples overlapping each other. "There are too many questions and too many possible answers."

Angry shouts forced their attention to the camp. Olet, jaw set in defiance, was up against a tree with three swords pointed at her throat.

"You know," Tigh stood and held out a hand to Jame, "if your warriors keep trying to kill each other, we won't have an army to fight with."

Jame rolled her eyes and allowed Tigh to pull her to her feet. "Some things never change," she muttered as she strode past Argis and Tas, who had been engaged in a bit of sparring. Tigh followed, raising an amused eyebrow at Argis and Tas.

"Take it back, or we'll take you back in a sack," Poylin said to an unrepentant-looking Olet.

"Take what back?" Jame walked around the angry scouts, put a finger on the bottom side of Poylin's blade, and pushed it up and out of the way. The other two scouts lowered their swords, but continued to glare at Olet, who straightened and grinned back.

"She called us deaf lambs because those Lukrians got lucky." Poylin pointed an accusing finger at Olet.

"Three of our best scouts getting captured by Lukrians," Olet said. "Maybe you're not as good as you think you are."

Jame crossed her arms. "Maybe the Lukrians used a potion developed for the Elite Guard that immediately renders them unconscious."

"I've never heard of such a thing," Olet said.

"It's all too real and it can be put on the tip of a dart." Jame relaxed a bit. "Now I want the three of you to fill Tas and Olet in on how this potion seems to work. All of us must be aware of the tactics the Lukrians are using against us."

The five Emorans straightened but held back their urge to protest.

Tigh hid an amused smile. "She's going to make a great queen someday."

Argis spun on Tigh, and then caught herself. "Yes, she is."

"WE'RE GOING THROUGH there?" Seeran stopped the wagon and stared at the dense tangle of vegetation on the edge of a mountain meadow and thick woods huddled against a bluff.

The Emorans grinned as they grabbed the vegetation and revealed it was sown onto rough wooden screens. Behind these screens was a tunnel constructed of branches and vines.

"Clever," Tigh said from on top of Gessen.

"You haven't seen anything yet." Jame's amused voice vibrated through her back.

Gelder took the reins and steered the wagon through the tunnel, while Seeran studied the screens.

"We tend this entrance like we tend our gardens," Argis said. "It's as important to our survival as the food we eat."

"Are we in Emoria?" Gelder stared into the heavy woods, broken only by the well-kept track.

A dozen Emorans stepped into view among the trees, their gray and green leather armor blending them into the landscape. Three formidable warriors strode onto the track and blocked the wagon's passage.

Jame tightened her arms around Tigh's waist, and her breath came out short and angry.

"It's all right," Tigh whispered.

"No it's not," Jame said through gritted teeth.

Tigh threw her leg over Gessen's neck and landed easily, then turned to help Jame down.

Jame glared at Tigh, not even trying to hide her anger. She'd play the game for now, but she planned to give her aunt an earful about it.

Tigh handed Gessen's reins to a scout and guided Jame around the wagon until they stood next to Argis.

The warriors unsheathed their swords and pressed the blades to their foreheads in homage to their princess. Tigh's sword hissed against the scabbard as she unsheathed it. The stillness was as tight as a bowstring. She turned to Argis and offered her the black-bladed sword.

Argis grasped the sword and held it aloft by the hilt and blade. One of the warriors stepped forward, and Argis delivered the sword to her. The Emorans then faded back into the woods.

Gelder broke the thoughtful silence. "Why did they take your sword?"

"I haven't been accepted by the Emorans as a friend, much less as a life partner to their princess," Tigh said. "An outsider has to earn the privilege to hold weapons in Emoria."

Gelder frowned a little. "It doesn't seem fair."

"Traditions come from a need to ensure survival. These kinds of precautions have allowed Emorans to survive through long generations." Tigh raised an eyebrow at Jame.

Jame took a deep breath. "I don't agree with the traditions in this particular case, but sometimes we must follow them for the greater good of the country."

Tigh's eyes sparkled, and she gave Gelder a ghost of a wink. "The sooner we get to Emor, the sooner you can work to amend these traditions."

IF COUNTRIES ARE a reflection of what threatens from outside their borders, then Emoria was a study in isolationism, Seeran mused. The route to the heart of the country was a series of concealed tunnels through narrow outcrops of stone and cleverly laid out trails that wound around rugged boulder-strewn landscapes.

They emerged from a shallow tunnel and entered a narrow, grassy valley with a rocky creek meandering through it. White cliffs climbed to great heights on all sides. The wall on the narrowest end of the valley was pocked with irregular openings, the largest fronted by cups of protruding rock. Two or three masked heads were just visible over the lips of these cups. Light from the late afternoon sun stretched long across the valley and spiked off the sword hilts and armor of the Emorans lining the uneven crest of the wall.

Seeran forgot to urge the patient pony forward, and the wagon crunched to a stop. Both she and Gelder, as if captured in a spell, gaped at the majesty of the outer wall of the city of Emor. Only the scant whisper of rumor spoke of Emor as being a city of stone, which was often dismissed as wild exaggeration. As had happened many times on this journey, the impartial recorder of places and events was abandoned, and a dreamlike haze settled over Seeran.

Without a word, Argis tugged on the horse's bridle and led the wagon down the well-maintained road.

STILL ATOP GESSEN, Jame looked around Tigh's arm at the place she called home. Stricken with another bout of apprehension, she fought the urge to beg Tigh to stop. The only thing that kept her going was how it would look if she showed anything but joy at returning to Emoria.

She had no problem feeling joy and pride as Tigh stared spellbound at the tenable wall of stone. She knew Tigh's military mind admired the details of it, down to the positioning of the entrance tunnel tucked to one side rather than dead center. It forced the enemy to be cornered with high walls on two sides. The outer bluff wall next to the entrance had pockets of hiding places Jame knew were equipped with arrows and throwing stones.

Argis stopped the wagon, returned the reins to Seeran, and signaled her to wait. She caught Tigh's eye. Tigh walked Gessen over to her.

"Please do your people honor and let them see you," Argis said to Jame. "Give them a tale to pass on to future generations."

"Why is this different from any other time I've visited home?" Jame asked, puzzled.

"Your presence gives us more than hope. It gives us the confidence we need to survive this latest threat to our existence," Argis said.

"I'm not the one they should be greeting as their savior," Jame said.

Tigh twisted to face her. "Argis is right."

"No, Tigh. Don't try to rationalize this," Jame said.

"If we succeed in beating down these rogue Guards, future generations will sing songs of the youthful exploits of a legendary queen," Tigh said.

Jame shook her head. "Just one of many ordinary queens."

"I don't think so," Tigh said. "It's your uniqueness that'll distinguish you from the other queens."

Jame put a hand on Tigh's arm. "They'll remember us both—if we succeed."

"Fair enough." Tigh swung her leg over Gessen's neck and landed next to a puzzled-looking Argis.

Tigh handed the reins to Jame and gave her a dazzling smile.

Unable to resist, Jame grinned back. She then raised her eyes to the walls crowded with Emorans and was possessed by the wild jolt of freedom she had felt when she rode her pony across the valley as a child.

"Give them something to cheer about," Tigh said.

Something tickled the child within Jame. The long dormant Emoran princess burst through with all the joyous memories of magical summer days.

Jame danced Gessen off the road into the shallow grasses as cheers filled the hollow with endless cascading echoes. Hundreds of swords flashed in the amber fingers of the dying sun. She resisted the impulse to gallop the restless horse to the city wall and took the time to etch the images and sounds into her memory. She knew this elation would fade back to a mundane reality. All the more reason to treasure this rare bit of joy.

Her feelings of apprehension gone, Jame, atop a war horse, cantered forward to the endless cheers of her people.

ARGIS AND TAS, caught in the euphoria, laughed and flashed their swords in the long tendrils of sunlight. The scouts and Olet, who had settled their differences during the trek in, loped through the grasses in Jame's wake, whooping and cheering her on.

Argis glanced around and then stared puzzled at Tigh, who stood as if in a trance. Her eyes, focused on Jame, glistened with pride and unshed tears.

"What?" Tas turned and followed Argis's gaze.

"I can't figure her out," Argis said.

"I can." Tas grinned. "Jame is her whole world."

Argis scowled. "It's not as simple as that. A warrior just doesn't give up what it takes to be a warrior. And I know she still has what it takes."

"She follows Jame, not the other way around," Tas said. "I don't know of many warriors who would do that. We're too stubborn and proud. The question is, does this make her stronger or weaker in a fight?"

"I guess we're going to find out," Argis mumbled as she signaled Seeran to start the wagon moving.

Years earlier, Jame had asked if she'd be willing to give up her life in Emoria to be with her as she pursued her arbiter career. She couldn't even respond to what she thought was an unreasonable question. Now she realized her stubborn selfishness and pride helped drive away the one thing she had wanted most in her life.

Seeran and Gelder stared open-mouthed at the spectacle on the wall of Emor. As the shadows thickened, torches blazed to life like overgrown fireflies, crisscrossing the wall and highlighting the women. The wall looked as if it had taken on a coat of living fire and shadows as all the concealed crevices and pockets of stone overflowed with masked, cheering Emorans. Still enraptured by the sight, Seeran shook the reins, and the wagon rumbled after the returning princess.

Tigh blinked as the wagon in front of her crunched in movement. She wiped away the tears with her sleeve and turned to Argis and Tas.

"Don't let the other warriors catch you crying," Argis said.

Tigh leveled an impassive gaze at Argis. "I don't cry in battle."

Argis straightened. "Emoran warriors don't cry. Ever."

Tigh raised an eyebrow. "Then fortunately for me, I'm not Emoran."

"That'll change if Jame has her way." Argis watched the capering horse and rider, the cheers a rhythmic chant of Jame's name.

"Then you'll have at least one Emoran warrior who cries." Tigh turned her attention to Jame's reactions to the chanting of her name. Jame danced Gessen around several times as if not quite believing her ears.

Argis stared in disbelief at the response of her people to Jame's return. The last time the valley had echoed with the chants of a princess's name had been seven hundred years earlier, when Hekolatis returned as the hero of Balderon. "How does she do that?"

Tigh grinned. "She's Jame. She can't help it."

Tas cocked her head at Tigh. "The Jame we knew used to draw people to her with her quiet, reasonable nature and her ability to tell stories."

Tigh shrugged. "Jame's an arbiter, she's used to taking charge. And it comes naturally to her because people are drawn to her. It's a gift."

"I thought the taking charge part was your job." Argis flicked a curious glance at Tigh.

"My job is to make sure the defendants—and sometimes their friends— behave themselves," Tigh said. "Peace warriors keep the peace, nothing more."

"If you say so." Argis increased her pace to catch up with the wagon.

JYAC DIDN'T KNOW what to think of this young woman trotting toward the wall. She'd been prepared to see the idealistic young girl who lived and breathed bringing peace and justice to the world. What she saw now was an Emoran princess. Even the foreign, well-worn clothing couldn't conceal the confidence and maturity in her bearing.

"What do you think?" Sark, Jyac's Right Hand, stood with her arms crossed and gazed over the valley. She had to raise her voice to be heard over the roaring, rhythmic cheers around them.

"I think life outside has changed my niece." Jyac turned to Sark. "But not necessarily in the ways we thought."

"Is that good or bad?" Sark raised a fair eyebrow, her light blue eyes twinkling in the direct light of the dying sun.

Jyac stretched her shorter, stockier body a little taller to watch Jame canter close to the wall. The studious girl she remembered wasn't visible in the laughing young woman prancing her horse down the length of the wall, setting off an echoing wave of cheers.

Yet, even in the midst of this show, the unassuming and self-deprecating Jame bubbled forth. The shock and surprise on her face when the Emorans chanted her name was genuine. Dancing the horse in circles as if to say, "Who me?" endeared her to her people even more.

Jame's eyes captured Jyac's as she paused in the cleared chalk-white ground. She replaced her delighted grin with a mature thoughtfulness and saluted Jyac with her staff.

Jyac pulled her sword from its scabbard on her back and returned the salute, setting off another roar of noise. The seriousness she remembered flitted across Jame's face before her attention returned to the chanting crowd.

"I think it's a good thing." Jyac felt more hopeful than she had in a long time.

Chapter 8

JAME DREW GESSEN up to the gaping, shallow tunnel into the city. She twisted around looking for Tigh and could barely make out the shadowed form of the wagon, too far away for her to wait. The traditional six-guard royal escort emerged from the tunnel, and a horse wrangler grabbed Gessen's bridle.

Jame realized nothing less than full ceremony was expected from her. She swung off the tall warhorse, the crunch of her hard-soled boots on the ground a contrast to the whisper of the Emorans' soft soles.

"Thanks, Gessen." She ran her fingers through the horse's coarse mane.

Gessen snorted and nodded. A horse handle grabbed her bridle.

"Take good care of her," Jame said.

"With pleasure, my princess." The handler grinned as she led Gessen toward the stables.

"My princess." The lead guard saluted, and the others snapped into formation.

Jame stepped between the two rows of guards. Before they disappeared into the torch-lit tunnel, she glanced back for a glimpse of Tigh. The darkness now hid even the wagon. She straightened and pushed away the last remnants of apprehension and entered her home after too long an absence.

She forgot how bright Emor was at night and shielded her eyes. The brightness was not so much from the number of torches lit in celebration, as it was from generations of study in the art of reflective light. The white rock was polished to near transparency around the torch sconces and in odd spots that reflected the sparking flames.

Emor was indeed a city of stone, carved in a horseshoe of bluffs rising high off the valley floor. The natural pocking of the soft stone served as an enabler for chambers and outcroppings connected by trails a little less treacherous than those frequented by mountain goats. Color tumbled from every possible crevice and ledge as fresco murals of legendary Emorans and their feats popped out of the shadows like giants.

Jame blinked away the sting of tears as her eyes adjusted to the brightness and tried to grasp the spectacle before her. Every place that could support a person, and some that really couldn't, was occupied by shouting women. Her ears popped from the pounding echoes in such an enclosed space. She finally focused on the woman who stood apart from a loose half-circle of Elders in the center of the main square.

Jyac still possessed the hard, muscular body of a warrior, even with a few lines etched around her eyes and the gray-streaked, golden hair. At that distance, Jame could determine if there was the telltale tightening of displeasure about Jyac's jaw. It had been the only way she knew she was in trouble as a child. Much to her relief, she saw nothing but delight and acceptance as Jyac stepped forward.

The royal guard backed away, allowing their queen and princess some privacy.

"Well met, Jame," Jyac said.

"Well met, my queen." Jame touched her staff to her forehead, then lowered it and grinned.

"You look well." Jyac grabbed Jame in a joyous hug and shouts and cheers cut through the night.

"I'm sorry I stayed away so long." Jame faltered from a wave of guilt.

Jyac pulled away and held Jame by the shoulders. "You did what you had to do. I see that now."

Jame turned at the sound of wagon wheels and stifled a grin at Seeran's and Gelder's stunned expressions as they goggled at the city and the spectacle of thousands of Emorans.

"We have Lukrian prisoners," Jame said.

"Really. How'd that happen?" Jyac asked.

"Long story." Jame rested her eyes on the one sight she'd been aching for since entering the city.

Tigh, blinking away the temporary blindness from the city brightness, emerged from the tunnel with Argis and Tas on either side of her.

"I know we have some things to talk about," Jyac said in Jame's ear, "but that can wait until tomorrow—after I've met your life companion and spent some time with her."

"That's all I ask for," Jame said. "Don't judge her before you know her."

She trotted to Tigh and nodded to Argis and Tas as they continued on to greet their queen. "It took you long enough to get here."

"You were the one on Gessen," Tigh said with puppy dog innocence.

Jame grinned and grabbed Tigh's arm. She pulled her into the circle of Elders, who had formed a tighter arc around the queen.

"Closing ranks?" Tigh asked.

"Just for show," Jame said. "Makes them feel important."

"If you say so," Tigh muttered.

Before Jame could utter the traditional introduction, Jyac stepped forward. "Well met, Tigh of Ingor."

"Well met, Jyac, Queen of Emoria." Tigh gave Jame a surprised glance.

"Thank you," Jame whispered.

She couldn't believe Jyac had greeted Tigh as if she were an invited guest and sending a pointed message to the Council and the rest of Emoria. Tigh still had to prove she was a worthy consort, but recognition was a good start.

"I see the changes in you. They're not what we expected," Jyac said. "Perhaps we've been hasty in our judgment of your life and companion." Her gaze lingered on Tigh who stood in deference to Jame. "I hope these changes don't include your appetite."

"Uh, no. I'm starving." Jame gave the polished cobblestones a sheepish look.

"That's good because the cooks have been working for days on those Ingoran dishes." Jyac laughed at Tigh and Jame's surprised expressions. "Come. We have much to catch up on."

The cheering rose up as they walked across the square to the palace caverns. It'd be long toward morning before the last echoes of celebration faded away.

THE ATTEMPT AT Ingoran food wasn't bad, but Tigh could never figure out why cooks thought they had to make up for the lack of meat with too many herbs and spices. She mentally took inventory of their mint supply in case the spicier concoctions bothered her later.

She re-crossed her long legs as she half-listened to Jame explain how they had acquired three Lukrian prisoners. She had spent most of the evening fending off an uncharacteristic exhaustion by studying the intimate eating chamber. This part of the palace cavern was near the top of the bluff, allowing odd glimpses of the outside through thin sheets of quartz filling in natural and a few unnatural chinks in the rock. The smooth-walled room had a circle of leather and cloth cushions with a low-lying wooden bar arcing in front of them. The entrance was cleared of both cushions and bar, where food could be delivered from the middle of the room to each woman. A small fireplace behind Jyac and Jame produced enough warmth for the cool cavern.

She snapped out of her hazy musings when she noticed everyone was looking at her.

Jame smiled. "I don't think you'll be giving away any big secrets by telling them how you knew when Argis passed by the door, since they know she'd have noticed if it had been open even a crack."

Tigh mentally thanked Jame and grinned at her expectant audience. "That's an easy one. I knew Jame would go barging ahead, so I just listened for a frustrated noise and hurried footfalls."

"Barging ahead, huh?" Jame squinted at Tigh with mock indignation. Tigh gave her an innocent look.

The others laughed.

"I see some things never change," Jyac said.

"Fortunately, Jame seems to be in the right hands for keeping her out of trouble," Ronalyn said.

Tigh was rather intrigued by this gentle dark-haired woman with soft brown eyes who, as Jyac's life companion, helped raise Jame.

"I don't get into trouble," Jame said. "We get into some interesting situations sometimes."

"Enough adventures for many long evenings of entertainment, I suspect," Jyac said.

Tigh stifled a yawn and flashed an apologetic look at Jyac.

"Tigh has had a hard few days, but that's a tale left for the light of day I think," Jame said.

"Eiget." Jyac raised her voice, and a muscular guard stepped into the doorway. "Please, escort our guest to her chamber."

Tigh looked at Jame.

Jame kissed her on the cheek. "Go rest. You're safe here."

Tigh smiled, then rose from the cushions. "Thank you for the fine meal, Queen Jyac."

"Thank you for bringing Jame back to us," Jyac said.

"Jame makes her own choices about where she wants to go. I only follow." She locked eyes for a heartbeat with a startled Jyac then stepped around the cushions and Sark on the way to the door.

Eiget kept glancing back at Tigh as she strode ahead of her. Tigh could only imagine the stories about Tigh the Terrible that were whispered after torches were extinguished in the barracks. Unfortunately, most of them were true.

She tried to pay attention to the maze of short corridors but a hazy aura remained draped over her brain.

A thick-muscled warrior entered the corridor and faced them with arms crossed. Stone-faced Eiget stepped behind Tigh, who stopped and waited.

The warrior made a show of looking Tigh up and down. She shot her hand out at Tigh to within a breath of her face. A braid of leather dangled from her fingers.

Without breaking eye contact with the warrior, Tigh took the braid.

The warrior sneered. "You look like you have as much backbone as a newborn lamb. It will be a pleasure making you whimper on the sparring fields tomorrow." She flicked one last look of disdain at Tigh and disappeared into the chamber she had come from.

Tigh tucked the braid into her belt and followed Eiget through a series of short shafts that jagged between small chambers. As they turned to cut through a sitting room, a warrior with streaming blonde hair and an impressive scar across the cheek blocked the opposite opening.

Tigh sighed and stepped up to the woman.

The warrior scowled and pelted the braid at Tigh, who caught it as it bounced off her chest. Then she turned and stomped through the opening.

Tigh tucked the braid into her belt next to the other one and flashed Eiget a quizzical look.

Eiget shrugged. "She's young."

Tigh entered the airy chamber that had been Jame's childhood refuge with sixteen leather braids dangling from her belt. Exhaustion overtook curiosity, and she piled the braids onto a side table. Jame would explain it to her tomorrow. She tugged off her tunic and boots and collapsed onto the bed.

JAME STOOD, HANDS on hips, bathed in the warm amber that streamed into the chamber from the torches that lined the outer corridor. Tigh was splayed out on the bed, still in her light shirt and leather leggings. She was so deep in sleep she didn't even twitch when the door opened and closed.

Jame picked the boots and tunic up off the floor. She scanned the carved out shelves that dominated a wall for a place to put Tigh's clothes and realized everything seemed to be as she had left them the last time she had visited. All her childhood trinkets and scrolls sat neatly where she herself had put them. She'd forgotten them but they hadn't forgotten her. An ache for that lost innocence crept over her, along with the knowledge she had never allowed a proper farewell to her life in Emoria.

She folded the tunic and put it on top of a pile of leathers she probably last wore when she was twelve. She stared at the heap of braids on a small table. She sorted through the bits of leather, recognizing, even after so many years, some of the designs woven into them with thick, colored thread. She counted them and glanced back at Tigh. Somehow she'd thought this wouldn't happen. Maybe she'd been kidding herself that Tigh would be treated differently from any other warrior.

Jame rummaged through their saddlebag and pulled out their sleeping shirts. She slipped out of her travel clothes and eased the soft woven shirt over her head, sighing at the warm comfort of it. She then sauntered over to the bed and studied the sprawled spectacle of long arms and legs.

The only time Jame had seen Tigh overcome with exhaustion was when she had caught a terrible cold, and they were laid up for a week in a dismal inn on the edge of nowhere. She pushed fearful thoughts from her mind, unlaced Tigh's leggings, and tugged at the snug leather.

"There's a beautiful woman undressing me. Should I be awake for this?" Tigh asked.

Jame gazed at Tigh with affection, and sleepy eyes blinked back at her. She pulled the leggings off, then crawled up the bed until she hovered over Tigh.

"How are you feeling?" She noted the lethargy and unfocused eyes.

"Tired," Tigh breathed out.

Jame ran a finger down Tigh's cheek, finding her skin cool. No fever, at least. "Do you think it's that potion?"

"Probably." Tigh closed her eyes in response to Jame's soothing touch. She opened them, and Jame was relieved to see a little more alertness there. "It's still working its way out of my body."

"I hope so." Jame brushed her lips against Tigh's. She realized this was the first time they'd been alone since rescuing Seeran. "Come on. Sit up, so I can get you out of that disgusting, dirty shirt."

"You certainly know how to sweet talk a girl." Tigh waggled her eyebrows as Jame pulled her up.

Jame knew Tigh's mild joking was a defense against feelings of uncertainty about the cause of the thick drowsiness. Tigh could barely lift her arms as she tried to free the shirt from her body.

"Let's get this on you." Jame pulled the clean shirt over Tigh's head and then one arm at a time. Unable to resist, she gathered Tigh into her arms, reacquainting her senses to the intoxication she always felt when she held her. It had been a long time, and her soul hungered for this closeness like her body craved food.

"What are those braids for?" Tigh mumbled against Jame's hair.

Jame heaved a sigh. "They're challenges."

"I gathered that." Tigh's breath tickled Jame's ear. "A serious challenge or a warriors-will-be-warriors kind of a challenge?"

Jame shook with laughter. "It's a kind of initiation. The typical backhanded compliment. They insult you to your face so you'll fight them. Then they'll only show you respect and accept you as one of their own if you beat the leathers off them."

Tigh nodded against the top of Jame's head. "It'll be a nice workout. I haven't had one in a while."

Jame raised her head and gazed at Tigh with affection. "Oh, you'll have fun all right. I just hope it'll help change the Council's mind about you."

"Uh, that reminds me." Tigh rubbed Jame's back. "They took away my sword. That might make the challenges a little one-sided."

"That's right, isn't it?"

"Why don't you take care of all the details and just tell me when and where I have to fight." Tigh brushed her lips against Jame's cheek.

Jame sighed. "That means I'll have to face the Council first thing in the morning."

"Just remember. You're not a young girl anymore." Tigh captured Jame's eyes. "You're an experienced arbiter. You've successfully argued the most difficult cases and have judged countless others."

"I know. My brain tells me this is what I do all the time, but this is different. I'm going to be arguing my own heart and my own happiness." Jame nuzzled against Tigh's muscular shoulder. "Just like I did when I was your arbiter."

"All the more reason why you'll win." Tigh put her chin on top of Jame's head. "No one can resist your impassioned arguments."

"I can always use tears." Jame smiled into the shoulder.

"It works on me every time." Tigh looked down. "Come on. Let's get under the blankets and get some sleep. Everything will be clearer in the morning."

DOZENS OF SOFT footfalls reached the edge of Tigh's dreamless sleep. She popped her eyes open. Sunlight filtered in through the quartz-covered crevices in the ceiling and . . . twelve spearheads were aimed at various parts of her body at close range. She remained frozen, staring at her masked, steadfast captors.

"Um, Jame." Tigh flexed the arm where Jame's head rested. She glanced at Jame, who was curled up on her side in contented sleep. "Jame!"

Jame's eyes fluttered opened and cast a curious look at Tigh. Her expression turned to puzzlement as she sensed that they weren't alone. She raised her head and blinked at the dozen figures surrounding the bed. With spears. Pointed at Tigh.

"What are you doing?" She rolled over and sat up.

"Defending the honor of our princess," the woman closest to Tigh's head announced with great dignity.

"Gindor. We're joined." Exasperated, Jame held her head in her hands.

"Only an Emoran joining is recognized within these walls." Gindor straightened to her full height, which was only a bit taller than Jame, and brought her spear to within a hand's span of Tigh's throat.

Tigh gave Jame an anxious glance.

"If that were true, why wasn't Tigh given another chamber last night?" Jame leveled a steady gaze at Gindor.

"The queen has always been too soft when dealing with you." Gindor returned Jame's gaze. "She let you study and pursue a life away from home because she could never deny you anything."

"That's not true," Jame said. "I fought to be allowed to follow my dream. And it's not my fault we weren't joined in an Emoran ceremony." She glared at the circle of women, a few avoided her eyes.

"We make our decisions for the greater good of our people," Gindor said. "We never expected you'd go against our wishes that you not be joined to this person."

"So you feel you can burst in here and arrest her for an archaic law that defends the honor of royal offspring?" Jame asked. "Someone I've shared my life with for nearly six years, and have been joined to for almost as long?"

The twelve straightened, never wavering in the positions of their spears.

"Yes," Gindor said.

Tigh turned her head to Jame. "Tell me again why it was a good idea to come here."

Jame ran a hand through her hair. "At least let us get dressed before you go through with this foolish charade."

"That's not the custom—" Gindor began.

"Custom?" Tigh shot a look at Jame.

"It's customary to parade the couple through the streets as they are found—usually naked," Jame said. "In this case, I don't think anyone will be surprised to discover we're sleeping in the same bed." She glared at the surrounding women.

"Let her up," Gindor said and the others stepped away from the bed, keeping their spears at the ready.

Tigh rolled her eyes, then gave Jame a questioning look. Jame squeezed her hand.

Tigh tossed back the blankets and eased her long, bronzed legs out over the edge of the bed. Keeping an eye on the spears, she stood and gave her shoulders a shake to settle the shirt that clung to, rather than draped, her upper thigh.

Twelve sets of eyes took in her tall, muscular body as she shook the hair out of her eyes, now focused and alert.

"Get dressed," Gindor said.

Jame climbed out of bed and padded to their saddlebags. She pulled out Tigh's softer set of leathers and handed them to her. As Tigh dressed, she rummaged the shelves for her Emoran leathers.

FOUR OF THE elders stepped into the corridor. Gindor signaled Jame and Tigh to follow them.

"They're not really going to parade us through the streets, are they?" Tigh fell into step beside Jame.

"I wouldn't worry too much if they do." Jame leaned close to Tigh's ear. "Everyone celebrated far into the night. I'd be surprised if the morning bell ringer is even awake."

The narrow, inner corridor emptied into the main gallery, and the four of elders who trailed behind, moved forward, two on either side of Jame and Tigh. As Jame predicted, the palace was unusually empty for that time of day.

Jame reacquainted herself with the openness of the main gallery and the chambers that flowed into it. The section of the palace they strode through lined the outer bluff wall. Fine-crafted panels of quartz, twice the height and width of a woman, lined the wall, forcing rainbows of light to dance across the polished stone floor.

They stepped out of the palace, and Jame adjusted her eyes to the dim early morning light. Full daylight reached the sheltered valley for only a few sandmarks a day.

Before they had a chance to progress across the square, a line of masked women stood, arms crossed, in front of them. Gindor eyed the newcomers with puzzlement and planted herself in front of the little procession.

"What's that about?" Tigh asked.

"Well . . ." Jame studied the women who stood in defiance before them. "It could be good or it could be bad."

Tigh shot her an exasperated look.

"What do you want?" Gindor demanded.

Argis stepped forward from the middle of the line, reached over her shoulder, and unsheathed her sword. "You're here to defend the honor of our royal princess. We're here to defend the honor of her life companion."

Never in Jame's life had she experienced a silence so profound or so satisfying. She thought back to another square. The prediction of a great Emoran warrior saving Balderon from being conquered again flashed clear in her mind as she watched Argis stand tall and defiant in front of the Council.

"Very well." Gindor's voice reflected an uncharacteristic lack of force.

The line of young Emorans moved aside to allow the Council to pass, and then fell into place behind them.

Tigh nudged a stunned Jame. "Is this good?"

"It's the most amazing thing I've ever witnessed." For the first time that morning Jame let a radiant sparkle lighten her mood.

Chapter 9

ARGIS STOOD IN the back of the Council chamber wondering, now that reality slapped her in the face, what possessed her to do this. She studied the tapestries hanging from the ceiling of the overturned bowl-shaped cavern and wanted to kick herself. She didn't have the oratory skills or even a compelling reason to defy tradition. All she understood was the absurdity of treating Jame like a cloistered princess and Tigh as nothing more than an ardent suitor. Her brief journey outside of Emoria brought home how narrow a world the Council draped around them.

Argis studied Jame, standing next to Tigh in the defendants' box, and had no doubt she could convince just about anyone of anything. But the Council wasn't just anyone. They clung to the old ways like a newborn to a mother, never accepting any reason as good enough to be weaned away.

She didn't have Jame's skill to stand up to the Council, but she remembered what Jame had told her when they'd been younger, when she had to defend Tas, who had gotten into trouble over a harmless prank. She had lamented that nothing she said would make any difference in saving Tas from punishment. Jame's response was—wise beyond her years—that sometimes just showing up made a difference. Astonishingly enough it had. The loyalty Argis showed to Tas, combined with the Council's respect for Argis as a future warrior, helped reduce Tas's punishment to a warning.

She glanced at Tas next to her and at Olet and the scouts, and realized just their presence made a statement more eloquent than any well-composed speech. Besides, Jame had flashed that radiant smile at her. That alone made the risks of defying the Council well worth it.

The Council lowered aged bones onto the cushioned chairs around a half moon table. The defendants' box, little more than a rectangle of ankle-high stones, was centered in front of the straight edge of the table. The black-bladed sword was on the table in front of Gindor.

Jame and Tigh gazed at the sword and exchanged glances.

The Council members pulled off their masks, revealing various shades of gray to white hair and strong faces lined with age. Gindor, seated at the center of the table, had white hair, but her face was almost smooth with large blue-gray eyes.

"It seems you've picked up some unexpected defenders." Gindor gazed at Tigh. "I'm surprised Argis thinks you have a right to pretend to be a joined couple."

"They're not pretending," Argis said, before remembering where she was.

She then re-gathered her resolve to defend Tigh. She pulled off her mask, strode around the table, and stood next to Jame who greeted her with a reassuring smile. Tigh's expression reflected curiosity, nothing more.

Argis was surprised to see a shocked fear in the Council's eyes.

"Maybe we should just let it be." Riglan, a thin, wrinkled woman with a long braid of gray hair, turned to Gindor.

"Coincidence," Gindor said. "We're letting our imaginations get the best of us."

Argis exchanged puzzled glances with Jame and Tigh.

"But what if it's real?" Poag's face creased in concern.

A low, hollow sound penetrated the stone. The shocked silence lasted a couple of heartbeats.

Argis rushed to the door with her small defiant band behind her.

POAG GASPED. "BY the waterfalls of Laur, it's happening."

Tigh grabbed Jame's arm. "What's going on?"

"It's the alarm—most likely an attack of some kind," Jame said.

Tigh stepped out of the box and strode to the table, eyes penetrating Gindor's soul as she could only stare back at her. She picked up her sword, then cast a glare around the half circle of women, daring them to utter a word. She was met with eyes wide with uncertainty and skin that matched the chalky walls around them.

Jame put a hand on Tigh's back, getting her attention. "Be careful."

"Always. You stay here." Tigh held Jame's eyes long enough to make sure she wouldn't fight her on this.

Jame nodded and brushed her lips against Tigh's.

Tigh pulled Jame into a brief hug and ran past the stunned Council into the square.

A wall of mist soaked her leathers. In the high mountain valleys, the weather was as changeable as an Emoran's mind, so the saying went. She squinted through the swirling fog, impressed by the activity where only a short time before was a silent emptiness. She spotted Argis in front of a small fountain at the center of the square, organizing the warriors who were still half asleep and pulling on their leathers and weapons.

Through the pockets of mists hovering against the bluff walls, Tigh could see the browns, grays, and greens of Emoran leather streaming up the narrow trails like huge mottled snakes. That meant the threat came from the forested lands stretching away from the tops of the bluffs.

"Tigh!" Argis waved Tigh over to her.

"What's going on?" Tigh asked.

"An army of Lukrians has made camp in the first meadow beyond that line of trees." Argis nodded upward. "They just appeared there this morning. Patrols and guard outposts extend to the edge of our territory, yet the first word we heard of the Lukrians was from an inner patrol—just now."

"What do you mean 'camp'?"

"Tents, fires, hundreds of warriors." Argis waved her arms. "Impossible is an understatement for Lukrians to enter Emoria and take over an open meadow without being seen."

"What about the outposts?" Tigh asked.

"We've sent runners out to them." She caught a series of reflected flashes from the top of the bluff and turned to Tigh. "Need your scabbard?"

Tigh loosened her belt a bit and slid the sword through it. "That'll do."

"Let's go see what we're up against."

GINDOR SHOT HER wrinkled hand out of the doorway and latched onto the arm of a startled scout. "What's going on?"

"An army of Lukrians is camped just beyond the trees," the scout sputtered.

"What?" Gindor ignored the scout struggling against her bony hand and scanned the chaotic activity of the city. "We send them an illuminated invitation or something?" She let go of the squirming scout, who stumbled away rubbing her arm.

Gindor stomped back into the chamber and glared at the elders hovering around Jame, giving her a proper greeting by the looks of it. What was their world coming to? Their best warrior, whose hatred for Tigh was as tangible as the rock around them, defied the Council to defend her honor. Her queen turned a blind eye on tradition and allowed a serious breach in the law. Lukrians marched through Emoria and set up camp as if it was a festival day. Now her own Council didn't have enough dignity to remember Jame's presence in Emoria was probationary at best.

"What's happening?" Jame asked.

Gindor glared at her. "Lukrians. An army of them has broken through our outer defenses and are camped in the meadow beyond the trees." She crossed her arms and continued to stare at Jame.

"Laur's waterfalls, how could that happen?" Jame asked.

"We've never had a problem with our defenses before." Gindor stepped around the table.

The other women backed away from Jame.

"Before what?" Jame narrowed her eyes.

Gindor planted herself in front of Jame. "Before today."

"I can't believe you're even suggesting such a thing," Jame said, anger flashing in her eyes.

"She was out of your sight for three days—up here in the mountains," Gindor said. "By all the accounts, she'd been transformed back into a Guard."

"She doesn't have anything to do with that army." Jame's anger pressed her voice into a low, even whisper.

"Do you know that for sure?" Gindor asked.

"Yes." Jame straightened. "And I don't need my eyes to see the truth."

"I admire your loyalty to your companion. I really do." Gindor relaxed the menace and pulled on her matriarchal mask. "But she's like a wild animal that's been tamed. You can only tame so much. The wildness is still at the core."

"You are so wrong," Jame said. "She's a gentle, kind soul who was turned into a wild animal to become an Elite Guard." Gindor frowned in surprise. "Don't decide the case until you have all the facts—the most important lesson of my training."

The black and white image of the Elite Guard shattered into too many shades of gray. Gindor met Jame's steady gaze, startled to find a strength she knew wouldn't be there if Tigh had a dominant hold on her. Argis's change of mind now made sense. "We have much to talk about."

"Yes, we do," Jame said.

A murmur from the other women drew their attention to a small scroll shelf hollowed out of the wall.

Gindor frowned. "What now?"

CLOUDS TENDED TO snag on the mountain peaks and settle over the high meadows, enveloping much of Emoria in evanescent blankets of moisture. Light drizzle accentuated the unease of the silent watchers concealed in the clumps of trees edging the expansive meadow.

Argis and Tigh studied the sprawled encampment from a lookout's nook at the top of a tree. Tigh focused her senses on the diffused air and sounds dislocated by the turbid banks of fog. With the exception of a sparse patrol on the outermost perimeter of the camp, the Lukrians showed no concern about being deep within enemy territory.

"How did they get this far?" Argis stretched her neck to get a better view of the large tent in the center of the camp.

Tigh, splayed out on her stomach on a nearby branch, tried to decipher as much as she could in the blotches of grays and whites. Her enhanced senses widened to encompass the meadow, the trees, and the swirl of snow where the ground rose to form a nearby rocky peak. She drew into her consciousness the reaction of the plants and animals to the visitors in the meadow in comparison to the silent watchers in the trees.

She blinked and whipped her head around to face Argis.

"What?" Argis asked.

"They're not real," Tigh said.

Argis stared at her. "What do you mean, they're not real?"

"I don't sense them there."

"Sense them? Don't we see them and hear them and smell their food cooking? What's there not to sense?" Argis asked.

"What else do you hear?" Tigh asked.

"What else?" Argis frowned a little.

"What do you hear around us, in the forest?"

Argis concentrated on listening. "I hear whispering. I hear someone moving around over there. Several warriors are walking over there . . ."

"Do you hear any birds or small animals?"

"Of course not. We're disturbing—" Argis frowned even more.

Birds twittering to each other and the movements of scurrying animals sounded out in the meadow—all over the meadow. A colony of mountain dogs created disturbances in the fog pockets. They showed no interest in the camp twenty paces from their frolic grounds.

Argis turned to Tigh, her expression inscrutable. "This war isn't going to be any fun if nothing about it is real."

Tigh quirked an eyebrow. "I never said the fighting wouldn't be real."

"How do we fight something that isn't even there?" Argis shifted in the small lookout notch and stared at the lively camp. "It sure looks real."

"First, we figure out what kind of reaction is expected of us." Tigh rubbed her chin on the smooth bark of the limb.

"Under normal circumstances we would attack."

"What would be accomplished if we ran into the meadow attacking something that isn't there?" Tigh asked. The Elite Guards' informal motto was "nothing is as it seems." Unfortunately, the luck it took to out think the Elite Guards was just as vaporous.

"We'd look pretty foolish," Argis said.

"What would that accomplish?" Tigh said. "There isn't anyone to witness the foolish action, and a story of that kind doesn't have to be true if it's told for the purpose of making you look foolish."

Argis rolled a twig between her fingers. "What exactly are you saying? We can't sit here all day waiting for something that isn't there to go away."

Tigh shrugged. "I say we do what they expect us to do. It's the only way of finding out what they're up to."

Argis stared at Tigh. "So we pretend that everything is as it appears and rush the camp?"

Tigh sat up and straddled the wide branch. "We play it by their rules." She surveyed the ground around the trees. "We attack their illusion with an illusion of our own."

Argis twisted the twig until it was sinew. "I thought you said the fighting would be real."

"Something tells me it will be."

"WE RUN INTO the field, yelling, then lob stones around the tents, but be careful not to hit the tents." Tas scratched her head. "And then we stay a hundred paces away."

"Then we wait and shoot at anyone who emerges from the tents and continually shower the tents with arrows." Mularke frowned. "Why don't we just shoot at the tents now?"

"Because, if Tigh's right, the tents are empty," Argis said. "Look. If we end up looking foolish, I'll rake the sparring fields and change the targets for two fortnights."

Tas and Mularke exchanged wry glances.

"We trust your confidence in Tigh's instincts," Mularke said.

The fog compressed into a thin layer knee-high off the ground while the warriors gathered small stones into their belt pouches and the archers took their places in the trees. The drizzle diffused into an uncomfortable cleaving mist as tension sparked through the trees from two hundred Emorans waiting for the signal.

"We're ready," Argis said.

Tigh raised her eyes as if searching the gray sky for whatever demented deity oversaw her destiny. For Jame. My life and everything I do, I dedicate to Jame. Give me a chance to place this victory at her feet.

"Command your force, Argis." She pulled her sword from her belt and pressed the flat of the blade against her forehead in a respectful salute.

Argis straightened, unsheathed her sword, and returned the salute. She then lifted the blade and waited until nine score sets of eyes were riveted on the length of steel before she slashed the air downward.

The trees edging the meadow awoke to the sound of battle yodels and the crunch of rushing boots against the brittle undergrowth. Threescore masked warriors crashed into the meadow, swinging slingshots. As soon as a stone hurtled through the air, they tucked the next one into the leather pocket and sent it flying.

An army of angry Lukrians didn't face them and charge.

The first lob of stones fell to the ground without obstruction.

Argis bounced with excitement. "Look at that. It *is* an illusion. And the ground is mostly stone just as you thought. How did you figure that out?"

"They had to pick a place where they'd be able to hear us attacking. Sound carries through stone better than dirt." Several figures clad from head to toe in red leather rushed out of tent openings. Tigh breathed a prayer of thanks to whoever watched over her destiny. "There."

"Archers," Argis barked.

She grinned as six score arrows arced into the sky and dove through the stretched leather of the tents. Dozens of red-clad warriors stumbled out of the tents with swords drawn. By the time they realized they were the rabbit rather than the hawk, their escape route was cut off by the constant menace of arrows.

A hundred paces away, Tas threw the slingshot to the ground and pulled out her sword. She whipped her body into a dance of ecstasy and whooped and bounced into flips while brandishing her blade in dazzling patterns. A cacophony of yodels rose in response to this display, followed by the flashing of threescore blades. The Emorans rushed forward and laughed as the satisfying clatter of steel against steel sang the song they lived to hear.

Argis ran several paces. She skidded to a stop on the water slick grass and cast a puzzled look back at Tigh. "What's wrong?"

Tigh blinked at her. A thousand responses spun through her mind. Each time she went into battle she fought her own demons along with the enemy. She gave her head a shake and studied the stone strewn ground. She was fighting for Jame now. For Jame's destiny. Their destiny.

She looked up at Argis. "Let's go teach these Lukrians the proper way to dance."

Argis grinned, and they trotted toward the camp.

Tigh watched as Tas swung her sword for the deathblow and looked startled as she met air where her opponent had been. Tas spun around and saw that her companions also fought air as the red-clad warriors disengaged and formed a concerted charge across the frolic ground of the mountain dogs.

Tigh stared at the score of warriors chasing after her. The way the lead warrior wielded her sword told her to keep away from those blades. She slung the first blade away, and then caught another while bouncing away from a near slice to her legs.

She flipped over their heads and landed behind them. No armor, not even her sturdy black leathers. She almost laughed at the irony as she deflected the blows from three blades. She snapped the head of the closest woman with an elbow. A quick shove with her knee sent the stunned Lukrian reeling into her two companions. Over their sprawled bodies, she sliced her sword against four more blades crunching down on her. She flipped back and got the inner two Lukrians in the chin with her knees and a quick flexing out of her feet sent the outer two flying.

Tigh landed on her back and winced as rocks chewed into her skin. Five Lukrians jumped into the air over her, and she rolled away from their free fall. She scrambled to her feet, kicked up a stone, and whacked it with her foot at the head of the warrior on top of the sprawled heap, and crashed her fist into the face of the first of four rushing hard at her. A low crouch sent the next warrior, unable to stop, stumbling over her. Tigh rolled onto her back and thrust her leg upward in time for a belly blow to the next warrior and a nice kick sent the winded woman against the fourth warrior.

EMORANS SWARMED AROUND Tigh as they gathered up the dazed and wounded Lukrians.

Argis stared at the damage done in just the time it took for them to catch up to Tigh and was beyond stunned. Never had she witnessed such control and inventiveness or such incredible speed. Tigh had been like a whirlwind uprooting the enemy. None left in her wake had been killed. Another mystery to the complex woman she had grown to respect.

She strode to Tigh, who was hitched up on her elbows watching the activity around her. Not even winded. Truly a disgusting sight.

"Make sure you clean their blades before taking them back to the city." Tigh nodded at the growing pile of weapons.

"Poisoned?" Argis hadn't even thought of that.

"It obviously has no effect on you." Tigh nodded at Tas, who tended a wounded warrior.

Argis frowned. "That's why they went after you. They knew you'd be here."

"It's not my place to question Emoran defenses or security, but I think it might be wise to consider a possible breach," Tigh said.

"Why does everything have to be so complicated?" Argis dropped cross-legged onto the ground, head in hands.

Chapter 10

POAG CRADLED A delicate crystal object in her hands as she broke from the cluster of women around her and walked to Gindor and Jame.

"Someone leaving us presents again?" Gindor peered at the object. "Looks like a shaggy goat."

"What do you mean, 'presents'?" Jame cocked her head to get a better look at the glass.

"These crystals have been appearing in the oddest places for, I would say, several moons now," Gindor said. "We seem to have a shy artist in our midst."

"Interesting," Jame said.

Gindor sighed. "We may as well go to the palace. Wait for word there."

"If that means the morning meal, I'm with you." Jame thought about Tigh rushing off to fight without eating.

She had never seen the city on alert with double guards at all posts on the wall and at the top of the bluffs. A nervous energy snapped against the air. Backup squads of warriors and archers gathered in a corner of the square in front of the barracks. Curious citizens mingled in clusters swapping bits of gossip. As far as she could remember, the enemy never had been this close to the city in such a force.

A woman dressed in loose-fitting Emoran leathers broke free from a knot of women chatting near the tavern. Jame had to look twice before recognizing Seeran.

"Have you heard?" Seeran asked as she skidded up to Jame. "I have to say, there hasn't been a dull moment since I met you two." She fell in next to Jame. "Where's Tigh?"

"She's gone to help," Jame said, smiling at Seeran's enthusiasm. "Have you eaten?"

"Actually, I just woke up. Who can even think about eating with all this excitement going on?" Seeran turned and gawked at the double line of lavender-draped acolytes to the High Follower of Laur, patron deity of Emoria. Each acolyte swung gleaming metal chains holding miniature waterfalls crafted from multicolored quartz.

"I was going to invite you to join me for some food, but if you find staying out here waiting for word more interesting . . ." Jame began.

Seeran pulled her eyes from the acolytes. "I guess I should eat something."

Jame stopped grinning. Jyac stepped into the square, followed by Sark and Ronalyn. Jyac nodded her approval as she scanned the activity.

Gindor straightened and met Jyac's eyes.

"I am not pleased," Jyac said in a low angry voice as the band of elders stopped in front of her. "Come in, Jame, I think you've suffered the company of these women long enough this morning."

Gindor leveled a frozen glare at Jyac. "We have much to discuss."

"I look forward to it." Jyac's voice was cold and smooth as the stone behind her.

"We found another crystal." Poag held up the delicate object.

After a few heartbeats, Jyac shifted her eyes away from Gindor to the crystal Poag cradled in her hands. She took it from Poag. "I'll add it to our collection." She held the crystal up to study it in the weak, misty light. "Thank you, Poag."

"My queen!" Poylin's voice came from a path above them. She rounded a painted and smoothed boulder that hid the entrance to the pathway.

"What's the word?" Jyac approached Poylin, followed by an anxious Jame.

"Argis sent me to tell you they are preparing to engage the enemy and have every confidence they will return in victory," Poylin said.

"To guarantee victory, take this back to her." Jyac handed the crystal to a smiling Jame and dug into her belt pouch for a leather braid laced with deep purple thread. "I challenge her to bring back victory."

Poylin took the braid. "We cannot fail now," she shouted, then turned and dashed to the overhead path.

"At least something's going right today." Jyac turned to Jame. "What . . . ?"

Jame stared at her through unfocused eyes. She felt her world fall away.

Poag caught the crystal as it fell from Jame's limp hands at the same time Jyac lunged forward to catch Jame in her arms.

"IT'S AS CONFUSING as Bal's maze down here," Argis muttered. Her torch lit another dark opening off one of the several small chambers they had explored.

They followed the snaking frozen waves of sand on the cavern floor and found evidence of the heavy tents that had been dragged through the tunnels.

"No doubt they came through this way," Argis said.

Tigh crouched down and studied a discolored patch on the shadowed ground. She put a finger on the spot and lifted it to her nose. "How are you going to stop them from doing this again?"

"Why'd they do it in the first place?" Argis frowned. "They could have come up through these caves and attacked us in the middle of the night, and we wouldn't have known what hit us."

"The answer lies in whoever created the illusion." Tigh brushed the sand from her hands and stood up.

Argis scowled. "More games?"

"At least you got to fight a little." Tigh arched an eyebrow. "I suggest you block all the passages. It'll be a lot more difficult for them to clean out obstructions in these dark tunnels than to break through whatever you put over the outside openings."

"I'll get the architect down here." Argis nodded. "What's that?"

The shadows hugging the uneven walls transformed into red-clad figures. The small band of Emorans drew their swords. Tas whipped her blade at the closest enemy, almost losing her balance without making solid contact.

"They're not real," Tigh yelled from the other side of the cavern.

Tas squeaked, dropped her sword, and pressed her hand under her arm. "Daughter of a shaggy goat. Don't touch them."

"Everyone out of here," Argis said.

The group backed to the middle of the cavern where the rope ladder to the surface dangled. Being only illusions, the counterfeit Lukrians made no move toward them, but their menacing stance was enough to make the Emorans uneasy.

Argis grabbed the ladder to steady it for Tigh's ascent, and soft laughter wafted from a tunnel. She pulled out her sword, ready to attack.

Tigh whipped around to face the tunnel the sound flowed from. Fear gripped her soul as a grim memory slapped her in the face.

She turned to a tense, alert Argis. "I know who we're up against."

"Is that good or bad?" Argis asked.

"Both." Tigh sighed and jumped onto the ladder. Argis sheathed her sword and followed her.

Tigh emerged from a hole hidden in the scattering of low rocks. The laugh continued to mock her memory as she offered a hand to Argis and pulled her from the earth. Never did she suspect this person as their enemy, even when the evidence practically screamed her name to her. That would have been pointing a finger at someone who had died at her own hand.

MOST OF THE Emorans who had battled that day had already returned to the city. The whooping and yodeling of celebration reached Argis's ears as they trekked through the forest. The usual elation she felt after a battle was tempered by the knowledge that they hadn't yet engaged their true enemy.

"Let's not spoil a good victory." Argis glanced around to catch her warriors' attention. "There are mysteries and questions to be sure, but right now, they're as intangible as Laur's magic waterfall. We fought well and caught the enemy at their own game."

The warriors grinned, and boastful words flitted amongst them, comparing tales that would grow bolder and wilder by evening's end.

As they descended into the city, Argis saw Jyac and Sark waiting in front of the palace doors and let the relief that she was able to bring home this victory soak away the uncertainties of the day. She strode to Jyac, followed by a frowning Tigh.

"I have met your challenge, my queen." Argis held out the purple-laced braid, which Jyac accepted.

"Well done, Argis." Jyac's eyes sparkled with pride. "As you can see, we couldn't stop the celebration from starting."

"I've never known anyone who could stop a warrior from celebrating." Argis grinned, looking around. "Where's Jame?"

Jyac and Sark exchanged enigmatic glances.

"Where is she?" Tigh's low voice was mixed with anger and concern.

"She's with the healer—" Jyac began.

"Healer? What happened?" Tigh looked around. "Where's the healer?"

"She's going to be all right." Jyac raised placating hands. "I'll take you to her."

"What happened to her?" Tigh asked as she and Argis flanked Jyac as they strode across the square.

"She met with a little accident—"

"Accident?" Tigh asked.

"It was that new girl, Gelder," Jyac said. "Kas was taking her to the upper stables. She saw her friend, Seeran, down here and leaned over a ledge where we put our offerings to Laur. A tribute—fortunately a wooden one—fell and hit Jame on the head. She passed out, but the healer thinks it was more from the shock of being hit in the head than from the injury itself."

"Did she get into this kind of trouble when she was young?" Tigh asked.

"She did have the tendency to be in the wrong place at the wrong time," Jyac said.

"She still does," Tigh mumbled.

WITH HER HEAD propped up on several pillows, Jame watched the healers tend to the minor wounds of the warriors returning from the upper meadow. A cacophony of excited voices competed as tales were slung back and forth of Lukrians made of mist, magic caves, and an unbelievable battle between Tigh and twenty . . . no, wait . . . fifty . . . at least a hundred Lukrians.

Tigh, without armor and wielding only a sword, downed them all in a matter of heartbeats and without receiving even the tiniest of scratches.

If Jame could shake her pounding head, she would have at the description of Tigh's idea of fun. She also felt a twinge of concern about why the

Lukrians ganged up on her like that. The only logical answer was not a happy one. She blinked back unexpected tears, refusing to let the emotional stress of the last few days overwhelm her. Tigh was in a vulnerable place among these unseen vipers who were trying to sap her strength and nip at her sanity. She shoved her feelings of despair into the deepest part of her consciousness. Tigh was her life. She would do anything to make sure her warrior was safe from harm.

"They may not be real, but they sting like the kiss of a whip." Tas's voice cut through the noise. She sat on a nearby pallet, wincing as the healer studied and prodded her hand before applying a cooling salve.

"What's not real?" Jame tried to lift her body, but she felt like a boulder had taken residence in her head.

Tas cradled her burnt hand and sat down on the stool next to Jame's pallet. "What happened to you?"

"My head got in the way of a falling tribute to Laur," Jame said.

"Ouch," Tas said. "I got this from one of those misty Lukrians. A group of them surrounded us while we were investigating the caves. Hidden in the shadows, they looked so real I took a swing at one of them. Some of the mist must have touched my hand because it stung like crazy."

"So they're more than a magical trick," Jame said.

"The ones up top seemed to be only illusion." Tas frowned. "We fought the real Lukrians in the middle of the illusions. They simply faded when we touched them. But the ones below ground were different. A kind of menace came from them."

"Sounds like we have a mystery on our hands." Jame pushed down the panic that had been an unwanted companion since she began her journey home.

Silence in the cavern heralded the entrance of Jyac followed by Argis and Tigh. As the warriors let out a cheer of respect for those who led them to victory, Tigh's only focus was on Jame.

Tas rose from the stool and drifted to a knot of warriors as Tigh approached.

"How's the hand?" Tigh asked.

"It'll be fine," Tas said.

Tigh nodded and dropped onto the stool. She gazed at Jame. "How come I'm the one who fought and you're the one who's injured?"

Jame smiled. "I try to share when I can. It's probably a mild concussion. The healer gave me something to help keep me awake until she thinks I'm all right."

Tigh nodded and studied the pattern woven into the pallet cover.

This quiet introspection told Jame something serious was bothering Tigh. "I heard you fought off only a hundred Lukrians. Getting soft in your old age?"

"Does it count that I wasn't wearing armor?" Tigh raised an innocent eyebrow.

"Not as much as if you'd been barefoot," Jame said.

"I'll try to remember to slice my boots off next time." Tigh took Jame's hand and brought it to her lips. "I suppose Laur owes you a tribute for a change."

Jame snorted. "Oh, right. Just after she replaces the waterfalls in her temple with washing pools."

"Some people do prefer bathing to showering," Tigh said.

Jame chuckled. "You now owe Laur a double tribute for that sacrilege."

Argis and Jyac, making the rounds among the wounded, stopped in front of Jame's pallet.

"Good to see you laughing," Jyac said, glancing at Tigh.

"I'm feeling better." Jame gave Tigh an affectionate look.

"Argis feels tomorrow is soon enough to discuss what happened today." Jyac turned to Tigh. "Is that acceptable?"

Tigh stood and pulled the black sword from her belt. "Whatever is acceptable to you." She offered the sword to Argis. "I don't have permission to carry this. Please keep it for me."

Argis stared at the sword and turned to Jyac. "Has she not earned the right to wear it?"

"She's earned the right." Jyac looked into Tigh's eyes. "As long as you wear it for Emoria."

Tigh straightened and pressed the flat of the blade against her forehead in a salute of respect. "You have my word."

Argis relaxed and grinned. "That's good news for the sixteen warriors anxious for you to meet their challenges. But not today. Today is for celebration."

"Why didn't you challenge me?" Tigh asked.

The chattering around them stopped, and Jame could feel every eye on them.

Argis looked Tigh up and down. "You've already met my challenge and won." She glanced at Jame, then back to Tigh. "You've proven to me that you're an acceptable consort for our future queen."

A stunned murmur rumbled through the chamber.

"Thank you, Argis," Jame said.

Argis nodded.

"Come." Jyac put a hand on Argis's shoulder. "It's time to celebrate our victory."

THE ONLY SOUNDS within the atrium were from the walls of water spilling over towering slabs of stone by means known only to Laur herself.

This chamber was the one place in the city where Tigh could get Jame away from the discordant revels of the Emorans. The festive noise aggravated Jame's throbbing head, and Tigh needed to think.

An acolyte occasionally drifted through the chamber to adjust the long slats of prismatic crystals along the walls so they continued to refract rainbows into the chamber as the sun drifted across the sky. Tigh felt like she was inside a giant kaleidoscope.

Besides smooth stone benches carved around the pools that rippled with the outflow of the waterfalls, the only other choice of seating was cloth-covered pillows, embroidered with countless renditions of waterfalls.

Sprawled on several pillows next to a pool, Tigh cradled Jame against her and let the warmth of their bond flow into her.

Jame sighed. "Pretty strange goings-on."

Tigh dipped a cloth in the pool and laid it on Jame's head. She then snaked her arms around Jame and pulled her closer.

"That bad?" Jame asked.

Tigh stared at the ropes of water skittering over rough patches of rock, flinging out curious patterns of droplets. "I know who we're up against."

Jame turned her head and winced.

"Easy." Tigh cupped Jame's head in her hands and eased it onto her shoulder.

"I thought we knew that." Jame relaxed into Tigh arms.

"I think they're following someone else's orders." The laugh in the cavern mocked her memories. Could it be another game of the rogue Guards to get to her by confronting her with her worst nightmare?

She had been newly elevated to the Elite Guards and was still learning to control the enhancements to her mind and body. The Guards needed a leader capable of dominating them and holding their respect. The only way to find this leader was through a test. Word had reached them that a wizard from the Umvian plains had been approached by the Northern leaders to create an enhanced warrior to go against the Guards.

General Rartrice strode into her cell before dawn one morning and awakened her with a shove of a boot against the cot. Before she had a chance to blink awake, Rartrice threw her leathers at her.

"You know where the Umvian plain is?"

Tigh nodded.

"You're to go there and find a wizard called Misner and kill her."

She remembered that jolt of anticipation of making her first kill hurtling through her. She was ready to run all the way to the Umvian plains, swinging her sword in abandoned ecstasy. Her life wouldn't be complete until that wizard's life was stolen with her blade.

The general laughed at her eagerness to fulfill this simple order that five other potential leaders of the Guard had failed to carry out.

"Who is it?" Jame's soft voice brushed against her ear.

Tigh drove away her memories and looked down at Jame. "When we were in the caves below the meadow, there was laughter coming from a tunnel. I've heard that laughter once before many years ago." She sighed. "There was a wizard who was trying to develop enhanced warriors for the North. I was given orders to go and kill her."

"I take it you succeeded." Jame wrapped her hands around Tigh's.

"Yes," Tigh whispered. "My first kill."

Somehow her mental conditioning had allowed her to work through the mind-numbing projections Misner drove into her brain like fire arrows. A part of her subconscious was able to keep track of what was real and what was illusion, leaving her body to follow the warrior instinct that propelled her forward to the kill.

The short, round wizard laughed at her and taunted her with the names of the five Guards she had killed. Perhaps the wizard's success at beating those other Guards made her too confident. Through burning muscles and illusions conjuring her worst nightmares, Tigh stayed focused on the diminutive wizard.

Tigh bellowed like an animal and crashed through the horrific illusions. She allowed her mind to give in to being frightened and be done with it. She'd either die or succeed and what she did at that point wasn't going to change her fate. Misner would never let her live. She swung her sword and lunged forth for the kill.

As Tigh collapsed from the psychological beating, the image of a head with startled eyes dropping several feet away from its body etched forever in her memory.

"So you saved us from facing a foe as formidable as the Elite Guard," Jame said.

Tigh blinked at her. "I thought I had. But she still seems to be alive."

"She was a wizard. She could have been close to death and may have revived herself through magic," Jame said.

"I decapitated her." Tigh wondered how that eager young Guard she saw in her mind's eye could be the same person cradling Jame.

Chapter 11

ARGIS WOVE MORE than walked across the midnight-darkened square. She flicked imaginary gnats away. Above her, the quartz-filled openings that speckled the bluffs danced with the light from victory parties within. Songs slurred from the celebrants in the tavern and from the balconies of the residences higher up the bluffs. Drunken laughter bubbled up from atop the gate wall in response to words that were too low for her to decipher. The clash of blades echoed from the barracks, accompanied by drunken cheers and calls. Three guards rushed across the square to break up the disturbance.

"All right, Tas." Argis's inebriated growl echoed off the bluff walls. "I know you're out here somewhere." She stumbled on an invisible stone and staggered around a bit. A wisp of laughter whipped her around too fast and she found the cobblestone ground much closer to her face than she would have liked.

The laughing materialized into Tas and Mularke. They tried to hold each other up but were chortling too hard to care as they negotiated their way to Argis. They collapsed onto the uneven stone next to her.

"Thought you swore off drinking so much." Mularke tried to slap Argis on the leg but missed and hit the ground. "Laur's waterfalls, I have to stop drinking so much." She held her stinging hand under her arm.

"Now we're a pair." Tas wiggled her burned hand.

"You're a pair all right." Argis winced and pulled her body up into a cross-legged position. "Speaking of, where are they?"

"You mean Jame and Tigh?" Tas slurred. "You sure have changed your leathers about them. When you asked me to stand with you in Tigh's defense this morning, I thought it was for Jame's sake. But after the battle today, I'm convinced you actually like her."

"I treated her as the enemy, and the first thing she did was save my life," Argis muttered. "I discovered I was wrong about her."

"She's not like I expected," Mularke said.

"She doesn't act like any warrior I've ever seen, but she certainly has the skills and the courage." Tas sliced her hands wildly in the air, and Argis and Mularke spluttered with ale-soaked laughter. "Is it true those blades had poison on them? The same stuff that turned her crazy?"

Argis nodded. "One nick and she would have been Tigh the Terrible."

"Scary." Mularke shivered.

"Speaking of . . ." Tas gazed at a tall figure with an arm wrapped around a shorter figure emerging from the Temple. "She's sober. We've been negligent in our duty."

Argis shot Tas a serious look. "She's been taking care of Jame."

Tas held up her hands in mock defense. "Sorry. Forgot. Sacred ground. Must tread lightly."

Mularke covered her mouth with her hands to keep from laughing.

Argis scowled at Tas for several heartbeats, then let the alcohol relax her. "I'll forgive you because you're drunk."

"You forgot to tell me about this strange ritual," Tigh said. "What's the significance of the battle leaders sitting alone in the middle of the square . . . in the middle of the night?"

Jame peered at the besotted trio. "It's an ancient time-honored tradition. Except they should be passed out by now."

Argis straightened. "We're having a very serious discussion."

Tigh raised an eyebrow. "Then that laughter must have been from someone else."

"Sometimes we can be seriously funny," Tas said.

Argis and Mularke snorted with laughter.

"How did you do that today?" Tas asked. "All that flipping and kicking. I've never seen anyone fight so much with their feet."

"It's a technique they taught us in the Guards," Tigh said. "It comes from a land far east of here."

"It can't be that hard if a bunch of passive quill-scrapers can learn it," Argis said as she leaned back on her elbows.

"I take it you're interested in learning it," Tigh said.

"It'll be your duty to teach us—if you become a citizen of Emoria." Argis kept a steady gaze on Tigh.

"When she becomes a citizen of Emoria." Jame pulled away from Tigh.

Argis was trying to get a rise out of Tigh and got one from Jame instead. Not like any warrior she had ever met, indeed. "I stand corrected."

"You're drunk so I'll forgive you." Jame relaxed and gave Tigh a nudge. "Someone has to stand up for your honor."

A shout came from the Council's chamber. A pair of Council guards rushed from the chamber entrance and ran to them, shouting disconnected words.

"Wait." Jame stepped in front of them, and they spoke at once. "One person, please. Wolfie, what's going on."

Wolfie, a stocky woman with wild, dark hair, took a calming breath. "We were outside the Council's door all night. They called a meeting, and from what we could hear, a rather heated dispute was going on." She glanced at Tigh. "Anyway, they were yelling at each other, then suddenly everything was as quiet as the Temple. We waited for the noise to start again but nothing happened. Finally we eased the door open a bit for just a look. They were gone."

"Maybe they went into one of the inner chambers," Jame said.

"We searched every room." Wolfie shook her head, causing the wild hair to fly. "As you know, the only way out is through the chamber door."

"I think we'd better have a talk with the queen," Jame said.

Argis scrambled to her feet, cursing. "I knew I shouldn't have had so much to drink."

"Go sleep it off, all of you," Jame said. "I have the feeling we're going to need you well and alert tomorrow."

JYAC WAS A see-it-to-believe-it kind of woman, and she didn't want to believe what Jame had told her. Still in her sleep shirt and a pair of cotton leggings, she strode across the square, trailed by a yawning Ronalyn. Tigh and Jame followed them, unable to keep pace because Jame's head still ached.

"I'm beginning to see some family resemblance," Tigh said.

"She's efficient. Like you." Jame lifted her chin a little but ended up grinning.

"This is too efficient, even for her," Ronalyn turned to them and whispered.

Jyac stopped at the entrance of the Council chamber and studied the curious scene. The chairs were pulled away from the table at odd angles. Papers and scrolls were scattered on the table. She located a scroll case leaning against a wall, gathered the scrolls, and rolled them into the case.

"Um, Aunt Jyac?" Jame stepped forward as Jyac, upon finishing her task, stood staring at the table, brow furrowed in thought. She laid a gentle hand on Jyac's arm. "Don't you think we ought to discuss what to do about this?"

"You don't understand." Jyac's expression was confused and overflowing with despair.

Jame took Jyac's arm, led her to a chair at the table, and sat down next to her. Ronalyn took the seat on Jyac's other side and put a comforting arm over her shoulder. Tigh roamed around the chamber.

"Now. What don't we understand?" Jame asked.

Jyac took a deep breath. "It was written that the Council would disappear one night."

"Written in the Emor Mysteries?" Jame asked.

"Yes," Jyac said. "After a battle with an enemy that was real but not real. That part made no sense . . . until today."

Jame frowned. "You don't really think those writings foretell the future, do you?"

"Not until today." Jyac laid the scroll case on the table and played with the leather thong attached to it.

Jame glanced up at Tigh, who had stopped poking around and watched them. "There are some logical explanations to consider before we decide we're at the mercy of predictions written a millennium ago."

"What logical explanations?" Jyac asked. "Maybe one or two things can be explained, but not everything at once."

"Tigh thinks that a wizard she, um . . . had dealings with many years ago is behind whatever is happening in the mountains and that the Lukrians are following her orders. We know that the wizard created the illusion in the meadow."

Tigh stopped her wandering around and sat cross-legged on the fire hearth.

"What is written in the Mysteries happens, no matter who may be behind them," Jyac said. "It would be different if it was an isolated incident. But two improbable incidents in a row?"

"Tigh and Argis have come up with a theory that's worth considering." Jame shot Tigh a look. Tigh gave her a short nod. "They thought it strange that, as soon as Tigh joined the battle, all the Lukrians went straight for her. Tigh guessed, rightly I might add, that the Lukrian blades were coated with the potion that, uh, affected her a few days ago."

Jyac turned to Tigh. "You fought them off without getting nicked? Impressive."

"Fortunately for her and us, her skill at evading sharp objects is very good." Jame gave Tigh an affectionate look. "The question is, how did the Lukrians know Tigh was here in Emoria?"

"That Meah person must have told them," Jyac said.

"She left Tigh for dead," Jame said. "But, as you say, she could have been lurking around as we crossed into Emoria, and saw that Tigh was alive. She then could have gone to a pocket of Lukrians hiding out near our borders and enlisted their help to try to cut Tigh down again. She also could have used the illusions of a wizard who was conveniently in the area. A wizard who had personal reasons for seeing Tigh dead." Jame caught Tigh's questioning expression as she presented an argument against the theory she was trying to put forth. "But, as you say, we're not dealing with an isolated incident here. We have a pair of mysteries written on scrolls that only the queen, the Council, and the High Follower of Laur are allowed to read."

"Go on," Jyac said.

"Let's look at what happened in this chamber." Jame caught the delighted twinkle in Tigh's eyes. Tigh loved to see her work. "The Council members are arguing, then suddenly there is silence. No sounds of surprise or struggle. Only a few heartbeats later, the guards look into the chamber and find it empty.

How could twelve women be disabled and dragged away in that short of time and with no visible place to go?"

"You have a theory?" Jyac asked.

"A theory that brings all the elements of this puzzle together," Jame said. "We were convinced we saw an army of Lukrians that weren't real. Is it too much of a stretch to convince a pair of guards that they don't see the Council members who are still in the chamber? An illusion can work both ways." She paused. "This is what I believe happened. At least twelve assailants entered the chamber from a hidden passage. If the enemy can create openings from underground caverns out on the meadow, they can certainly find a way into Emor. Let's say the assailants and the opening to the hidden passage are concealed by illusion. They position themselves behind the Council members and prick them with a fast-acting sleep potion."

"Fast-acting sleep potion?" Jyac asked in disbelief.

"It was used to capture the Guards after the Wars," Jame said.

Jyac and Ronalyn tossed startled glances at Tigh who sat by the fire.

"Anyway, they subdue the Council members, then cover them with the illusion of invisibility. The guards enter the chamber as the assailants are removing the Council members, but the guards can't see them. They wait until the guards have checked the inner chambers, then take the Council away through the hidden passage."

"Even if it is as you say, it still doesn't change the fact that the predictions in the Mysteries are coming true," Jyac said.

"If the enemy can enter the city unseen, they can find the Mysteries and read them," Jame said.

"Why would anyone create such a masquerade?"

"What do these predictions lead to?" Jame captured Jyac's eyes, seeing a flicker of fear there. "Not something good, I suspect, or your reactions to them coming true would be different."

"You're right. It's not a pleasant destiny for the Emoran people." Jyac nodded and raised respectful eyes to Jame. "What a clever niece I have. Your mothers would have been proud."

"Thank you." Jame briefly closed her eyes at the reminder of the mothers she never knew. "The Elite Guard's greatest weapon was the ability to weaken the enemy through fear and mental torture before they raised a sword in battle. There's no doubt we're up against rogue Guards most likely led by a powerful wizard. If their goal is to cause panic, then we must not panic. If their goal is to cause fear, then we mustn't show fear. We fight back with mental warfare of our own. Then we do everything we can to smoke them out of their underground hiding places and stop them before they cause another full out war."

Jyac stared at Jame as the strong words penetrated. "According to Argis, rumors of their strength have already reached beyond the mountains. How can one small nation be expected to stop them?"

"Because the Elite Guard cannot be defeated by the strength of an army." Jame almost laughed at Jyac's confused expression. "All it takes is the ability to out-think them. And fortunately for us, we have Tigh, the most elite of the Elite Guard. That's why they want to destroy her. They know she can destroy them."

"It sounds implausible." Jyac wrapped her hands around the scroll case. "But then, this whole situation is implausible. We'll meet with the military leaders tomorrow, and you can present your theory."

"Thank you, Aunt." Jame smiled as she caught the affectionate sparkle in Tigh's eyes.

"A thorough search will be made of these chambers for a hidden passageway." Jyac glanced around. "Finding it will help your argument."

"We'll get through this." Jame put a reassuring hand on Jyac's arm. "We'll create our own destiny."

"It is written in the Mysteries that a princess will lead a victorious campaign against a half-crazed wizard." Jyac took Jame's hand into hers. "I don't need the Mysteries to tell me you're the only one among us who is a master of creative strategies. I'm putting you in command of the campaign against this wizard."

A stunned Jame shook her head. "No. I can't do that."

"Ask Tigh," Jyac said.

Jame took in Tigh's encouraging grin. "On one condition. I want Tigh to work out the battle plans."

"I can agree to that," Jyac said.

JAME FELT THE sun filtering in through the quartz windows in the roof of her cave chamber. She opened her eyes, and was pleased to feel only a slight tinge of the ache from her close encounter with a tribute to Laur. Poor Gelder. The girl had been so mortified that she had injured her princess. But those kinds of accidents happened in a city like Emor.

Jame glanced at Tigh sprawled next to her and grinned. This morning was much better to wake up to than the morning before.

The Council. Missing. Jame stifled a chuckle at Tigh's question before they fell asleep, about whether that was good or bad. She ran a gentle finger over the slight tension in Tigh's brow.

Tigh's face scrunched and shook a little at the touch, but she didn't wake. Jame frowned at this sluggish reaction. Despite her miraculous display in the previous day's battle, she knew Tigh wasn't up to her usual physical alertness.

Jame pulled up to lean against the stone wall that backed the bed, pleased her head had lost the aching heaviness. She squinted at the remnants of her childhood that filled the niches in the wall and couldn't believe she possessed so many things. Their importance in her life had diminished as she'd drifted away from her roots. Her first braid for mastering the staff, her first warrior leathers, her first battle braid.

She had forgotten about that. She had been a part of a patrol that was ambushed by a band of raiders. For their victory in the skirmish, she received a nice scar just above the elbow and the battle braid. A heady prize for a fifteen-year-old, but, even then, she hadn't felt the pride that Argis felt when she'd won her first battle braid. She never had the heart for it.

The bed shook as Tigh rolled over with a groan that sounded a little too much like an admission of pain. Tigh blinked her sleepy eyes open and grimaced.

"You all right?" Jame put a hand on Tigh's shoulder.

Tigh gingerly pulled into a cross-legged position and arched her back. "I landed on some rocks yesterday. There are probably some nice, ripe bruises back there."

"Just bruises?" Jame lifted the back of Tigh's shirt and winced at a pair of dark purple patches. "Ouch."

"If you're gentle about it, I'll let you put salve on them." Tigh gave Jame a sheepish look.

"My big brave warrior. What am I going to do with you?" Jame bit her lip to keep from laughing.

Tigh raised a saucy eyebrow. "Anything you want."

Jame trotted across the chamber to their packs.

The rapid patter of boots sounded in the corridor. She gave the door a quizzical glance, but continued to rummage through Tigh's pack for the salve.

More footfalls rushed by, and Tigh climbed out of bed. She ran a hand through her disheveled hair and opened the door as four women passed by. She grabbed the closest woman.

"What's going on?" Tigh asked.

"Something happened at the Temple," the young guard said.

"Something," Tigh said.

"I don't know what it is, but the acolytes are upset."

Tigh let the woman go and stepped back into the chamber. She closed the door behind her.

"What's happening?" Jame walked up to her with the jar of salve.

Tigh shrugged. "Something happened at the Temple. The acolytes are upset."

Jame sighed. "Let me get this salve on you before we see what's going on."

"It could be important."

"It's not more important than you," Jame said.

By the time they stepped outside the palace, the square was filled with women focused on the Temple. The lavender-robed acolytes were huddled near the Temple walls.

"What happened?" Jame asked.

Kas, the Horse Master, turned around. "We don't know. No one will tell us anything. But the acolytes are upset."

Jame led the way around the perimeter of the crowd. Argis and Tas, both a little pale but looking alert despite their overindulgence the night before, greeted them with frustrated expressions.

"They won't let us in, and no one will tell us what's going on," Argis said.

"So," Tigh eyed the flustered and sobbing acolytes huddled together, "all we know is the acolytes are upset."

Jame shot her a look and then focused on Argis. "Who's inside?"

"Panilope, of course, and Jyac and, of all people, Hallie," Argis said.

"Hallie?" Jame cast a puzzled look at the Temple door.

"Who's Hallie?" Tigh asked.

"Our dowser," Jame said. "Come on, Tigh. Let's go see what this is about."

"Good luck," Argis called to their backs.

Much to Jame's surprise, Eiget, the guard at the door, let them pass without a word.

They stood in the doorway for several heartbeats taking in the silence. Not a drop of water could be seen or heard in the chamber. Even the stones at the bottoms of the pools were dry. They walked into the chamber and peeked around the waterless vertical slabs of stone.

"This isn't an illusion." Jame held her hand out to where there should have been sheets of cascading water.

Tigh stepped behind Jame and wrapped her arms around her. "There's always an explanation," she whispered against Jame's hair. "We can't let them think there isn't. Remember your own words. 'If their goal is to cause panic, then we must not panic. If their goal is to cause fear, then we mustn't show fear.'"

Jame turned around in Tigh's arms. "I didn't know you were paying attention."

Tigh laughed. "Don't you know by now I can't help but listen to your voice?"

Jame's breath caught at this unexpected admission. "Really?"

Tigh grinned. "Remember, it was your voice that captured me from the very beginning."

Muffled voices rose up from the next chamber.

Jame sighed. "I think we'll continue this discussion later."

Tigh released Jame and let her lead the way into the rainbow chamber.

Panilope, the High Follower of Laur, draped in a robe of intense purple, leaned over a smaller, older woman who dangled a weighted string over one of the natural drains for the circulating water. Jyac stood in the middle of the chamber watching them. All three looked up.

The buds of hope that Jame had seen the night before were gone from Jyac's eyes—her face was set in grim shock as she approached them.

"This is in the Mysteries," Jame said.

"Yes." Jyac glanced around the waterless chamber, then captured Jame's eyes. "Do you think a wizard could do this? Suck the water from the Temple until it's dry? The prophecies are coming true. There's no doubt about it now."

Chapter 12

JAME TURNED TO get Tigh's reaction to Jyac's words, only to find Tigh not paying attention. Tigh had a hand on one of the stone slabs that supported the cascading waterfalls, and her brow was creased in concentration.

Jame exchanged glances with Jyac and placed a gentle hand on Tigh's other arm, getting her attention. "What is it?"

For an answer Tigh took Jame's hand and pressed it against the stone. Jame felt a strong trembling.

"It's water," Tigh said. "This cavern is surging with it, we just can't see it, hear it, or feel it."

"What is this nonsense?" Hallie demanded as she and Panilope joined them. "There isn't any water here, not even deep in the caverns below." She shook her dowsing medallion at Tigh.

"A good illusionist never does anything halfway," Tigh said.

Jyac threw up her hands in frustration. "You still think the wizard is behind all this?"

"I can detect a faint scent of water and hear the whisper of splashing and gurgling," Tigh said. "We must allow the voice of the possible overtake the screams of the impossible. A single act can break an illusion of this kind. The illusions in the meadow faded to nothing as soon as they were penetrated. To get to the real enemy, we simply pretended the imaginary Lukrians didn't exist."

She turned to Panilope, who fidgeted with a silver vessel. "I want to receive a water blessing."

The others stared at her as if she had received one too many blows to the head.

"Water is necessary for a water blessing," Panilope said.

"Pretend there's water flowing down this stone." Tigh waved her hand over the upright slab. "Go through the motions of preparing a water offering."

Panilope looked at Jyac and Jame for guidance.

Jame put a comforting hand on Panilope's cloth-draped arm. "Tigh has an understanding of the enemy we're up against. She wouldn't ask you to do something without a purpose to it." She turned to Tigh to double-check her sincerity. Tigh's wicked sense of humor surfaced at the oddest times.

Tigh raised an eyebrow at her.

"I guess it's better than doing nothing." Panilope held the small vessel between her hands and approached the dry slab. She gazed at the polished stone and moved her lips in a silent preparation for the offering. After a few heartbeats, she turned to Tigh. "Please come and accept your offering." Tigh stood next to her. "Tigh of Ingor, Laur welcomes you to her Temple."

Panilope thrust the vessel forward. Her shocked fingers, drenched in water, reacted and the vessel splashed into the pool.

The roar of water startled Jame after the silence.

"It *was* an illusion," Jame cried in wonderment. She caught Jyac's thoughtful expression. "What?"

Jyac approached a pool and ran a finger across the water's surface. "A few heartbeats ago I was without hope, because what was written about how the waters of Laur were restored sounded like a miracle." Her quiet voice captured everyone's attention—even Panilope, who was knee deep in water, fetching her blessing vessel. "But now I see it was just a test for the outsider who is going to help save Emoria from whoever is threatening our borders."

Jame nodded. "This is also in the Mysteries."

"It's confusing to read," Jyac said. "The miracle of the flowing water is followed by a passage that is more of a parable than a prediction. The person who performs the miracle is accused of trying to destroy Laur by pretending to be more powerful than the deity. The Emorans imprison her and fight the enemy on their own . . . and lose."

"It's a warning, not a prediction," Jame said.

"I think so," Jyac said.

"One more attempt to use the Mysteries to destroy Tigh is thwarted," Jame said, resting a chin on her fist.

"She's thinking. Not always a good thing," Tigh said, glancing at Jyac.

Jyac emitted a delicate snort of laughter.

Jame narrowed her eyes at them before returning to her thoughts. "Maybe the parable has something to it." She turned to Tigh. "It's plain that anyone who can perform this kind of miracle in Laur's own Temple, under her very nose, figuratively speaking, is too powerful to have running around."

Tigh frowned at Jame.

"What are you saying?" Jyac sounded shocked.

"She should be imprisoned for the safety of our people." Jame sauntered up to Tigh. "What do you think?"

"Could we make it a dry prison cell for a change? Maybe one that doesn't have a cold draft?" Tigh gazed down at Jame with eyes soaked with innocence.

"Hmm. That does take some of the fun out of it . . . Whoa." Jame found herself in the air, cradled in Tigh's arms, and held over the pool of water. She looked down at the water, then at a smirking Tigh, then down at the water and searched for words of reason. "It would make an awful messy splash if you dropped me."

Tigh shrugged. "The acolytes can clean it up."

"Dry and warm. I think I can manage that," Jame said. "Now put me down."

"One more thing." Tigh pulled Jame's head close enough to put her lips to her ear. "I want a roommate."

Jame tried to keep from grinning. "You do, do you?"

"It gets lonely in those dry, warm prison cells." Tigh's voice sent shivers through Jame.

"Do you have anyone in mind?"

"You'll do." Tigh turned around and put Jame on the ground. Jame thanked her with a slap on the arm.

Jyac wiped away her amused expression. "Get that worked out?"

"Yes." Jame wrapped an arm around Tigh's waist. "We're going to pretend to hold Tigh under house arrest. It may be in the Mysteries, but I don't think our foes think we'll actually do it. Let's give them something else to consider while we start preparations to attack. If we think we can win if Tigh is imprisoned, we may as well look like we're ready to fight."

Tigh grinned. "You just want to get me into a warm, dry prison cell for a few days."

Jame grinned back as Jyac just shook her head.

"HOW EXACTLY DID Misner know Tigh would figure out the illusion in the Temple?" Seeran didn't raise her head as she scribbled the incredible account of the last couple of days.

Tigh, seated cross-legged in front of the fire, looked up from her maintenance on her armor and smiled but did not answer.

"Good question." Jame grabbed a challenge braid from the small table next to her and threw it at Tigh, who let it bounce off her forehead. "Good catch."

Tigh picked up the braid and studied it. "Tall, red-head, not bad looking."

Jame threw a half dozen more braids at her. "How did Misner know you would figure out the illusion in the Temple?"

"It is written." Tigh shielded herself from another volley of braids. "Much of our Guard training involved solving seemingly impossible puzzles. By comparison, the illusion in the Temple was an easy one." She picked up a braid. "How can I meet these challenges if I'm under house arrest?"

Jame grinned. "Maybe we can make it a part of your reward for gaining the acolytes' undying gratitude."

Tigh scowled. "You enjoyed that didn't you?"

"Until I had to pull them off you," Jame muttered.

"You're cute when you're jealous," Tigh said. "They were too . . . um, lavender for my taste."

Jame noticed that Seeran was scribbling away in her journal.

"You're not writing this down, are you?" Jame asked.

Seeran blinked up at her. "Of course. You two have a very unique, but entertaining, way of talking to each other."

Jame and Tigh exchanged bewildered glances.

Tigh shrugged. "We talk like anyone else."

"Rarely does an historian have the opportunity to hear everyday conversations between heroes," Seeran said, getting twin looks of exasperation. "I know, I know. You're not heroes."

"We're just doing what needs to be done," Jame said.

"Because you're the best ones for the job," Seeran said.

"For this particular job, yes," Jame said.

"So you restore the waters of Laur, and they show their gratitude by putting you under house arrest," Seeran said.

"Actually, that was Jame's idea," Tigh said as she returned to her task.

Seeran shot Jame a startled look.

"We're trying to outsmart the enemy by pretending not to fall for one of their tricks," Jame said. "You see, in the Mysteries, the Emorans are defeated if they imprison the outsider. The logical moral of the parable is that the Emorans will win if Tigh remains free. So we confuse Misner by imprisoning Tigh."

"Argis is so frustrated by all this game playing she spent the day sparring. I think there are more injuries from her sparring than from the battle yesterday." Seeran dipped her quill into the ceramic ink jar. "So that's the story up to now?"

"That's it." Jame nodded. "And if you think Argis is frustrated, just wait until Tigh gets out on the sparring grounds to meet those challenges. I just hope the enemy makes their next move fast or we'll have a very frustrated warrior on our hands."

"I'll just have to find other ways to work off that excess energy," Tigh said with utter innocence.

Jame turned to her, but her attention was back on the armor.

Seeran blinked between them, an embarrassed blush rising up her cheeks.

Jame picked up another braid and studied it. "Do I detect a different kind of frustration?"

Tigh feigned surprise. "I thought maybe you'd want to sort through some of your things here. Clean out some of the stuff from your childhood."

Jame laughed. "Right. I know how much you love puttering around and tidying up." She turned to a curious Seeran. "I have to use all kinds of bribery to get her to do the simplest chores in our place in Ynit."

"You have a place in Ynit?" Seeran asked.

"A small house in the arbiters' quarter," Jame said. "It's home until we settle here for good."

"Why not Ingor?"

Tigh looked up from her work and cleared her throat. "Have you ever been to Ingor?"

"Uh, no." Seeran shook her head. "But I hear it has stunning architecture. It's supposed to be the most beautiful of cities, perched on hills overlooking the Nirlion Sea."

"It *is* beautiful," Tigh said. "A city built from the riches of well-to-do merchants. Not the kind of place for a poor arbiter and her warrior."

"Even with your family there?" Seeran asked.

"My family had different ideas of a career for me," Tigh said. "They thought I could just put being a warrior behind me and go back to the family business."

"I thought . . . I mean," Seeran stammered.

"You thought I was cut off from my family and disowned?" Tigh raised an eyebrow. "Merchants are a different breed. They have dealings with all kinds of people. War is big business, and merchants can't afford to take sides or be bothered by questions of ethics or morality. I'm actually of more value to my family now because of what I know about war and because of the knowledge acquired as the companion of an arbiter."

"Interesting," Seeran said.

"Lucky for me, Tigh's spirit is more Emoran than Ingoran," Jame said.

"I'm the lucky one." Tigh winked at Seeran.

A gentle rap drew their attention to the door.

"Come in," Jame said.

A young girl, holding a tray, pushed opened the door and walked in.

"The queen has sent the midday meal for you, my princess, and for the prisoner." The girl cast shy eyes at Tigh.

"Thank you. Just put it on the table there." Jame got up from her chair and wandered over to inspect the tray. "Thank the cooks for the wonderful Ingoran food."

The girl's delighted smile almost overwhelmed her delicate features. "The cooks will be happy to hear that, my princess," she managed to stammer before skipping out of the chamber.

Jame turned to Seeran, who was gathering up her things. "I think bringing Tigh here will have a positive impact on Emoria."

"You just want to get them thinking more like you. So it'll be easier for them to understand you when you become queen." Tigh cocked her at head Jame.

"That, too. But they don't need to know that." Jame tried to pretend to be serious but she couldn't help grinning. "Now you better get over here and get some food before I eat it all."

JAME SQUINTED INTO the late evening sun as she stood, flanked by Argis and Mularke, atop the gate wall. Despite the seriousness of the threat to Emoria, she felt more relaxed than she had in a long time. Two days of keeping her willing prisoner company made her think they should take a few days off for themselves every once in a while. A small smile played on her lips as she ruminated about how wonderfully attentive a relaxed Tigh could be.

"There." Mularke pointed at a movement at the far end of the valley.

They watched as a small band of women shimmered into view.

"So they just appeared in the forest?" Jame shaded her eyes and picked out Gindor, walking beside an apparent stranger draped in delicate, dancing cloth.

"The patrol had just passed a small clearing," Argis said. "They heard noises behind them and went back to investigate, and there stood the Council and that woman."

A quick patter of footfalls heralded the arrival of Jyac and Sark to the overlook. They shaded their eyes and stared out into the valley.

"They seem to be all right," Argis said.

Jyac turned to her. "That's good to hear. Do we know who this stranger is?"

Mularke shook her head. "The scout said she doesn't look like she's from around here."

Jame studied the foreign clothing. "I'd say she's from the Oheria Gulf coast."

"That's hundreds of miles from here," Jyac said. "You had a big case there. Several years ago."

Jame gave her a wary look. "You heard about that?"

Jyac laughed at Jame's expression. "We heard about it. I hear it's an interesting place. Very exotic."

"Compared to here, it would be considered exotic," Jame said. "Their dress is more suited to the warmer weather."

"Why is someone from the Oheria Gulf coast here? With the Council?" Sark, always the practical thinker, stood with arms crossed.

"Only she has the answer," Jyac said.

"There are many strangers in these mountains who are trying to do us harm," Argis said. "We must be cautious with this one."

Mularke frowned. "How will we know for sure if she is friend or foe?"

"We have Tigh to determine that," Jame said. "She still has many of the skills from when she was a Guard. One of them is knowing if someone is telling the truth."

"That's right," Argis said. "She knew when that Meah woman was lying to her."

"I just hope the Council has forgotten about treating her like an unwanted interloper," Jyac said. "At least they'll be happy to see her imprisoned. Even if it is a ruse."

"Imprisoned in Jame's chamber," Argis said. "We could all wish for such a punishment."

To cover her embarrassment Jame slapped Argis on the arm.

Jyac smiled at them.

High, excited voices wafted up to them from the valley as the Council members, rambling along like they were out for a pleasant walk, jabbered and gestured at the patrol.

"They don't look like they've been through too much of an ordeal," Jyac said.

"You can bet they're going to be raving mad about . . . let's see, how lax we've become in our security, how we didn't find them and rescue them . . . and you can be sure they'll throw in everything else they've been complaining about since Laur was a child before we hear the end of it," Sark said and covered her ears for emphasis.

"Unless this seemingly miraculous return has changed their dispositions, be ready for a steady tongue-lashing for at least a season or two," Jyac said.

Jame leaned over the wall for a better look at the stranger strolling next to Gindor. She talked with her hands as much as with her voice, and the folds of the thin shimmering fabric she wore caught the long rays of the dying sun. Gindor appeared to be immersed in the stranger's words. That alone signaled there was more to this stranger than someone who had wandered too far from home. Gindor's distrust of anything not Emoran was as much a part of her as her own skin.

"I suppose we'd better be at the gate or else they'll have one more thing to torment us with." Jyac straightened and led the way down the switchback to the city square.

Argis leaned into Jame's ear. "Do you think this is written in the Mysteries?"

Jame, keeping an eye on her footing, shook her head. "I don't think so. We won't know for sure until I can speak privately with Jyac."

"If it's not written . . ."

"I know," Jame said. "It might be enough to turn our chances around. Give us an advantage for a change."

They looked up at the commotion as twelve bedraggled women in surprisingly good spirits emerged from the tunnel. Heads poked out of doorways, and women wandered out into the torch-lit square to see what had disturbed their quiet evening.

"In case you hadn't noticed, we were kidnapped," Gindor said upon seeing Jyac.

Jyac stifled a sigh and strode to the twelve women.

Jame rolled her eyes. How they disappeared was truly a mystery. They had searched every patch of rock in the Council's chambers for a hidden tunnel or even evidence of recent disturbance and found nothing. Tigh determined that the escape route was concealed with a spell rather than an illusion, since an illusion would break as soon as it was touched.

"We couldn't figure out how you were taken," Jyac said.

"Right out from under your noses. While you were drunk with celebrating." Gindor waved a hand at the gathering crowd.

"Not all of us were drunk and all the guards were on duty," Jame said.

"You, my girl, have no voice here until we say so." Gindor shook a bony finger at Jame.

"If we hadn't listened to her voice and the voice of her partner, there might not have been an Emor for you to return to." Argis strolled up to Gindor.

"Introduce us to your friend," Jyac said.

To Jame's surprise, Gindor stopped her confrontation with Argis and turned to the tall woman.

The stranger pulled the cloth draped over her head down onto her shoulders, revealing thick, curly dark hair that reflected a reddish tint in the deepening torchlight. Her skin was sun touched, as was common to the folks from the Gulf coast. Gentle, curious eyes, the same color as her hair, blinked back at them.

"This is Goodemer, a wizard from the Maymi Peninsula," Gindor said with near reverence. "She found us after we managed to escape. Fortunately for you, we still have our wits about us and can act like warriors when called upon to do so. We lost our way in the caves and when we finally found an opening to the outside, we were on the other side of Jacalore Peak. Three good days walk from here. After we had traveled a bit, we came upon Goodemer. She told us she was sent here to investigate the news a rogue wizard was up to no good in these mountains."

"How did you know that?" Jame asked Goodemer.

"Wizards can feel other wizards at work. It's a way to keep any misuse of our power in check," Goodemer said in a voice that flowed like a sweet melody from the accents of her native land. "There are one or two rogue wizards we've tried to find over the last several seasons. One seems to have settled in these mountains and is causing terrible havoc in the natural force."

"She found a shortcut through the mountains for us," Gindor said. She seemed to trust this wizard, despite every reason to be wary of her.

"I'm Jyac, Queen of Emoria, and this is my niece, Jame," Jyac said. "This is Sark, my Right Hand, Argis, Master Warrior, and Mularke, Master Archer."

Goodemer laid gentle eyes on each Emoran and then returned her attention to Jame. "I've seen you before. You saved those children from being sold into slavery and broke up the underground criminal activity in Maymi. I am honored to be in your presence." She performed a gracious bow to a stunned Jame.

"I was just doing my job," Jame mumbled.

"It seems we have much to discuss." Jyac cleared her throat. "We welcome you as our guest, Goodemer. We also want to stop this wizard."

Goodemer grinned in delight and followed her hosts to the palace.

Chapter 13

JYAC SANK INTO her favorite chair in front of the fire in her private sitting chamber. She pointed to the chair next to her, and Jame sat on the edge of it.

The return of the Council tore a hole in Jyac's faith in the Mysteries, playing havoc with her ability to focus. She couldn't turn away from her beliefs because a single incident didn't happen the way it was written. This was not the time to be incapacitated by a faltering faith.

"That was not the way that the Council was to return to us," Jyac said.

Jame nodded. "I gathered as much."

"They were to reappear one morning asleep in their own beds." Jyac made the decision to tell Jame what she had just learned from Gindor.

She tried to accept that if these incidents were forced events from the Mysteries, then the whole situation was false and had nothing to do with the Mysteries at all. Leaving the one truth Jyac knew she had to follow. A princess would defeat the wizard.

"Gindor overheard the Lukrian guards grumbling about their mysterious leaders. The Lukrians wanted to trade the Council for our prisoners. They thought that was the reason for kidnapping the Council in the first place."

"Makes sense," Jame said.

"So they weren't very happy when they found out the Council members were to be returned to Emor unharmed," Jyac continued.

Jame frowned and turned puzzled eyes to Jyac. "Since the Council has read the Mysteries, they knew they would be returned unharmed. Why did they bother to escape?"

"It seems the Lukrians were plotting to go against their leaders and even discussed moving the Council to a hiding place until they could agree on a prisoner exchange." Jyac smiled at Jame. Nothing got past that sharp mind. "The Council saw an opportunity to escape and took it."

"So the illusion of the Emor Mysteries has been broken," Jame said. "That means their present strategy has been foiled."

"Maybe buying us a little time," Jyac said with cautious optimism.

"All we need is a crack to slip through." Jame grinned. "That was a favorite saying of a professor of mine. To learn all the family secrets, one must find where the mice get into the house. Our mouse hole is the Lukrian village."

Jyac steepled her fingers. Jame always had a mind for strategy, making it all the more sad when she turned away from her warrior training. The same trait served her well as an arbiter, but to Jyac's mind, it was wasted on such passive activities. "There's also this wizard from the south."

"If she's as she says, we'll have the cat to go with the mice." Jame leaned back in the chair.

Jyac gave Jame a sidelong glance. "Can Tigh really tell if she's truthful or not?"

"I've never known her to be wrong," Jame said. "It has something to do with the heightened senses of the Guards."

"So we add another animal to your menagerie." Jyac's expression turned to amusement.

"The panther and the fox." Jame nodded. "We were given those nicknames by the people of Ampiston. We reminded them of a storyteller and warrior from their ancient stories."

"I'd like to hear that story sometime." Jyac, knowing Jame's modest nature, would have to think of creative ways of coaxing what appeared to be an adventurous life out of her. "It's time to join the others for the evening meal."

"Tigh will be pleased she can join us." Jame's eyes twinkled. "She doesn't like being shut up for any length of time. Two moons in a narrow cell in Ynit just about drove her crazy."

Jyac gazed at Jame. "I'd like to hear about your experiences with the Guards someday. I think it may not have been such a bad learning experience for a princess."

TIGH, JUST HAPPY to be out of Jame's room for the first time in two days, settled into the cushions of Jyac's private dining chamber. Not that the opportunity to laze around with Jame wasn't pleasant. It had been a while since they had reaffirmed their love with such depths of intimacy. A grin tugged at her mouth as she glanced at her tablemates. Sark and Ronalyn chatted, and Argis sipped from her mug of spiced tea.

"I hear you're getting let off for good behavior." Argis sat up from her slouch and put both elbows on the table.

Tigh was thankful Jame wasn't there to comment on just how good her behavior had been over the last couple of days. She answered with an expressive lift of an eyebrow.

"The warriors are itching for you to meet their challenges." Argis made a show of studying Tigh. "But if you think you need a couple of days practice after lazing around indoors . . ."

"I got plenty of exercise," Tigh said.

"I don't think fighting off Jame counts," Sark said.

Tigh shifted her eyes to Sark. "Whatever Jame wants, Jame gets. I know better than to put up any resistance."

Sark grinned. "Are you rested enough for the challenges?"

"Completely invigorated." Tigh grinned.

"Looks like some things never change." Argis kept steady eyes on Tigh.

Tigh gazed at Argis. It took every bit of control she had to keep her jealousy below the simmering point. Jame had told her that no one could get away from reminders of past relationships or disputes or moments of indiscretion in a close community like Emoria. Argis was testing her, reminding her that she had to share her cherished intimate memories of Jame with someone else. Someone who she now called friend.

She lifted her mug of spiced tea. "Here's to Jame. The most remarkable person I've ever met."

Argis looked startled, then she grinned and raised her mug. "Here's to Jame."

Sark and Ronalyn joined in the toast.

"So the challenge is on for tomorrow?" Argis relaxed back into the cushions.

"Just name the time," Tigh said.

"One at a time or all at once?" Argis asked.

Sark sputtered her tea.

"Your choice." Tigh put down her mug.

Sark whipped her head around to Tigh. "Warrior humor, right?"

Argis arched an eyebrow. "You didn't see her fight."

"I heard about it." Sark sucked in a breath.

"I'll let the challengers decide," Tigh said.

Argis turned to the door as Jyac and Jame walked in.

Jame plopped down next to Tigh, wrapped her arms around her, and gave her a warm hug.

"You're in a good mood." Tigh picked up the hot kettle with her free hand and poured the aromatic tea into Jame's mug.

"Hmmm. Thanks." Jame disengaged from Tigh, took the mug in both hands, and sipped the steaming tea.

"Where is our guest?" Jyac turned to Ronalyn.

"Probably still bathing." Ronalyn grinned. "She couldn't stop marveling at our warm, running water."

Tigh kept her thoughts to herself, as she did earlier when Argis told her of the stranger who had accompanied the Council back to Emor claiming to be a wizard. She wasn't in a position to question Jyac's decision to allow this stranger to be treated as a guest in the palace. She just hoped she could detect if the woman meant harm to the Emorans or not.

"She's from the Maymi peninsula," Jame said, leaning into Tigh.

"Where Meah's from," Tigh said.

All eyes turned to them.

"I think it's just a coincidence," Jame said. "This wizard knew me from when we had visited there."

"When that young man sculpted the statue of you surrounded by thankful children. If I remember correctly, it's now displayed in the Gardens of Trinagol." Tigh watched in delight as the blush blossomed on Jame's cheeks. "She made quite an impression on the Maymians." Tigh looked around Jame at Jyac.

"So it seems." Jyac chuckled.

Jame squirmed. "I was just doing my job."

"Convincing the slavers a wagon could fly was beyond inspired," Tigh said.

"I had to think of something," Jame said.

"I think most of us would have been a little less dramatic," Tigh said.

Jame crossed her arms. "It worked, didn't it?"

"It not only worked but it ensured your place in Maymian history." Tigh grinned. "It's your own fault for being hailed a hero. You gave them too good of a story to ignore."

"And what were you doing during this creative subterfuge?" Jyac directed a pointed look at Tigh.

Jame rested her chin on her hand and gazed at Tigh. "Yes. Tell us what you were doing."

Tigh fiddled with a piece of flat bread. "I was backing up Jame."

"Backing up. Is that what you call it?" Jame turned to her audience, already captive, and recounted a harrowing tale of how their attempts to foil the slavers kept failing and their only chance of freeing the children was a final act of desperation before the slavers sailed away. A story of impenetrable swamps, flying slavers, and brave children left her audience stunned into silence.

"Is this what you do all the time?" Argis finally asked.

"Oh, no. Not at all," Jame said. "Our lives are generally quiet. Almost boring. Traveling from place to place. Judging local cases."

Jyac chuckled. "Your personal historian seems to know a lot of stories that don't sound very quiet to me."

"Things are always exaggerated." Jame shrugged and dipped a sliver of bread into a bowl of sweet mountain fruit chutney. "Personal historian?"

"I think Seeran has been doing her bit to contribute to the growing legend of their future queen," Tigh murmured in her ear. "It seems she knows more about us than she let on."

"For what it's worth, we've been very pleased and proud of what you've done with your life." Jyac took Jame's hand into both of hers. "I'm going to talk with Gindor tonight. Get her to put aside her objections to Tigh, at least until we overcome our enemies."

"Good luck," Argis said.

"I think my luck will hinge on how our guest and Tigh react to each other." Jyac turned to Tigh. "Gindor seems to trust this wizard, and you're the only one among us who can determine if she is friend or foe."

Tigh nodded. "I will do everything I can to help."

NOTHING IN HER limited experience in Maymi could have prepared Goodemer for the wonder and sophistication of the palace at Emor. The clever ways of providing light had her thinking that one of her wizard colleagues had lent a hand in the illumination until she studied the light source closer. She couldn't believe the airiness of the guest chamber. The polished white walls glowed orange in the reflected torchlight.

For all their fabled fierceness, the Emorans appeared to have a sophisticated culture. Goodemer didn't quite know what to make of the twelve women who called themselves Emorans, since the only exposure she had to them was Jame and brief glimpses of the Emorans who visited Ynit during Tigh's rehabilitation. She certainly didn't expect a comfortably furnished room, replete with a waterfall of warm water flowing into a quartz-lined pool.

The nice guard told her the waterfall was a gift of Laur, their patron deity. *The Maymians should think about adopting this deity for some relief from their hot, humid climate.* She got out of the pool and dried herself with the linen cloth. Light wool leggings and tunic had been laid out on the bed. She fingered the soft fabric and wondered if they were woven from the wool of the shaggy goats she had seen frolicking on the steep mountain slopes. They were definitely much warmer than her filmy clothes.

After slipping into the warm wool, she added her belt pouch and a silver amulet of a wolf's head that she wore around her neck. She spent a few moments stilling her mind, knowing her first battle in these mountains would be against the Emorans' distrust of her.

"I don't know if I can do this. What if I can't convince them I'm a friend and not a foe?"

She listened to the cascading water, expecting no answer and getting none. Her mentor had faith in her ability to perform this daunting task. She just had to see through her natural modest impression of her skill. Sighing, she walked to the door and pushed it open. Eiget, lounging against the opposite wall, straightened.

"This way." Eiget led Goodemer through a baffling maze of carved and painted corridors and small chambers. Goodemer, ever curious, gawked around like a child in a confectionery shop.

At the end of a narrow corridor stood a doorway covered with hanging leather strips rather than a light wooden door. Eiget stepped to the side of the opening and signaled Goodemer through. Careful not to show the nervousness roiling around inside of her, she nodded to Eiget, pulled aside the leather strands, and stepped into a cozy chamber. She was relieved to see a small party, four she had already met and one she knew well, if only from a distance.

"Enter, enter." Jyac waved her in and pointed to an empty space opposite Tigh and next to Argis. "Please sit."

"Thank you," Goodemer said and dropped cross-legged onto the cushions.

"You've met Jame, Argis, and Sark," Jyac said. "This is my consort, Ronalyn, and Jame's partner, Tigh."

Goodemer bowed her head to Ronalyn and Tigh, her eyes lingering on Tigh. "I've seen you before in Maymi. The story of your bravery and compassion has become a favorite among my people." She decided it was not the proper place to speak of the other time she had seen Jame and Tigh when she was a young apprentice in Ynit. She had spent most of that time lost in an adolescent fascination with the pair.

Tigh bowed her head in acknowledgment of the compliment.

"Goodemer is a wizard," Jyac said. "She's here to investigate the doings of a certain wizard in these mountains."

Argis poured spiced tea into Goodemer's cup and pushed a basket of flat bread and a bowl of chutney within her reach. "We're curious about this investigation."

"We seem to have a common goal of wanting to stop this wizard before she can do great harm," Jame said.

Goodemer nodded as she took a sip of the warm liquid to calm her nerves. This was the toughest part of her assignment. Her mentor always joked that wizardry would be simple if they didn't have to deal with people. So much energy went into turning distrust and hostility into a working alliance. Up to that moment it was all just theory to her.

"She's been a rogue wizard for many years," Goodemer said. *Gain trust by giving information freely*, her mentor's voice echoed in her head.

"Is she called Misner?" Tigh sat forward, pinning Goodemer with her compelling eyes.

"Yes." Goodemer tilted her head. "How do you know that?"

Tigh crossed her arms, holding Goodemer's gaze. "I had some . . . dealings with her. Several years ago."

"Dealings?"

"I was sent to kill her," Tigh said. "I thought I succeeded. Time has proven me wrong."

Goodemer tried to swallow, but her throat was too dry. "May I ask why you were sent to kill her?"

"The Northern powers wanted her to create an army that could defeat the Elite Guards," Tigh said. "Five Guards before me were sent to kill her. She killed them. When I faced her, she taunted me with their names and played havoc with my mind. I somehow fought through that and sliced off her head. Something fed back from the blow and knocked me unconscious for over a day. When I came to, what was left of the wizard was still there, so I had no reason to doubt she was dead."

"It would have been an easy enough illusion." Goodemer felt her nervousness slip away.

"Why would she pretend to let me kill her when she had killed the other Guards?" Tigh looked around the discreet kitchen helpers who put platters of food on the table.

Goodemer gazed with delight at the feast before her then raised her eyes to Tigh. "Why is she playing games with your people?"

"Tigh is not Emoran, and we were attacked before she ever visited Emoria." Argis scooped a thick meaty stew into a small bowl. "Eat up. Jyac presides over an informal table."

"Thank you." Goodemer watched how the others filled their plates and bowls and took a little of everything within her reach. Traveling introduced her taste buds to some interesting treats. She noticed a different type of food in front of Tigh and Jame. "Do you follow a special diet?"

Jame looked up from her plate. "Tigh is Ingoran. I cook according to their customs because it's easier than preparing two different things for every meal."

"This is very good. Different from the food in Maymi." Goodemer smiled at Jyac.

"Thank you. We take pride in our cuisine," Jyac said.

They ate, keeping the conversation to inconsequential matters and exchanging cultural differences. The spiced tea had turned into spiced wine at some point, and Goodemer relaxed in the presence of these seemingly benign women. She thought how strange that was. They should have been treating her with suspicion. She was a wizard after all, capable of creating great mayhem even as she ate.

"I'm curious about one thing," she said. "I have to admit I was expecting to be treated with a little more suspicion, being a wizard and all."

Six sets of eyes were on her, lifted forks and cups forgotten. She blinked at them, realizing the wine might have loosened her tongue too much.

Tigh sucked in a breath and cleared her throat, bringing Goodemer's attention her way. "A part of our training in the Elite Guards was to learn how to detect deception in others. I haven't felt any deception from you."

"How do you know I'm not covering my deception with an illusion?" Goodemer asked in a friendly challenge.

"Illusion only works when the illusion is unexpected," Tigh said. "We've learned in the past few days not to trust anyone or anything, so naturally we were looking for deception from you. Your illusion would have been shattered immediately and I would have seen it."

Goodemer cocked her head. "You understand the ways of the wizard?"

"I understand what I've observed," Tigh said. "What I don't understand is the total lack of deception coming from you. Everyone has something to hide, and there's always a degree of evasion when we talk with others, especially strangers."

"Wizards can't lie." Goodemer, once again, found all eyes on her.

"What do you mean—can't?" Jame asked.

"We take an oath on the staff of Hatliz, swearing we can only tell the truth."

Jame frowned. "What happens if you don't speak the truth?"

"We die." Goodemer shrugged.

A shocked silence dropped over the chamber. All eyes shifted to Tigh.

"She's telling the truth," Tigh said.

Jyac sat back with a catlike grin. "Well then. That changes everything. Welcome to Emoria, Goodemer. I think we may be able to help each other."

JAME HEARD THE gathering crowd before rounding the last switchback and walking the final long incline to the fields above the city's south cliff. Unlike the tree-covered northern rim, an extended meadow spread away from the southern rim before it rose into the distant snowy peak.

Tigh stopped walking. and Jame almost collided into her.

"What . . . ?" Jame looked around Tigh. "You're going to have a bit of an audience."

Tigh scowled at her, and she hid a smile behind a hand.

"Is this good or bad?" Tigh took a few steps away from the edge of the bluff, allowing Jame onto the grass.

"They're smiling and laughing. Sounds like a celebration to me." Jame grinned as a joyful jolt ran through her body.

Tigh raised an eyebrow. "But what are they celebrating?"

"The initiation of a new citizen of Emoria." Jame laughed at Tigh's stunned expression. "The challenges are for you to prove your worth. You've done that in battle, no less. Now the challenges are to prove your solidarity with the other warriors."

Tigh's face lit up. "So I can have fun?"

"Have fun. Give them a show." Tigh's delighted grin was a gift Jame treasured.

The groups of women shifted as Tigh and Jame strolled to the center of the circle where Jyac was in an animated discussion with Argis.

"Probably trying to figure out the order of challengers," Jame said.

"Unless they've decided I take them all on at once." Tigh flashed innocent eyes at her.

"And why would they think of doing that?" Jame gave Tigh a knowing look. She sighed at the guilty child expression she could never resist. "Warriors."

Tigh grinned.

Jame quickened the pace across the centuries-hardened sparring fields and archery ranges that splotched the meadow outside of a well-kept ceremonial circle. The circle was large enough to hold much of the population of Emor around its perimeter. Most Emorans' strongest memories were of events as witnesses or participants within the ceremonial circle. In celebration or in mourning, receiving a first braid or witnessing a severe reprimand, it all happened on that high meadow.

Jyac and Argis stopped their discussion and watched Jame and Tigh approach.

"Good morning," Jame said.

Jyac nodded. "Good morning. A good morning for a challenge or two or sixteen."

Argis and Tigh rolled their eyes.

"I'm glad we were able to keep the city entertained." Jame glanced around the circle.

"Looks like we're going to get more than our blades trade worth," Argis said.

Jame followed her gaze back toward the city. The Council, in full ceremonial garb of supple intricately embossed leather, trampled across the meadow, faces set and determined.

Jame turned to Jyac. "I thought you were going to talk to Gindor."

"She wouldn't see me," Jyac said.

Within a heartbeat the only sound in the meadow was the breeze playing with the grass and the soft crackle beneath the Council members' boots. From long years of practice, the Council formed a ring around the foursome standing in the middle of the larger circle.

"That woman is not allowed to carry a sword in Emoria." Gindor pointed to Tigh. "We have not accepted her presence here."

"I've had enough of this bothersome, daughter-of-a-shaggy-goat talk about tradition!" Every head whipped around as an angry Tas strode out from the crowd, rotating her sword with negligent skill.

Gindor looked too shocked to come up with a reaction before an indignant Tas stood before her. "You know better than to challenge the Council."

Threescore warriors, including the challengers, emerged from the stilled onlookers, with swords drawn and ready to stand for what they thought was right, over the Council's old-fashioned traditions.

Jame turned to Jyac and wondered why she wasn't surprised to see her smiling.

Chapter 14

GINDOR SHOOK AN accusing finger at Jyac. "You put them up to this to make it look like what was written in the Mysteries."

"I did no such thing," Jyac said. "Our warriors have enough sense to see when you're using tradition as an excuse."

Gindor glared at Jyac, then broke away from her place in the Council ring and strode to her. Argis unsheathed her sword to protect her queen.

"You dare speak to me about tradition?" Gindor's voice dropped low and menacing.

Jyac straightened, presenting a calm, controlled demeanor. "Traditions are created to protect our society from threat and from losing its identity. A princess taking a consort from outside the community only departs from tradition, it does not break any of our written laws. Other princesses have taken consorts from outside our borders. The law states a princess must be joined in an Emoran ceremony, it does not forbid her from being joined in a ceremony of another culture. The fact that you refuse to acknowledge her joining doesn't make it any less real according to our laws. And the fact that you refused to approve her joining to an outsider doesn't make your words law. And as for the matter of bearing arms, I think Tigh has proven she is an asset rather than a threat to our society."

"The Council has the last word on the interpretation of the law," Gindor said. "Jame has brought a potential threat to our society by entering into a union with an unstable and menacing woman whose deeds are worse than any stories from the Book of Horrors. It is our responsibility to protect Emoran society. Especially when our people are sometimes too blind to see the true threat."

Jame strode up to Gindor, not even trying to hide her anger. "Show me the proof she is a threat. Tell me what you've heard in the last few years or seen in the last few days to support this accusation. You have no argument. I'm an arbiter for the Southern Districts and Emoria, by treaty, is under my jurisdiction. Let me advise you, as your counsel, you have no case."

Two shocked heartbeats later, the citizens of Emoria erupted in deafening support for Jame. Argis stepped forward behind Jame's right shoulder. At the same time Tas strode through the opening in the Council's circle and stood behind Jame's left side. Their swords rested on their shoulders in a show of casual menace.

Gindor kept a steady eye on Jame, stepped back, and crossed her strong arms. The spectators fell into silence. After several heartbeats of studying an indignant Jame she raised her eyes to Jyac. "Spoken like a true princess of Emoria." She returned her attention to Jame. "You're right. We have no evidence against Tigh. Everything points to the fact she's been fully cleansed and she lives a life dedicated to peace and justice. The Council met last night and decided to accept Tigh into our society and recognize your joining, if you agree to an official Emoran joining before you leave our territory again."

Jame reined in her anger. "Excuse me for being a little confused, but didn't you just say you haven't accepted her presence here?"

Gindor straightened. "It's not official until we make the announcement."

The Council loved keeping everyone off balance, and Jame decided this was one time they needed to be confronted about it. "I thank the Council for accepting Tigh into our society." She paused to give her next words the appropriate weight. "But I have a problem with the tactics you used today. You made the decision to allow Tigh Emoran rights, yet the first thing you did was fling threats at everyone when all you had to do was make the announcement."

"You must see it from our point of view," Gindor said. "You didn't know of our decision, yet you were going against our law by letting a stranger bear arms in Emoria. It doesn't matter she wore a sword to fight for Emoria. She made the honorable decision to give up the sword after the battle but no one accepted it. The question of the joining may be more a part of tradition than law. The ban on strangers bearing arms in Emoria is law, and no matter how silly it seems to enforce it sometimes, we have to continue to take it seriously. We needed to remind you that a law has been broken."

"Perhaps a less dramatic reminder next time might be wise," Jame said.

Gindor studied Jame. "Perhaps. We'll take your words under advisement." She raised her eyes to Jyac, and her grim features transformed into a grin. "Now, Jyac. I think you have a challenge to oversee."

GOODEMER, STILL PONDERING the curious scene involving the Council, followed Eiget to the other two strangers in Emoria. She was thankful to be encased in warm Emoran leathers since the chill of the morning was as cold as it ever got in Maymi. Eiget had explained what the confrontation with the Council was about and the ensuing challenge was not a serious fight. "Warriors' idea of fun," was the way the taciturn guard put it.

Just as Goodemer and Eiget joined Seeran and Gelder, wild drumming started up, signaling the challenge was about to begin.

Jame, Jyac, and Ronalyn lounged in low chairs, slung with shaggy mountain goat skins, on a platform built of meadow stone. Tigh stood on one side of the circle and the sixteen challengers casually lounged on the opposite side. The low morning sun shimmered as the dew vaporized, casting the scene into an ethereal tableau.

"What's she doing?" Gelder nudged Seeran.

Goodemer turned to Tigh as low murmurs of speculation filled the air. Tigh tugged off her boots and put them aside. Goodemer then looked at Jame, who threw up her hands and appeared to be uttering some colorful phrases.

Seeran shrugged. "I don't know. Maybe it's some Elite Guard ritual."

Jyac stood and raised a hand. The women silenced their excited twitters. "Sixteen of our warriors have challenged Tigh of Ingor, life companion of Jame, princess of Emoria, to a battle of skill. The rules of engagement have been agreed upon between the challengers and the challenged. Tigh of Ingor will take on all the challengers at once, in any fight formation chosen by the challengers." A shocked murmur rose and fell as Jyac waited. "The only weapons will be swords. Because there are sixteen challengers and only one challenged and the intent is to show skill and not to do harm, three touches of aggression will constitute a defeat."

Goodemer exchanged incredulous looks with Seeran. Surely Tigh would receive three blows before she could strike sixteen three times over.

Jyac nodded to Tigh and settled into the low-slung chair.

TIGH SHIFTED HER gaze to Jame, who glanced down at the bare feet, then raised an eyebrow at her. Tigh replied with a quirky grin and a shrug.

Jame shook her head a little before yielding to Tigh with a grin. Tigh gave her a dazzling smile.

Tigh, feeling the cool, dewy grass against her bare feet, strode to the center of the circle. The damp air tickled her skin, waking up her body, opening her mind to the thrill of balancing on the sharp edge of her warrior skills. She studied her adversaries. Much of their present state of mind was visible through the language their bodies spoke. She instructed her own body to take their nervousness and relative inexperience into consideration to ensure no serious injuries happened on the field that day. Jame needed every warrior to be whole and ready when they faced their adversary in the mountains.

Eight warriors stepped forward and separated into two lines of four.

Tigh lifted each foot and checked the soles. The warriors stopped their advance in surprise. Tigh grinned and sprinted toward them. Three paces away, she dove into a somersault and kicked both feet out, collapsing the legs of the two closest warriors. She then rolled to her feet behind the warriors.

She tapped a tall blonde on the shoulder. The blonde whirled her sword around, and Tigh slapped her hands against the flat of the blade. The blonde sailed over Tigh and released the blade. Tigh leapt straight up and shot her legs out parallel to the ground, kicking to two warriors that had been behind the blonde in the stomachs.

Tigh arched her back and landed on her feet in time to whack the blades of the three remaining warriors with the hilt of the sword. She then flipped the sword, grabbed the hilt, and ducked. Four swords crashed above her as she rolled free, leaving the sword in the grass for its owner to claim.

The remaining eight warriors, recovered from the startling quickness with which their comrades received their first touches of aggression, whooped and yodeled as they rushed forward.

Tigh sprang to her feet and ran toward the oncoming flashing swords. She caught a nice soft patch of dirt with her toes and catapulted into a casual flip over them. Before they had a chance to turn around, she scuttled down the line, slapping each one on the arm, then plunged sideways, causing two warriors to crash into each other.

GOODEMER PUT HER hand to her mouth as she stifled both amusement and amazement at Tigh's skill. The crowd around her shifted and strained to decipher what looked like a mad free-for-all. Sixteen warriors chased and slashed at the capering Tigh, as she teased and slipped away from them like a fabled mountain sprite. Blades flashed and crashed and bare feet caused creative havoc and aching bruises. Blood sprayed from an unlucky nose, a mumbled apology lost as the crowd roared. One by one the warriors stepped away from the fray, one holding a leather rag to her nose, another limping, another flexing her hand. All looked stunned by Tigh's unnatural fighting ability, her body whirling like a snow devil and as quick and unerring as a slick-coated panther.

The last three challengers faced the barefooted, aggravating, daughter of a shaggy goat with expressions of unflinching determination.

"The honor of Emoria is on their shoulders," Seeran said.

Goodemer nodded with giddy anticipation.

Tigh took the slight breather to plop down onto the grass and pluck a small stone from the sole of her foot.

The warriors rushed forward and prepared to whack Tigh with the flat of their blades.

They whacked each other and never saw a flying Tigh, who introduced their backs to the hard ground. The roaring crowd hushed as the three climbed to their feet. They faced Tigh and whipped their swords into a salute before turning and joining their fallen comrades.

TIGH FROWNED AND faced the platform with a hopeful expression. "I forgot to use my sword. Can we do it again?"

She was answered by the hiss of a sword sliding along a leather sheath. She whirled around to face the warrior who dared challenge her skill.

She expected Argis or Tas and hid her surprise. Gindor stood ten paces away, twirling her sword, a mocking smile creasing her aged face.

"Let's show these baby lambs how to fight." Gindor's voice came out as a purr, and she straightened to her full height—head and shoulders shorter than Tigh.

Jame and Jyac, looking apprehensive, were on their feet. Some laughter rose from the crowd but most watched in silent anticipation.

Tigh knew Gindor more than made up for her height with a fluid quickness and incomparable skill. The stories told of her encounters with brigands and skirmishes with the Lukrians bordered on exaggeration, yet the fear and respect she commanded was a legacy from that time.

Tigh did not laugh. She turned to the platform to gauge Jame's reaction to this challenge. Their eyes met long enough to tell her she had to be careful with Gindor.

Tigh's weapons instructors had been hardened veterans of wars, past what many considered their prime but still possessing the ability to push the younger, stronger warriors to exhaustion. She gazed at Gindor and drew her sword.

"We're both honorable warriors. We don't need rules of combat to have a nice friendly fight." The bold words rolled from Gindor as her eyes flashed with anticipation.

"As you wish." Tigh rested her blade on her shoulder.

GINDOR STROLLED AROUND Tigh, who turned to follow her path. "That was quite a spectacle you just put on. Don't they teach warriors to stand up and fight anymore?"

"They taught us how to survive a fight with as little injury as possible." Tigh kicked up a small stone, caught it on the flat of her blade, and bounced it a few times before bunting it away.

Gindor rushed forward with her sword raised and clashed with the black blade. She hopped backward, startled. She had known Tigh would counter the blow, but she expected her to be caught off balance. Tigh, she discovered, was both quick and unhurried at the same time, with no excess of movement. She narrowed her eyes. Tigh put her opponents off guard by pretending to get distracted away from the fight. Clever.

To test Tigh's handling of her weapon, Gindor traded a series of strokes with her. Nice. She nodded with approval. "Now do you think we can do something a little more fun without any fancy playing?"

"Play? Me?" Tigh pointed to herself with one hand, while flipping her sword in the other.

"Yes, you." Gindor almost laughed at the warrior-child. She swung her sword, and the meadow rang with flourishes of parries and thrusts.

TIGH KEPT HER mischievous streak in check and concentrated on simple sword work. She was impressed by Gindor's skill as they worked together in a smooth, deadly dance.

Each stroke made it obvious Gindor practiced regularly. Muscles bulging from strained arms and legs held as solidly as those of a warrior in her prime. The joy of battle glinted in her eyes, and a wild grin brightened her usually dour features.

Tigh realized she was face to face with her own future. Too old to be a warrior. Giving up something that was as much a part of her as her soul. Not having the reflexes to protect Jame.

Tigh frowned at the surprise in Gindor's eyes as she backed off from a parry. She looked at her shoulder. The leather was ripped between the light armor plates. A thin line of blood marred the exposed skin.

Tigh straightened and flipped her blade in a respectful salute to Gindor.

A puzzled murmur wafted across the meadow.

"You have a strange sense of honor," Gindor said.

"You drew first blood. The victory is yours," Tigh said.

Gindor kept hold of Tigh's eyes for a bit longer. "You just beat sixteen warriors at once without even getting hit. How does an old woman get in a nick like that one?"

Tigh gazed at the ground. "You reminded me of my greatest fear."

Gindor nodded. "Growing old."

"Not being able to protect Jame someday."

"If you ever feel that time has come, don't be foolish and refuse to recruit a younger warrior for the job," Gindor said. "Our history is filled with too much unnecessary tragedy because of a warrior's pride."

Tigh nodded at the kind of lecture her grandmother loved to give and sheathed her sword. She shook her arms out and settled her thoughts. "I hope I'll have the wisdom to do that when the time comes."

Gindor straightened and whipped her sword into a salute. "I think we should have had more confidence in Jame's ability to choose the right companion. Perhaps we were wrong to reject her choice based only on rumor and campfire stories. We can't wander through our past to try a different path. We can only find a new path to follow into the future. I believe Emoria needs you and Jame to join us on that journey."

"Whatever path Jame takes, I'll follow," Tigh said.

SOMETIMES TIGH ACTED like a bashful child, especially after engaging in something she knew Jame didn't quite approve of. Jame found it sweet, and she greeted Tigh with a twinkling grin.

She wrapped her arms around a sweat-soaked Tigh. The knowledge that she would never have to choose between Tigh and Emoria spread a warm feeling through her soul. All the carefully worded arguments and pleas she had composed for her ultimate confrontation with the Council had been a waste of mental energy. Sometimes Tigh's way was better. Sometimes.

Around them, women gathered in chatty knots while others followed the persistent drumming and wound braids of rhythmic dance steps across the meadow. Once the challenge was officially over the atmosphere had dissolved into a festival in honor of the newest citizen of Emoria.

"Good work." Jame coaxed a dazzling smile from Tigh. "I suppose they want you to play with them some more."

Tigh responded with a sheepish shrugged. "You don't mind?" She brushed her lips against Jame's cheek.

"I'm delighted they've accepted you," Jame said.

"They want me to show them a few fancy moves, then they'll drag me off to the tavern," Tigh breathed in her ear.

"Emoran ale is stronger than most," Jame said. "According to legend, it's distilled from the souls of ancient Emoran warriors."

Tigh chuckled. "You have such quaint traditions."

"I'm sure Ingor has its share of quirky customs." Jame inspected the sword cut on Tigh's arm. The shallowness was a tribute to Gindor's control and skill.

"It's just a nick," Tigh said.

"My idea of a nick has never quite agreed with yours," Jame said. "But I have to agree on this one. Your sleeve, however, is a different tale." She flicked the torn leather flap.

"One of the hazards of being a warrior," Tigh said. "Hard on the wardrobe."

Jame saw the three guests of Emoria move away from a knot of women and trudge across the grass toward them. She noticed Tas strolling next to Eiget. "That's strange."

Tigh turned to see what had caught her attention, then looked back at her for enlightenment.

"What's Tas up to?"

Tigh returned her gaze to Tas. "Uh, don't know."

Jame whipped around to an innocent-looking Tigh. "How come I don't believe you?"

"I'll explain later," Tigh muttered as Seeran, Gelder, and Goodemer stepped within listening range.

"Tonight. If you're not too drunk." Jame laughed at Tigh's mock indignation. "Yes, you." She turned to the others. "Did you enjoy the challenge?"

"I feel so honored. So honored," Seeran stammered out. "It's like being caught in the time of legends and myths."

Jame laughed. "Emoria is hardly mythical. We like to call it Paradise with Wasps."

"That's because of our tendency to greet newcomers with the sting of the sword," Tas said.

"I feel fortunate I was spared such a greeting." Seeran grinned at Tas.

Tas stepped next to Seeran. "If you'd like, I'd be honored to explain some more of our traditions to you." She scuffed the toe of her boot into a soft patch of dirt, her eyes trained on the puffs of dust.

Jame exchanged a quick glance with Tigh. The greatest foe of a warrior's boldness was the emotion of the heart.

"The honor would be mine," Seeran said.

"If you don't mind, I'd like to visit the stables," Gelder said. "Kas promised she'd let me help with the horses."

"Take that as a compliment," Jame said. "Kas is very particular about who she lets near those beasts."

"Give Gessen a few extra strokes," Tigh said. "I'll try to visit her tomorrow."

"I'll make sure she's nice and shiny." Gelder grinned as she trotted away.

"I'd better get over there." Tigh nodded at the cluster of warriors watching her with expectant eyes. "See you later." She pulled Jame into a one-armed hug and then strode toward the now grinning group of warriors.

Tas and Seeran had already wandered off, leaving Jame and Goodemer watching with amusement as two lines of dancers nearly collided.

"Would you like to join me for a bite to eat?" Jame asked.

"Only if I can try some of that interesting-looking Ingoran cuisine," Goodemer said.

"I'll send someone to fetch the food," Jame said. "I don't want to miss Tigh playing with the warriors."

Chapter 15

"THIS IS IT," Argis said in a slurred voice.

Tigh held the torch as Argis felt for the hidden door latch in the carved wall blocking their way.

"I can't believe we're doing this," Mularke muttered, before taking a nip from an ale skin.

"Got it." Argis straightened and pulled on one of several carved handholds. The stone pivoted to reveal an opening, and a puff of cool, stale air touched Tigh's senses.

Tigh held the torch into the deep blackness. "You've been in here before?"

"When I was young," Argis said. "Tas and I stumbled on it when we were looking for somewhere to hide after we put indigo in the ceremonial waterfall."

Mularke giggled. "You two were in so much trouble for that."

Tigh cast an amused glance at Argis. "What was Jame doing at the time?"

Argis grinned. "She masterminded the plot."

"And got you to actually do it." Tigh stepped into the long-forgotten chamber.

The walls extended far beyond the light from the torch. She sniffed, detecting an unexpected freshness and water.

"What do you remember of this cave?" Tigh asked.

"Not much, except it was large and dark." Argis shrugged and wandered around within the range of the torchlight. "It's a nice cave. I wonder why we've never used it?"

Tigh dug her boot into the sandy ground to reveal a darker color just beneath the surface. "Water. Probably floods."

Mularke nodded as she took fire from Tigh's torch with a taper that all Emorans carried, and lit a small oil lamp she had picked up in the corridor. "The water that feeds Laur's waterfalls is on the other side of that wall."

Tigh illuminated the craggy wall. She picked up a set of markings that didn't look natural.

"What's that?" Argis stumbled over to the markings and peered at the circular design.

Tigh ran a finger over the brown substance. It didn't smudge or rub off. "Wizard marks." Mularke joined them. She put a chin on Argis's shoulder as she stared at the design. "This is where the illusion in the Temple was created."

The three exchanged looks as they allowed the words to penetrate their ale-soaked brains.

Mularke scratched her head. "That means the enemy . . ."

JAME STEPPED INTO her chamber and sensed that Tigh wasn't there. The fire crackling in the fireplace was the only noise that reached her ears. It was late—closer to dawn than dusk. She had spent the evening learning about Goodemer and their enemy, gathering as much knowledge as possible for her to present her case. That was how she approached the daunting responsibility of leading the Emorans to a victory against the wizard in the mountains. She decided to prepare the facts and evidence as if she were putting together a defense. After all, she had never lost a case.

She ran a hand through her hair and frowned at the empty bed. She knew she wouldn't be able to sleep knowing Tigh was probably passed out somewhere. Tavern first. If Tigh wasn't there, she could follow the trail. Emor had a discreet, well-organized security—So much so, it was difficult to move around the city without being observed.

She entered the tavern and tried not to breathe in the odorous cloud of stale ale and leather. She stepped around passed out warriors and avoided the wild uncontrolled movements of the few who clung to consciousness. The long tables were packed together, and she took her time peeking under the furniture and into the darkened corners of the domed cavern.

She approached the bar where Teniar, a battle-hardened white-haired woman, was cleaning up for the night. "Have you seen Tigh?"

Teniar glanced up from her task and straightened. "My princess," she murmured in a voice made rough from years of barking orders to novice warriors. "She was here. These young pups couldn't get enough of her. Bragging about how she busted their shaggy-goated noses or flipped them onto their worthless behinds."

Jame arched an eyebrow. "The ale flowed freely?"

"They were pressing drink on her all night." Teniar waved a scarred hand. "But between us, I noticed she'd slide every other full mug in the direction of one of her table mates."

Jame frowned. "So she wasn't falling down drunk when she left?"

Teniar scratched her nose in thought. "She left with Argis and Mularke. They'd been having some kind of discussion about hidden caves around the city. Argis was drunk but no worse than usual. Mularke was stumbling around a bit, but that's Mularke. Tigh seemed to be relaxed, the most sober of the three, I think."

"How long ago did they leave?" Jame felt a chill that had nothing to do with the cool night air wafting through the open tavern doors.

"Let me think." Teniar put down her rag and gazed at the door. "Probably about two sandmarks ago."

Jame squinted at the tall sand clock behind the bar. "Do you have any idea where they could have gone?"

"Not really. But, by the sound of their discussion, it sounded like they were going somewhere specific," Teniar said. "You know how focused warriors can get. Just add a bit of ale and you have them making bets on who can hit Laur's eye at two hundred paces in the dark. And they can't live another heartbeat until they meet the challenge."

"If they went off on some crazy warrior bet two sandmarks ago, they'd be finished by now," Jame said. "Thank you, Teniar."

"They probably couldn't stop betting." Teniar gave her a sympathetic look.

"It's hard to get them to stop once they get started." Jame nodded and walked onto the quiet square. She concentrated on the silence, opening up her senses like Tigh had taught her to. She stared into the deep shadows near the Temple. Two women, holding each other up, staggered into the torchlight.

She strode toward them. Argis and Mularke. Their sober, pain-filled expressions told her their condition wasn't from drunkenness. She broke into a trot and got to them in time to stop Argis from pitching forward.

"Jame," Argis said in a raspy voice. "It's our fault. We're so sorry. So sorry." She sank to her knees, sobbing, breaking the old code that warriors never cried.

"What happened?" Jame managed to push sound through her arid throat.

Mularke put a trembling hand on Argis's shoulder to steady her own weak body. "We were showing Tigh a cave. A close one just beneath the Temple. We found some strange markings—wizard markings, according to Tigh. The next thing we knew we were waking up, and Tigh was gone."

Panic and fear crashed through Jame's mind, making her lightheaded. But she couldn't give in to it. Tigh was in trouble. "Guards!"

Shadows appeared and footfalls clattered from several directions.

"What happened?" Tas asked.

"We think Tigh's been captured," Jame said. "Mularke will tell you where they were when this happened. Get two squads of scouts and try to find out how whoever took her got into the cave, and then follow where they went."

A guard ran to the bell stand outside the barracks. She pulled back a metal shaft suspended on rope and let it go. The shaft bounced on the bell, sending a deep rumble through the city.

Several other guards ran into the barracks shouting, "Rouse the scouts, no time to lose!"

Tas helped Jame get Argis back onto her feet.

"They need to see a healer," Jame said. Tas nodded at a young eager guard to take charge of Mularke.

In a matter of heartbeats, the square was filled with torches and scouts, pulling on leathers and weapons. Shouted commands quickly brought order to the chaos as the leaders of two squads of scouts approached Jame for instructions.

Jame explained to them what had happened and the location of the cave. "Be careful. Approach everything as if it's a deception, from the solid rock wall to the ground you step on. If anything is covered by only illusion *that* will break it." She turned to a wiry guard with alert eyes. "Go wake Goodemer. We need her here."

The guard grinned and sprinted to the palace.

"If the passage out of the cavern is hidden by a spell, Goodemer will find it," Jame said. "Stay alert, they can take you down in a heartbeat with darts covered with a potion."

The scouts stormed through the Temple door, and Jame was alone. It took every bit of strength she had to keep the tears, pooling in her eyes, and a dark despair wrapping a thick fog around her mind, from taking over. Tigh was in trouble, and she wouldn't rest until Tigh was safely back with her.

TIGH NOTICED HER hands were bound in front of her instead of in back and the pallet she was on was filled with down rather than straw. She moved her legs and discovered her feet were loosely tied together. The dank chill of a cavern or the stale and unwashed odors of a prison cell were absent. Muffled voices touched her ears. She concentrated. One of the voices was Meah.

Meah, Tigh sighed. She was in trouble. Her foggy mind drifted to how she was captured. Jame was going to kill her for being so careless. At least Argis and Mularke wouldn't be mistreated because the Lukrians wanted their people released.

She cracked open her eyes and assessed the tidy chamber. The furnishings suggested a private sitting room. She opened her eyes wider. A fire burned in a stone fireplace, giving off enough light to illuminate a puzzle that kept getting more and more confusing. She tensed at the sound of footfalls.

"Misner is tired of hearing about your people." Meah's voice was distinct and close. Tigh squinted at the door. The wood was too thin to stop sound from coming through. Meah and the person she talked to must have just entered the neighboring chamber.

"What kind of honor does this wizard have that she won't let us get our warriors out of the hands of the enemy?" a weary yet strong voice asked.

"She doesn't care about your quaint sense of honor." Tigh could hear the scowl in Meah's voice. "There's only one thing she wants right now."

"The great warrior, Tigh." It sounded like an old argument. "We deliver Tigh, Misner delivers Emoria to us."

"Your honor will be more than restored when you have the Emorans bowing at your feet," Meah said.

"Misner must be patient. Now that the Emorans know we can enter their city unseen, they're on extra alert. Tigh is rarely where we can easily capture her." Tigh was impressed by how the Lukrian worded her statement so it wasn't a lie. "I still don't understand how Misner can deliver Emoria to us and not be able to capture Tigh herself."

The soft pacing of boots replaced words for several heartbeats. "Misner has a tendency to treat people like sheep." Was there a trace of bitterness in Meah's voice? "I guess she didn't think you'd figure out that little inconsistency."

"Go on," the other woman said.

The sigh from Meah sounded genuine enough, but Tigh would have given anything to see her face. "What I'm about to tell you must not tell anyone. I'm risking my place in Misner's circle by saying this to you. But you need to know it to follow her orders without question." Meah hesitated for a heartbeat. "Misner's magic doesn't work on Tigh."

The shock of the words struck Tigh like a sword blow. Several blank pieces of the puzzle gained meaning and slipped into place.

"What do you mean—doesn't work?" The Lukrian sounded incredulous.

"Many years ago, Tigh was sent to kill Misner," Meah said. "She somehow was able to fight through her magic. Misner became so weak she barely escaped with her life. To get away, she created one final illusion of her death at Tigh's hands. It took her many long years to recover from what Tigh did to her."

Tigh pulled out the memories of that horrific encounter on the Umvian plains. She slipped the explanation into the holes left by the ensuing questions of how she defeated Misner and realized her mentors had tried to pull an answer out of her she didn't know she possessed. She had no doubt she had defeated Misner's magic, but it was a warrior's belief that anything could be defeated with enough savage force.

"Tigh was a Guard then," the Lukrian said. "Surely that power has been cleansed from her."

"Five Guards possessing power and skill equal to Tigh's were easily defeated by Misner." Meah's voice was a little distant. One of the five had been Meah's lover. Tigh wondered if Misner was aware of this. "Misner believes whatever defeated her had nothing to do with the Guard enhancements."

"Why hasn't Tigh just confronted her and stopped her?" the Lukrian asked.

"Tigh doesn't know how she defeated Misner." Meah's voice betrayed her amusement. "She thinks she killed her by whacking her head off."

"All right. Your explanation is outrageous enough to probably be true," the Lukrian said. "I can see why Misner wants Tigh out of the way."

"Her patience has been stretched much farther than she likes." The cold warning was back in Meah's voice. "She wants Tigh. Do everything you can to deliver her. Soon."

Soft footfalls faded away, leaving Tigh focused on the silence. Several heartbeats passed and then the door opened.

JAME WATCHED GOODEMER wander around the cavern muttering words that didn't sound encouraging and felt a pang of disappointment. She realized she had hoped Goodemer would enter the cavern and in an impressive, colorful display, tear down Misner's illusions so the scouts had a chance to rescue Tigh. Goodemer's methodical study of the markings, and her casual poking of odd places in the rocky wall grated on Jame's heightened anxiety. Too many sandmarks had passed for hope of catching Tigh's abductors.

Tas strode into the cavern. "Argis and Mularke are all right. Aggie said that the combination of the alcohol and whatever knocked them out might take a while to wear off."

"Glad they're all right," Jame said.

"Clever, clever," Goodemer muttered.

"What?" Jame could no longer hold in her frustration.

Goodemer blinked at her audience. "Several spells have been woven together in such a way that an attempt to unravel one weaves the other spells tighter." She ran a strong hand over a rough patch of rock. "It's a rather clumsy weave, but works well enough."

Her eyes had a wicked glint in them as she wrapped a hand around her wolf's head amulet. Soundless words formed on her lips as the head of the wolf incandesced for a scarce heartbeat.

"If this is any indication of Misner's abilities, I don't think we have much to worry about."

A yawning darkness replaced the rugged wall. The astonished scouts put hands on their belt knives before observing a grinning Goodemer.

Jame and Tas rushed to the tunnel.

"You did it," Jame said.

Goodemer peered into the darkness and held out her amulet. "She makes up for clumsy weaving with excessive redundancy."

"Huh?" Tas stared into the dark.

Jame rolled her eyes. "She means that Misner has compensated for her less than perfect spell weaving skills by repeating the weave within the tunnel."

"Oh." Tas knitted her brow. "You mean she leaves a little trap like this every so often in the tunnel?"

Goodemer sighed. "Excessively so."

"Then how do the Lukrians get through?" Jame asked.

"All they need is a token that acts as a key, so they can pass through without breaking the spells." Goodemer rubbed her chin.

"Exactly how excessive are these spells?" Jame cocked her head at Goodemer.

"Hundreds I would say," Goodemer said. "And they have to be unraveled one at a time. Sometimes superior skill isn't all it takes to beat another wizard, especially a clever wizard like Misner."

"So Misner is not a proficient wizard?"

"If this spell is any indication, her skills are mediocre at best." Goodemer rubbed a fingertip on the wolf's head.

"Then why would the Northern Territories ask her to create a rival warrior to the Guards?"

"She was probably the only wizard who agreed to do such a thing." Goodemer shrugged. "It's against our covenant to engage in actions that do physical or mental harm. If we allowed that kind of behavior, no one would trust us to do our traditional work. To ensure we can't deceive those we're helping, we take the vow of truth. We would die on the spot if we attempted a deception. Wizards like Misner are castoffs from our society before they complete their apprenticeship. They never take the vow because it's a part of our initiation ritual."

Anxious footfalls pounded in the outer corridor. Poylin ran into the cavern and skidded on the powdery sand. She handed Jame a long, heavy object wrapped in soft leather. "This was delivered to the Northern outpost by a shepherd on horseback."

Jame pulled away the leather and gasped as she stared at Tigh's sword. A piece of parchment, held in place by a thin strip of leather, was wrapped around the hilt. She took a deep breath to steady her trembling hands, pulled the tie loose, and removed the parchment. She handed the sword to Tas and unrolled the stiff scrap.

A single word was traced, signed with a graceful solitary letter. Unexpected yet intriguing pieces hovered over significant parts of the puzzle that was their enemy.

THE WOMAN STUDYING Tigh was tall and possessed a battle-hardened body. Like the Emorans, she was encased in a patchwork of red leather and armor that covered as much of her body as not. The woman ran a powerful hand through white-streaked auburn hair and eased onto a low-slung chair several paces from her.

"If I'd known Meah was going to toss that little shock bomb at me, I'd have chosen a different place for our conversation." Her voice hinted at a gnawing frustration. "Perhaps it's for the best. I'm Kylara, by the way. Regent-General of Lukria."

"Why didn't you turn me over to Meah?" Tigh's voice was raw from the potion still playing havoc with her alertness.

"Because you're the only one who can convince the others I'm telling the truth." Kylara rested inscrutable hazel eyes on Tigh.

"Others?" Tigh said.

"Emorans," Kylara said in weary resignation.

"What truth?"

Kylara contemplated Tigh for several heartbeats. "The truth about how I made a decision that led my people to be used by an insane wizard. I was in the Regulars."

Tigh raised an eyebrow in surprise.

"We interact with the outside world a little more than the Emorans, and we've never been above fighting in the major wars." Kylara shrugged. "Anyway, I was the leader of the Gold Corps under Meah's command."

"You were in the battle of Halt," Tigh whispered as shadowy memories of that horrific night battle assaulted her tired mind.

"Yes," Kylara said. "Several moons ago, Meah showed up here in Lukria. She told us a wizard in the mountains had heard the Emorans were planning to invade our territory, and she'd help us fight them off for a few favors in return. Originally, these favors were to help train the small army the wizard was building. A defense force, she called it, nothing more. To keep people from wandering too near to the wizard's stronghold."

"The rumors were already abroad by then that she was building an army to re-take the Southern Territories," Tigh said.

"We're sometimes cursed by our isolation. We rarely hear rumors until long after they've run their course," Kylara said. "Shortly after we agreed to help, Meah came to us with another offer. She said if we did everything the wizard asked, she'd deliver Emoria to us. We told her we'd never accept a territory we hadn't fought for. We were assured the wizard would do enough to enable us to capture Emoria on our own. We agreed." She flicked apologetic eyes at Tigh. "Many traditions are too strong to give up, even long after their foundations have crumbled and washed away. We've been at odds with Emoria since before our written history. The idea of finally defeating them in battle is as much a part of our life as the blood in our bodies."

"She wanted you to raise money for her army," Tigh said.

Kylara flashed a startled look.

"You were selling everything you could get your hands on," Tigh said. "When Misner showed you how to enter Emor undetected, you stole things that wouldn't be immediately missed but would bring in a great deal of money. Like Emoran ceremonial swords."

Kylara gave her a half smile. "You did more in Balderon than rescue your scouts. It was frustrating, but we were sworn to our bargain with Misner. We first sent our scholars into Emor to read their Mysteries. I'd gotten used to Guard mind games during the war and convinced our Council that mentally breaking down the Emorans would ensure victory against them. Your Council destroyed that deception when they escaped."

"The deception was broken before that," Tigh said. "We saw through the army in the meadow."

Kylara nodded. "We were wondering what went wrong."

"So why am I here?" Tigh shifted a little.

"We're being used by a wizard who has no honor," Kylara said. "She wanted to continue the silly mind game instead of exchanging your Council for the prisoners. We began to question our alliance with this person."

"She didn't allow you to free the prisoners through the tunnels."

"You have no idea how frustrating it's been not to be able to reach them." Kylara looked at her hands. "Now we've learned Misner is moving her army to Balderon valley. She has this insane plan to take over the Southern Territories—starting with Balderon. As far as she's concerned, only one obstacle stands in her way. You."

Tigh pondered this for several heartbeats. "So, she used your traditional animosity toward the Emorans and my relationship to Jame to draw me here."

"Yes. It took me a long time to figure out what she was really after." Kylara straightened and rose to her feet. "We've been dishonored by our dealings with this insane wizard. Our only honorable path is to destroy Misner." She whipped out her knife and cut the rope between Tigh's hands. "Our paths lie together."

Chapter 16

DARK, RESTLESS FLASHES of deep fears and horrors subverted her tranquil sleep. Her subconscious mind gave way to desperate images as she fought the growing anxiety . . . Something tickled her cheek.

Jame's arm flew up in reflex only to be caught in a gentle but firm grip. She popped her eyes open, and it took just a half-heartbeat for her restive dream to vanish. She wrapped her arms around Tigh, squeezing so tight that Tigh grunted. The low chuckling in her ear revealed a good mood, meaning hope.

Jame pulled back and looked into gentle, affectionate eyes. "How . . . ?"

Tigh glanced at the door and nodded. A stranger, in Emoran leathers, stood watching them. "That's Kylara, Regent-General of Lukria."

"What?" Jame pulled away from Tigh, slipped off the bed, and approached the leader of the traditional enemy of Emoria. She smoothed down her leathers, having collapsed onto the bed fully clothed early that morning.

Kylara stood tall but her eyes sparked like a skittish horse.

"Well met, Kylara." Jame bowed her head. "Thank you for returning Tigh's sword and for your note."

"Well met, Jame." Kylara returned the bow. "I was hoping you'd understand the note. I couldn't risk writing down too much. At least not until I talked with Tigh."

"Note?" Tigh strolled up to Jame.

"Kylara sent a note with your sword," Jame said. "It had the word 'truce' and the letter 'K' on it."

"Did you show it to anyone else?" Tigh asked.

"I showed it to Jyac. She was wary but struggled to keep an open mind." Jame faced Kylara. "Come, let's sit down. I think we have some things to discuss." She pointed to the pair of chairs in front of the fireplace.

Tigh went to rummage through their saddlebags for some herbs for tea. She then brought the fire back to life and set a heavy kettle full of water on a shelf in the fireplace.

Kylara cleared her throat and settled into the chair. "Thank you for allowing me to present my case."

"That's my job." Jame smiled and flashed an amused glance at Tigh, who sat cross-legged on the hearth waiting for the water to boil.

"And that's the only reason I feel this may work," Kylara said as she held Jame's eyes.

"Just remember. By speaking to me, you have put yourself in my care. It's my sworn duty as a peace arbiter to make sure your case is fairly presented and judged, and it's Tigh's sworn duty as a peace warrior to protect you." Jame settled into her accustomed job with surprising relief.

Kylara chuckled. "I'd forgotten about that. It's hard to see beyond the Emoran princess."

"I understand. And thank you, by the way, for releasing Argis and Mularke and returning Tigh unharmed." Jame took the steaming mug that Tigh offered and handed it to Kylara. She then accepted her own mug and settled back into the chair. "Now why don't you tell me why you're here."

Kylara told the story of how the Lukrian's become associated with Misner. Many of her fears and concerns tumbled out, and Jame realized Kylara entrusted her with her honor and her life.

An expectant silence settled over them as the last of Kylara's words seeped into the thick rock walls.

Jame's thoughts raced as she sought the best way of presenting Kylara to Jyac and the Council. Then she mentally banged her head on the wall. Like Kylara, she was having problems getting past the Emoran princess. This wasn't any different than any other case she had either judged or presented.

"I'll write up your statement and present it to Jyac," she said. "We don't have much time to waste so it might be best if I can convince her to at least be reasonable before arranging a meeting between you. You and Tigh—"

Jame turned at a gentle rap on the door. The door opened, and she heard the hiss of steel against leather. She rolled her eyes upward to whatever divine imp oversaw her destiny.

ARGIS SENSED THE stranger before she saw her, and the sword was in her hand, ready to defend her princess to the death if need be. Poised to strike, she glanced from Jame to Tigh, then to the stranger, all three frozen and staring at her.

"Put the sword down, Argis." Jame's voice penetrated her confusion.

"Who is she, and how did Tigh escape?" Argis remained tense.

Jame glanced at Tigh.

Tigh stood and strode to Argis. She jabbed Argis's wrist, and the sword hit the woven mud catcher in front of the door with a thud.

"Why don't you come and keep our visitor company while I write up her statement?" Jame stood.

"What's going on? Who is this . . . ?" Argis got a good look at the stranger and dove for her sword.

Tigh snatched up the sword, backed away, and wagged a finger.

"This is Kylara, Regent-General of Lukria," Jame said. "She's also in my protective custody."

Anger and confusion chased each other through Argis's mind. "What's she doing here?"

"She's here to call a truce between Lukria and Emoria and to help us defeat Misner," Jame said.

"Truce? And you believe her?" Argis asked.

"Yes," Tigh said.

Argis whipped around to face her.

"Jame could win any case she argued using her compelling personality alone, but she refuses to take a case unless whoever she defends is truly innocent of what they've been accused of. Fortunately, I can help her with that. Kylara is sincere in wanting a truce."

"Kylara let you and Mularke go when, by right, she should have taken you prisoner," Jame said. "She returned Tigh's sword instead of keeping it as a badge of honor. And she wrote a note accompanying the sword that conveyed her wish to call a truce. She had the opportunity to turn Tigh over to Meah and didn't take it. Do you know what she would have gotten in return for that simple act?"

Argis stared dumbfounded at her and shook her head.

"Misner promised to deliver Emoria to the Lukrians."

"What?" Argis asked.

"And we know Misner could have done it, given her ability to penetrate Emor with ease," Jame said. "So why don't you sit here and let Kylara talk to you?"

"She's the enemy, Jame." Argis's voice cracked from frustration.

"Why?" Jame ambled over to Argis and crossed her arms.

"What do you mean, why?" Argis ran a hand through her hair.

"Why are the Lukrians the enemy?" Jame put up a hand before Argis could speak. "Think about it. We've been skirmishing for years, but can anyone remember why? Isn't it time to leave behind what has been long forgotten? We have a chance to defeat Misner and gain a valuable ally. Should we turn our backs on this opportunity because of something that happened countless generations ago? Or should we show we've grown as a society and put aside petty disputes for the greater good of the world at large? Because that's what this is all about. Once again, Emoria has a chance to save the world from a powerful, ruthless force. It'll be the Kuntic wars all over again, with a new Hekolatis rising up to stand beside the old. But we can't hope to succeed without the help of the Lukrians." Jame turned to Kylara. "Our animosity toward the Lukrians is traditional." She turned back and captured Argis's eyes. "We've spent the last few days liberating some of our traditions from

Emoria's dusty foundation. This can be the dawn of a new age for Emoria. But we must have the strength and courage to make it happen."

"I've got to think about this," Argis muttered to the floor.

Jame took the stupefied Argis by the arm and led her to the chair. Kylara followed with her eyes, not relaxing until Argis settled back. "Kylara, this is Argis, Master Warrior. Chat a bit while I prepare the statement."

As Jame backed away, Tigh took her place on the fire hearth and poured another cup of tea. Argis and Kylara eyed each other for several heartbeats.

"So," Argis finally said, "tell me why you're going against Misner."

PRIDE. A STRONG, satisfying feeling. Especially in a situation so volatile that a single, minor action could undermine the spell that Jame had cast upon the hushed crowd gathered around the ceremonial circle as the day faded into night. Standing straight and unmoving, Jyac swept her gaze around the transfixed women as the last of Jame's ardent plea floated away on the gusts of the evening breeze.

Jyac stepped forward next to Jame, who looked astonished at the reception of her words. "You of all people shouldn't be surprised that they accept your judgment in this matter," she said in Jame's ear. "You're the wind of change for Emoria, and they all want to be caught up in your wake."

Jame stared at Jyac. "I can't believe this is all that is needed for them to lay down generations of hostility toward the Lukrians."

"The Lukrians are not much different from us," Jyac said. "We share the same sense of honor and tradition. I think our people were feeling a reluctant sympathy for the way the wizard used them. We could very easily have been in their place."

Jame sighed. "We'll know in a few heartbeats, won't we?"

A disturbance near the city bluff caused a wave of tension to flow over the silent gathering of women.

Kylara strode past her traditional enemies, flanked by Argis and Tigh.

Jyac noted that her people were more curious than vengeful. Tigh and Argis had spread the word that Kylara had fought in the Grappian Wars in one of the Elite Guard's own regiments. This was enough to pique the curiosity of these warriors to want to witness Kylara's fighting skills.

Jyac, followed by Jame, stepped from the stone platform and strode to the center of the circle, following the tradition for peaceful confrontations with the enemy to be witnessed by the people of Emoria.

Kylara stopped several paces in front of Jyac.

"Well met, Kylara, Regent-General of Lukria." Jyac bowed her head.

"Well met, Jyac, Queen of Emoria," Kylara said with a bow.

Jyac closed the space between them and held out her arm. Kylara met her steady gaze and clasped her hand around the offered forearm. Jyac let the solid contact penetrate her senses for several heartbeats before releasing her grip.

"Kylara, Regent-General of Lukria, you have presented a truce between our peoples to fight an enemy who could destroy both our territories." Jyac raised her voice so the surrounding women could hear her words. "The Council has allowed this truce to take place under the following condition: we must engage in a symbolic battle to bring our traditional hostilities to a satisfying conclusion. In this way, we can maintain our honor while resolving our differences. Do you accept this condition, Kylara, Regent-General of Lukria?"

"I accept the conditions of this truce, Queen Jyac." Kylara's voice rose on the breeze.

Jame stepped between the two women. "The rules of combat have been agreed upon by the combatants. Drawing first blood ends the competition and the hostilities between Emoria and Lukria will be resolved in favor of the country that draws first blood. It's been agreed that this will end all hostility and aggression between Lukria and Emoria. It has also been agreed that Tigh of Ingor will judge the combat, and her word will be the final decision."

An excited rumble threatened to shake the ground as the anticipation of a fight that promised to become legend penetrated the crowd. The sky was almost full dark, and the amber glow of thousands of torches added to the magic that crackled in the thin mountain air.

TIGH SLID NEXT to Jame. "You were wonderful," she breathed in Jame's ear. "I think this will work."

"I hope you're right," Jame said.

"Reach out with your senses. Your people are ready for this change." Tigh then straightened and nodded to Argis, who stepped forward to escort Jame back to the royal platform.

"I'll try to believe." Jame looked back at Tigh who gave her a warm, affectionate smile.

Tigh turned to the leaders of Lukria and Emoria and pulled out a sword tucked into her belt. Kylara's sword. She had carried it for her since they had entered Emoria. She impaled a soft patch of dirt, allowing the sword to stand freely, and backed away.

A tense silence ensued while Kylara strode to her weapon. Tigh backed far enough away to be out of the intense focus of the two older warriors.

Kylara pulled her sword from the ground, rested the blade on her shoulder, and made a show of scrutinizing Jyac. They were both canny warriors, well-versed in the patient probing of an opponent's skills. Tigh knew they were more inclined to wait for the other to make the first move. Kylara was bound to give in to the honor of a queen on her home ground and raise her blade first.

With a relaxed flip of her sword, Kylara stalked around the equally loose Jyac, both looking as though they were ready to start a friendly conversation rather than a deadly battle. Jyac slipped her sword from its sheath on her back. The blade flashed in the flames from tall stone lanterns within the circle.

The first clash of blades all but echoed off the distant mountain peaks as the crowd held a collective breath. Several more clashes sounded as they tested each other's strength and movement.

"It's good to see the Queen of Emoria stays battle ready." Kylara slid past a sideswipe, then whipped her blade around, only to have it parried by Jyac's quick anticipation.

Jyac grinned. "With Lukrians lurking about my borders, it seemed a prudent thing to do."

Kylara pushed Jyac's blade away from her vulnerable side, spun around, and caught Jyac's rebound with the momentum of her blade. "I can see where your niece gets her ability to sweet talk a wolf into becoming a lap dog."

Jyac leapt up, avoiding a swipe to the legs, plunged in the opposite direction of Kylara's sword, and rolled to her feet to the side and a bit behind Kylara. Kylara whirled around in time to feel the sting of a ready sword against her own.

Rapid parries of jarring steel against steel set off a fireworks display of flame-touched reflections off the polished metal. Caught hilt-to-hilt, faces close enough to smell remnants of the evening meal, steady eyes met, and Tigh could see a surprising respect for each other.

They pushed apart and broke into a brilliant dance of flying blades and nimble steps.

"I have a niece," Kylara said as she feinted to one side before making a swift reverse, but was not quick enough to catch Jyac off guard. "She has also turned her back on the ways of the warrior."

Jyac glided past Kylara's arcing sword and danced out of range. "Where do you suppose we went wrong?"

Kylara faced Jyac with poised sword. "Perhaps they are reflections of a new world . . . a new society."

The pair circled each other, flipping and waving their swords.

"Perhaps," Jyac said. "Should we, as elders show the way?"

The roaring crowd dropped to silence as Jyac and Kylara stopped circling and faced each other.

Kylara nodded. "It is our duty."

Never breaking eye contact, they lowered their swords until the tips nuzzled the slick grass. The rustle of leaves and the crackle of the torches rose up to meet the silence as the two leaders whipped their swords into a salute.

Several heartbeats passed before the Emorans realized the battle was over. That, by some miracle, these two proud leaders chose to give up victory for a peace without conditions. The wall of cheering exploded from the circle of spectators.

Tigh stepped between the two combatants and motioned them to her. Kylara and Jyac sheathed their swords, walked to Tigh, and clasped forearms as the burden of generations tumbled off their shoulders.

Rapid footfalls brought Argis and Jame into the center circle of light. Jame wrapped her arms around Jyac.

"It's your fault, you know." Jyac patted Jame's back.

"What do you mean?" Jame pulled back confused.

"We decided we had to set an example for the next generation," Jyac said. Tigh grinned. "They chose peace."

Jame laughed. "You're not hearing any arguments from me." She released Jyac, and then snaked an arm around Tigh's waist. "What is it?"

"Sometimes miracles need a little help," Tigh said in a low voice.

Jame frowned and looked to where Tigh was staring. Goodemer stood with a grin that was ready to engulf her face.

"You think she had something to do with this?" Jame asked.

"I could feel it. Like I was able to feel Misner when I fought her," Tigh said. "I didn't know it was unusual to be able to feel spells. It took being captured and an admission from Meah to tell me more about myself than I ever knew."

"I'm glad you have that gift." Jame gave Tigh a loving squeeze. "If only to prove these people I thought I knew couldn't change so suddenly overnight."

"I think it would have happened, even without a wizard's help," Tigh said.

"I guess we'll never know."

Kylara and Jyac were already halfway across the circle back to the city, so they joined the trailing Emorans, off for yet another night of celebration.

Chapter 17

TWO DAYS LATER, Tas was picking at the shoulders of the red leathers that had been scavenged for the handful of Emorans who had volunteered to go to the Lukrian camp huddled around the caves inhabited by Misner. After quietly freeing the Lukrian prisoners, Jyac and Kylara agreed to exchange representatives, as a show of good will and to erase the last remnants of distrust between the two countries.

"Do you find these shoulder pads uncomfortable?" she asked Olet.

"Actually, they're rather comfortable." Olet focused her attention on Tas's shoulders. "They're made for someone with broader shoulders." She tugged and shifted the leather. "How's that?"

Tas flexed her upper body. "Better."

Hard, hurried footfalls sounded outside the entrance of the large tent they were in. A serious, sturdy woman rushed in. "Everyone up, Misner wants to review the troops."

Two score warriors who were sleeping off night duty didn't hesitate to voice their objections, even as they groggily pulled on their leathers and weapons.

The fair-haired woman spotted Tas and Olet in the back of the tent and strode up to them. "I'm Tindal, Master Warrior."

"Tas, and this is Olet," Tas said.

"Misner likes to play Supreme Commander," Tindal said. "Just follow what the others do and you'll be fine."

"Yes, Master Warrior," Tas and Olet said, as they straightened and saluted with their belt knives.

Tindal gave them a long, appraising look before she nodded and strode out of the tent.

"I think she has Argis beat," Olet said

"Can't wait to see them try to out-warrior each other," Tas said.

"Fourth Regiment," a stocky Lukrian with a powerful voice barked into the tent opening. "Out to the review grounds."

Tas was impressed by the Lukrian warriors' quickness as they ran out of the tent and trotted to the expanse of open fields surrounding the camp. In step with her Regiment, she had to concentrate on keeping her feet moving as her stunned senses took in the dusty mass of humanity streaming from the half-dozen camps around the edge of the well-trodden fields. She fell into place in the back line of their Regiment and fought to shake off the shock of the enormity of Misner's army.

The Lukrians, being a ready-made defense force, held the place of honor as the personal guard to Misner. The other Regiments lining the field were recruits and mercenaries. The number of soldiers had to be in the thousands. She and Olet exchanged wide-eyed glances. Never had she seen so many people in one place, much less a well-armed and disciplined army.

"We're supposed to defeat this?" Olet whispered as the five-hundred horse cavalry, kicking up tufts of dust, cantered to their place across the grounds.

"Tigh knows what we're up against, and she thinks we can do it," Tas muttered back.

"You think she knows the army is this large?" Olet darted uncertain glances at Tas.

"She once led an army this size," Tas said.

"Fourth Regiment! Stand at attention!" the rough-voiced group leader barked as Tindal trotted her horse past them.

Within heartbeats, the field was silent and still except for the fluttering of the narrow banners displaying the colors of each regiment. Enough time passed for the dust to settle and the breeze to chill the sweat-soaked skin of the fully armored troops.

A noise from the Lukrian camp tickled the edge of Tas's hearing. She concentrated on keeping her eyes on the back of the head in front of her. No order had been given to pull on their masks. In Emoria and, she was sure, Lukria, masks were required for all formal military ceremonies and reviews. She shifted her gaze to the rows of troops across the field and thought how Seeran would love to witness this. She pledged to remember as much of this experience in the midst of the enemy as she could, just to see the delight in Seeran's eyes.

Tas stiffened as barked orders and numbers of regiments sounded from the direction of the caves. Misner was on the field. She stood for what felt like a whole sandmark before a cluster of horses and riders appeared on the edge of her vision. A shout, and the Regiment next to hers pulled out their swords and whipped them into a sharp salute.

Before she even had time to think, "We're next," their group leader shouted "Fourth Regiment" and gave the orders to salute. Fortunately, Tas was concentrating on performing the salute in rhythm with the Lukrian in front of her. If she had raised her eyes before she safely executed the move, she would have surely faced a Lukrian dressing down.

Five black-clad figures sat atop tall war horses. Tas shivered at the cold that wafted off these creatures. She realized they were not monsters but women, arrogant and confident, sweeping their stone-hard gazes across the Regiment and dismissing it with a sneer. She remembered Tigh saying something about how certain enhancements for the Guards were rejected because they made them detectable. That coldness would certainly not go unnoticed. By the waterfalls of Laur, her mind clenched in horror, Tigh used to be one of them.

She calmed her pounding heart and shifted her gaze to a round, diminutive figure on a pony. The woman's head was bent in a discussion with Tindal, and she couldn't see her features, but she knew this was the mad wizard.

Misner raised her head and turned to the indolent brown-eyed Guard on her other side. Tas stared in shock. She expected an insane, cold monster, not a sweet-faced, motherly woman with gentle eyes.

"Very nice, Tindal." The soothing, light voice, loud enough for the regiment to hear, sweetly touched her ears. Then the small group trotted down the line to the next regiment.

"Welcome to Misner's army." The young warrior on the other side of Olet winked at them.

GOODEMER FIDGETED WITH the leather bracer on her forearm and wondered how anyone could get used to wearing something so tight and unforgiving. She didn't think there was enough leather and armor in the known world to make her look like a warrior.

"That looks great on you," Jame said as she wandered into the armory.

Goodemer snorted.

Jame raised an eyebrow at Argis, who was hefting swords. "What do you think?"

Argis stopped and looked at Goodemer. "I think you do our leathers justice."

Jame turned back to Goodemer. "You don't think you look good in our clothing?"

"I look ridiculous." Goodemer glanced down at herself.

Jame grinned. "You may feel ridiculous but you look fine."

"I'm not a warrior." Goodemer stared at the weapons of war hanging from the walls and piled under leather covers on the floor.

"But that doesn't mean you can't look like one, and you have to blend in with the rest of us." Jame turned to a low opening in the back of the cavern. Tigh emerged, cradling a rough wooden ball. A thick layer of dust and cobwebs fell away from the ball, telling a tale of long neglect.

"Do you still have the catapults for these?" Tigh asked Argis.

Argis rubbed the back of her neck as she thought. "Maybe. We have odds and ends of things from when we battled the invaders from the east. The stuff in those balls has probably rotted by now."

"We can make more." Tigh shrugged. "What's important is the mechanism to propel them."

"I'll get someone on that." Argis nodded and strode out of the chamber.

"I just got a report from Tas," Jame said as Tigh put the filthy ball on the floor and dipped her hands into the water the smithy used for cooling metals. "She says Misner's army is roughly four thousand foot soldiers and five hundred on horseback. Think we can handle them?"

Goodemer gasped in alarm. "By the Children of Bal."

"Has Tas seen any of the leaders?" Tigh asked, testing several of the swords lying about.

"While Misner was reviewing the troops, Tas saw five Elite Guards," Jame said.

"Five," Tigh said.

"She also mentioned she could feel the cold coming off them, like what we felt from Meah in Balderon," Jame said. "You have a plan?"

"I think so." Tigh gazed at Goodemer. "That was a neat spell you used on Kylara and Jyac."

Goodemer almost tripped on a bundle of spears as she stepped back startled. "What do you mean?"

"The spell you used on Kylara and Jyac was clever," Tigh said. "Very subtle."

Goodemer stared at her, cursing her inexperience at getting around the truth. "How do you know I had anything to do with that?"

"I've recently learned I can detect when a wizard is casting a spell." Tigh spun a staff. "But I don't seem to be able to detect spells that have already been cast."

"I've heard of that gift," Goodemer said. "It's extremely rare. So you can sense even the minor spell I used on Kylara and Jyac?"

"Yes. It felt quite tangible to me," Tigh said.

"That's how you defeated Misner," Goodemer said. "Whatever allows you to sense the spells also makes you immune to them."

"Her spells felt pretty real to me." Tigh rested the staff on her shoulder.

"Of course, you were able to feel them and understand what they were trying to do to you, but you also resisted them," Goodemer said, her astonishment now replaced by excitement. "Since magic doesn't affect you, I can channel it through you."

"Why would you want to do that?" Jame asked.

"So far I've been able to mask my presence from Misner," Goodemer said. "The bit of magic the other night was not enough to break through my mask and capture her attention. There will be some point when she'll become aware of it, and that could ruin our attempts to take her down. My magic has to be carefully coordinated with your actions or I'll give everything away too soon.

But if I can channel the magic through Tigh, I'll be able to maintain the mask, and Misner will never detect it."

Tigh and Jame stared at Goodemer for several heartbeats.

"Is this something that's been tried before or just theory?" Jame asked.

"The great wizard, Gryplor, is said to have defeated a rogue wizard by channeling through a small girl who was immune to magic," Goodemer said. "It can work."

"Sounds good." Tigh nodded, then arched an eyebrow at Jame.

"Is this going to harm Tigh in any way?" Jame asked.

"Only resistance to channeling may cause harm." Goodemer turned to Tigh.

Tigh grinned. "I have no reason to resist."

SEERAN SAT AT the little table tucked in the corner of the airy gallery turned war room. Her intent scribbling in her journal was the only sound echoing through that part of the palace. She had to call upon all her powers of memorization to capture the intricate detail of the plan Tigh had laid out for the battle leaders. The casual mixing of magic with troop placement sounded like an impossible plot from a novel. But this was real. She stopped her scraping of quill against parchment in mid-word. Tas was in enemy territory. She knew the small warrior had the tendency to get into dangerous situations, but she had been shocked when Tas volunteered to go behind enemy lines.

She forced herself to concentrate on the amazing tale she had the good fortune to witness. Scholars didn't let personal feelings get in the way of objective observation. Besides, Tas will have quite a tale to tell when she returned.

JAME WATCHED TIGH, still bent over the scattering of maps on the stone table in the middle of the gallery. The battle leaders had long gone to bed, not knowing when their next opportunity for rest would be. She felt a rare uncertainty radiating from Tigh. The intent frown and the resigned sag of the shoulders told her that Tigh had more than a few worries about her plan.

She nodded to Seeran, who blinked up from her work, and padded around the table. She studied the maps until Tigh came back from wherever she was and turned to her. "Looks . . . interesting." She was glad to see the furrow between Tigh's brows relax.

As the Supreme Commander of the campaign to stop Misner and her army, Jame knew the general outline of the plan, but she left the detailed placement of individuals at any given time to the person who had commanded the decisive battle of the Grappian Wars.

Tigh nodded. "It'll be interesting all right."

"Where will Argis be?" Jame asked, peering at the different colored lines and matching small blocks of wood.

"Here." Tigh laid a finger on an artistic rendering of a hill. "And Mularke will be here, and Kas with her horse troops will be next to Argis, here." She indicated a line of trees.

"Where will we be?"

"In these caves." Tigh tapped the place. "Kylara convinced Misner to allow the Lukrian regiments to be the rear guard for the main army. Her excuse was they could scour the area for Emorans who might be trying to get to Misner. In reality, they will keep close behind the main army and make up the third side of our little box."

"And the fourth side is Balderon, hopefully armed and ready, thanks to our swift-footed scouts," Jame said.

Tigh grinned. "All we have to do is disable the Guards and Misner right before the signal to attack is made."

"And we know how to find the Guards and we have the potion to disable them, thanks to Tas." It really did seem possible. Jame cocked her head. "Maybe the army will surrender without any bloodshed."

"Then Argis won't have any fun." Tigh messed up Jame's bangs.

"So, everything seems to be falling into place," Jame said. "What's bothering you then?"

"We're dealing with a set of events that have to happen between two places that are a good four days' march from each other. Too many things can go wrong." Tigh sighed. "I had a long talk with Goodemer. We have to get into Misner's stronghold and wait for her to cast the spells that will make her army invincible. If we stop her too soon, the Guards, who will be in some kind of contact with her, will be suspicious. So we have to stop her as she's preparing the spell."

"Why doesn't she just cast the spell over them now?" Jame asked. She frowned at Seeran, who was jotting down their conversation.

"She'd alert every wizard in the area of what she was up to," Tigh said. "I don't think she's willing to take that chance."

"It'll work," Jame said. "Misner doesn't know we know what she's up to."

"That's the only thing we have in our favor." Tigh's eyes drifted back to the map.

"So." Jame wrapped an arm around Tigh. "Are you going to stand here and stare at these maps all night?"

Tigh cast an amused glance at her. "Depends."

"I happen to know a nice warm bed that's big enough for two." Jame nuzzled Tigh's shoulder.

Tigh snaked her arm around Jame. "If you can't think of anything better, I guess that'll have to do."

Jame playfully punched Tigh's shoulder. She then found herself in the air, cradled in Tigh's arms.

Tigh bounced on her toes and launched them into a quick flip over the table.

"Show off. Good night, Seeran." Jame waved at a wide-eyed, slack-jawed Seeran, as Tigh strode into the corridor with her beloved burden.

CARVED OUT OF the natural landscape, Emor tenuously clings to life, and the absence of most of its inhabitants is a disturbing reminder of how civilizations can slip to dust in just a short span of time . . .

Seeran, seated cross-legged on the wide stone ledge of the fountain in the center of Emor, looked up from her writing at the first noise she'd heard that morning that wasn't nesting cliff birds. A small band of reluctant heroes emerged from the Palace to embark on the kind of adventure she had only dreamed of witnessing firsthand. Except, she'd discovered, reality had a way of mixing living dreams with nightmares.

She could only blame herself for forgetting the first rule of being a historian—never get emotionally involved. But she couldn't help it. The Emorans had captured her heart and soul, and for the first time in her life she'd found something greater than her love of history.

She jumped to her feet as the group approached. "Good luck."

"Thank you, Seeran." Jame stepped forward and took Seeran's hand. "I'll try to bring back a story that will make you the envy of Artocia."

"Just bring yourselves back," Seeran whispered, lowering her eyes, not wanting to give in to the pressure of tears.

"No fear." Jame gave her hand a gentle squeeze. "Tigh and I have made a promise to each other." Seeran raised her eyes. "We promised that we'd have a long life together after we've given up being on the road. And we always keep our promises to each other." She turned to catch Tigh's tender, affectionate look.

"I wouldn't want to have Jame angry with me, would you?" Tigh asked.

"I guess not." Seeran smiled, fighting hard to keep the tears back.

"See you soon, Seeran," Tigh said, and they continued across the square, followed by a pensive Jyac.

Goodemer, looking oddly at home in her warrior gear, paused in front of Seeran. She fished from her belt pouch a small amulet with the image of a wolf pup engraved on it. "In case some magic strays this way, just wrap your hand around this and think about those things you love the most. This will protect you." She glanced around and leaned closer to Seeran. "It will also protect a loved one, if you speak protective words to it."

Seeran blinked up at Goodemer with a profound sense of thankfulness and relief. "Thank you."

GOODEMER SMILED AND hurried to catch up with the others who waited for her at the door to the Temple. Sometimes being a wizard wasn't such a bad job as long as she never lost sight of the individuals around her. Small magic was as powerful as attention-getting, flashy displays, and more often than not, much more satisfying. Her mentor would call her a mushball, and she would most amiably agree.

Goodemer had yet to set foot in the Temple and was surprised at the feat of engineering that allowed the continuous flow of water. A little mental probing told her that no mortal magic was involved in this impressive aquatic display. Any deity who could provide warm water for indoor bathing was well worth cultivating.

JYAC TOOK JAME by the arm and led her away from the others to the altar at the end of the main worship hall.

"My faith in the Emor Mysteries gives me the confidence that we'll be victorious." Jyac studied the floor, polished by generations of worshipers. "But the side of me that's your aunt can't help but feel apprehensive about all this." She lifted proud eyes to Jame. "You left Emoria an idealistic girl. The road you chose to follow returned to us a strong, likable young woman as prepared for leadership as any Emoran princess. Be careful and come back to us safe and victorious. Let no harm come to your partner. She has won the hearts of our people and will be a worthy consort for their future queen."

"Thank you." Jame wrapped her arms around Jyac. "Tigh has led campaigns many times greater than this one and has never lost. We'll succeed because she has the ability to focus on not being defeated. She can pluck more tricks from her bracers than a street magician. I've placed my life in her hands more times than I can count, and she's always kept both of us from harm. This time will be no different."

Jyac nodded. She prayed that Misner's power hadn't grown strong enough to overpower Tigh, even with Goodemer's help. She wished a more experienced wizard had been sent to deal with the rogue Misner. She just had to trust the decisions of that secretive society.

The small group entered the neglected chamber where Tigh had been kidnapped.

Goodemer had practiced channeling magic through Tigh by breaking the spells in the tunnel during the four days since they had learned Misner's army was on the move. She had discovered the Lukrians could pass through the spells without a problem, but the Emorans couldn't penetrate them without being in physical contact with a Lukrian. Jyac prayed Goodemer was right, or the mission was doomed before they left the city.

"Good luck and may all of Bal's Children be with you." Jyac clasped each of them on the shoulder. "May the waters of Laur flow through you and safely bring you back to the mother head waters."

"We follow the waters' journey to victory and back," Jame said.

As the unlikely trio of wizard, arbiter, and warrior disappeared around the first bend in the cavern, Jyac fought back the urge to follow. One of the hardest parts about being queen was being left behind to wait while others set off to fight for the fate of the country. She turned and trudged back to Laur's Worship Hall. She hated waiting more than almost anything.

Chapter 18

"HAVE YOU EVER seen anything like it?" Kas whispered in awe.

She was sprawled, with Argis and Mularke, on her stomach on a windy hill with only knee-high grass as cover. The night-darkened Balderon valley was spread before them. Far to their left, the torches sparkled along the thick impenetrable walls of Balderon. In front of them, close enough to hear voices and to detect the main ingredients of the stews bubbling in the numerous cauldrons, was Misner's army.

Misner's troops had spent most of the day setting up camp within sight of Balderon. Confident that no one would dare go against them, they didn't even send out patrols to scout the area. Tigh had predicted this behavior. This arrogance was a part of the Elite Guards' psyche. The Guards were invincible, and they made sure everyone knew it.

Argis sucked in the chilly night air. To her shock, she'd found herself hoping to disable the leaders so they wouldn't have to engage this terrifying force in battle. Never in her life had she turned away from the opportunity to fight. Her soul longed for the edgy rush she felt when her sword became an extension of her body as she danced with the enemy. She had waited all her life to be in this place, leading her army to victory. Now . . . She gazed at the neatly spaced watch fires surrounded by shadowy soldiers. Now the whole camp confounded her imagination by its immense size, and she realized she'd be satisfied if the victory came without bloodshed.

"To think Tigh used to lead an army four times this size," Mularke said in awe.

Shouts from the camp signaled a changing of the watch.

The grass crunched behind them, and they put their hands on their dagger hilts.

Kylara dropped to the ground and slithered up next to them. "I've got some news. Have you noticed there are only four command tents down there? There are five Guards. One is missing."

"Which one?" Argis asked.

"I've seen all but two out there," Kylara said. "They don't like to show themselves if they can help it. I haven't seen Patch or Meah."

"Meah." Argis dropped her chin onto clenched fists. "I hope she's still not playing with Tigh."

Kylara rubbed a weed between her fingers. "They do have a bit of a history together."

Argis nodded. "They were friends."

"More than friends," Kylara said. "Meah was obsessed with Tigh back then. That's one of the reasons Misner recruited her. It seems Meah has been holding some kind of grudge against Tigh for a long time."

Argis frowned as the conversation in the Balderon safe house tickled her memory. "Meah had been cleansed, which means she was at Ynit the same time as Tigh. Was this relationship still going on at the end of the War?"

"Close to the end, at least," Kylara said. "Meah was one of several commanders under Tigh by that time. You have to remember the Meah you've met was not the one I served under. She was like most of the Guards, arrogant and ruthless to be sure, but also a good commander. Tigh was the monster. She was many times worse than this wizard-enhanced Meah, if you can imagine it."

Argis and Mularke exchanged wary glances.

Argis certainly could imagine it after witnessing Tigh's brief relapse. "I was just thinking things must have cooled down between them by the time they were returned to Ynit for cleansing because Jame was close to Tigh from almost the beginning." She was sure Jame would have mentioned Meah if she'd been more of a presence in Tigh's life while in Ynit.

"Sounds like a reason for a grudge to me," Kylara said.

Argis nodded. "We don't have time to send back a warning that one of the Guards is at large."

"I know." Kylara stared at the endless enemy camp. "It's never easy, is it?"

THE SPIDERY NETWORK of caverns beneath the Phytian Mountains was illuminated with permanent fire spells, and maps, showing the intricate routes, were etched at each intersection of chambers and tunnels. Jame ran a hand over the inscriptions and wondered how many years Misner ruled these caverns without anyone knowing she was right below their feet.

"This way." Tigh peered down a wide tunnel.

As always, Goodemer went first. Cunning spells hid traps and treacherous openings so the travel was slow as she found and unraveled the spells one at a time.

They walked a few paces into this new tunnel. Goodemer shook her head and waved her amulet over the ground. A circle of finger-length spikes protruded from the floor before them.

"That would have been painful," Jame said as they eased around the spikes.

"Are you sure Misner won't be able to detect your magic?" Tigh asked as they continued down the tunnel.

"As long as my mask is in place, she can't detect me," Goodemer said. "The little magic it takes to break these spells can't be distinguished from the stray magic that's always charging the air around us."

"Stray magic?" Jame asked.

Goodemer shook her amulet at a rock wall, revealing a shadow trigger—a mechanism that clicked into action when a shadow passed over it. She snapped her fingers, and a half dozen darts flew out and skittered on the ground. "Wizards don't make magic, we simply learn to harness the magic that exists around us, all the time. If you can detect magic it cannot harm you. Tigh can detect magic."

"But I can't detect a spell that's already been cast." Tigh frowned as they paused for Goodemer to set off another shadow trigger that catapulted several stones into their path.

"That's because the magic in a cast spell is dormant until the circumstances are in place to awaken it and set off the spell. These caverns would be extremely noisy with magic if the spells weren't protected in this way. So noisy it could confuse the spells, and unpleasant and unwanted things could happen." Goodemer revealed a gaping hole in the middle of the path.

Jame stared into the dark hole as they skirted it. "Isn't this protection a little extreme? It seems to me setting off just one of these spells would stop someone."

"Several backup spells aren't unusual, but this obsessive repetition betrays an unstable mind," Goodemer said. "They're also attempts to make up for being a mediocre wizard at best. A mad and mediocre wizard is a dangerous foe to go up against."

"Now's not the time to have second thoughts," Tigh said.

"Not second thoughts," Goodemer said. "We just have to be alert to her weaknesses and use them against her. Just as you do when you fight."

"If I recount what I can remember of my last meeting with her," Tigh said, "do you think we can figure out how I was able to get the upper hand and beat her?"

Goodemer grinned. "We can certainly try."

"KYLARA JUST TOLD me there are only four Guards out there." Tas entered the ring of light at one of the watch fires that illuminated the Lukrian camp on the barren, narrow strip of land between the foothills and the mountains. She held a plate filled with stew and a hunk of bread and plopped down on the grass next to Olet and the other four Emorans masquerading as Lukrians.

"We saw all five of them leave." Olet frowned. "It wasn't hard to miss them at the head of their regiments. They can make snow shiver."

"All the regiments are out there," Tas nodded in the direction of Balderon, "but only four command tents are set up."

"So what does that do to our plans?" Wolfie asked, her wild hair catching the firelight and shadows.

"We stick to the original plan," Tas said. "If we can't stop all five, at least we can get four of them."

"I wonder which one is missing," Olet said.

Tas shrugged. "We'll find out tomorrow."

They scrambled to their feet as Tindal approached. Lukrian or not, they had grown to respect this no-nonsense Master Warrior. She was tough but fair and never mentioned their Emoran origins. More importantly, she made certain the other warriors in the Lukrian regiments treated them with civil respect.

"They plan to attack Balderon at first light," Tindal said. "Kylara will enter the main camp with an escort of twelve, including you six. You must do what needs to be done, and all but one of you will rejoin the escort when Kylara is ready to return."

"What about the missing Guard?" Tas asked in a low voice.

Tindal pondered the question. "There's a possibility she may be in camp by the time we get there. We're scouring the area for her, in case she's thinking of making trouble. The Guards play mind games, and Misner may have some tricks for tomorrow. We can't be certain of anything we think is going to happen. We have to stay alert and be ready to adapt. I'm hoping we won't have to implement the backup plan, but we must be prepared for it."

Tas straightened. "We'll do whatever it takes to stop them."

"Good luck on your mission," Tindal said. "Show us Lukrians that legendary Emoran ability to sneak up on the enemy in a field of snow and have to tap them on the shoulder to let them know you're behind them."

The Emorans grinned. A challenge from the enemy was enough of a blow to their honor to succeed or die trying.

TIGH EMERGED FROM the cave, blinked up at the half-moon lit sky, and determined it was closer to dawn than dusk. The Lukrian camp, fifty paces in front of them, was quiet except for a handful of guards posted around the perimeter.

Jame wrapped her arms around Tigh. "You're going to have to wear Emoran leathers for the joining."

"Hope they're more comfortable than they look." Tigh brushed her lips against Jame's cheek.

"I'll make sure they're cut to fit you perfectly." Jame nuzzled Tigh's neck.

"Is that a promise?" Tigh murmured in Jame's ear.

"It's a promise." Jame captured Tigh's eyes. "And I always keep my promises to you."

Tigh reaffirmed their bond with a gentle kiss. "Time to go play with Misner."

GOODEMER STUDIED THE opening in the craggy bluff beyond the Lukrian camp tents. She raised her eyes and wished her mentor were there to whisper words of guidance. *Take one step at a time and work with whatever is at hand.* She blinked out of her reverie and turned to her companions, who watched her with expectation.

"The magic in this place is disturbed and unstable," she said. "It's as if she can't quite control what she's trying to do. That, in itself, can be extremely dangerous."

"Let's go and stop her then," Tigh said with a wolfish grin.

Goodemer followed Tigh and Jame to the edge of camp. She wished it was as simple as strolling into the cavern and beating up Misner. She paused and gave that thought another look. An idea wove an intriguing pattern in her mind.

As they approached a Lukrian guard, Tigh flashed with her fingers the code that allowed them safe entry into enemy territory. The tall, slender guard straightened and nodded as they walked past her.

Goodemer paused at the mouth of the cave, held her amulet, and gently probed the wards and spells spilling out to them like a pile of string after a kitten was tired of playing with it. The magic was confusing and not particularly effective. Too much magic pulled into too many spells at once was more messy than useful. She didn't have the time to push the magic aside. "There are too many spells. We'll need a Lukrian to get through them."

"Wonder if we can convince someone to volunteer." Tigh ran her eyes over the all but deserted tents. Her head snapped back, and she stared into the cave.

Goodemer shivered from a chill flowing out of the cave.

They backed away from the opening as the blackness materialized into Meah.

THE OUTER GUARDS signaled the small band on horseback through the lines. The camp was awakening, although still dark, and the aroma of oat gruel permeated the air. The thirteen riders trotted through the camp to a ragged hide tent where they dismounted and tied their horses to a nearby picket line.

Kylara poked her head through the tent's opening, relieved that there was a lone occupant seated at a small table, illuminated by a single lamp.

"Come in, old friend." A silver-haired, war-hardened woman looked up from the book she was reading.

Kylara nodded to six of her escort to remain outside and entered the low-pitched tent accompanied by the Emorans. "Good evening, Yanajin." She walked to the older woman, and they clasped arms.

"Please sit." Yanajin nodded to the chair opposite her. "Relax while your friends relieve us of a handful of trouble."

"Are there still only four?" Kylara asked as she settled into the goat hide chair.

"As of a half sandmark ago, yes," Yanajin said. "One can't do the damage of five, so the odds are still with us."

Kylara shrugged. "It'd still be better to know where the fifth one is, and what she's up to."

"Ah, but that would make this game of war too easy and predictable." Yanajin grinned.

Kylara turned to the waiting Emorans. "Good luck to you, and get back here as swiftly as you can."

"We'll be back before you know it," Tas said, flashing a feral grin.

THE FOUR EMORANS slipped through the back slit of the tent and paused to make sure no one looked in their direction. Tas met each set of serious, intent eyes before they disappeared in four separate directions.

Tas strode past the kitchen fires where soldiers were lining up for what passed as the morning meal in Misner's army. She would be happy if she never again saw another bowl of the pasty stuff they had the audacity to call porridge. Across the camp, the dark shadows draping the ground came alive as regiment after regiment responded to the insistent shouts of their group leaders to wake up and get their bellies filled.

If they didn't succeed, they would have to actually fight this formidable army. They had to win. For Emoria, and for the odd reason that she wanted to present Seeran the story of a lifetime.

Her target was in sight. Tigh was right. The imposing tent made from white goat hides was not guarded. A part of the Elite Guard mystique was they feared no one and all but dared anyone to try to sneak up on them with the intent to do harm.

Tas strode past the tent and felt the cold radiating from it as if it were made of ice. A meal line snaked close to the front of the tent and the light from the kitchen fires sank the darkened sides and back into deeper shadow. She circled away from the tent and approached it from behind. She then disappeared into a shadow and dropped to her stomach.

Making no more noise than the wind, she pulled herself to the tent's edge. She worked a hole around the seams that held the hides together with her knife, while listening for sounds inside.

A cold arm shot through the hole so fast, Tas froze for half a heartbeat before fumbling open her belt pouch and pulling out a sharpened dart. The steely fingers wrapped around her throat, freezing her skin. She got her hand up and pricked the arm with the dart.

Tas gasped to bring both air and warmth back into her throat. She pushed the arm through the slit in the tent, grasped the wolf pup amulet around her neck, and held it until her fingers tingled.

One down. She prayed to Laur that the other three were successful.

"WE DO SEEM to meet in the oddest places." Meah grinned with wicked delight. The frozen tension snapped in the thin mountain air.

Tigh turned to Goodemer. "Is she real?"

"She's real." Goodemer nodded, not taking her eyes off the cold menace.

"Have you finally figured out whose side you're on?" Tigh crossed her arms, ignoring Jame's startled glance.

"I've always known whose side I'm on." Meah strolled out of the cave. "My side." Her night-deepened eyes swept over Jame.

Tigh raised an eyebrow. "Misner never found out about Ocarla?"

Meah's haunted eyes captured Tigh's. "No."

Jame was taken aback by the raw emotion in Meah's voice. It touched old memories from her time during the cleansings in Ynit. She had witnessed Guards teeter between being ruthless warriors and the gentle souls that were their true selves.

"I have only one question." Tigh took a step closer to Meah.

Jame was shocked to see Meah struggle not to take a step back. Whatever had been between them went beyond the knowledge that Tigh had the means to disable her. Meah betrayed a frightened awe of her former commander.

Tigh put her hands on her hips. "Why have you waited until now to take your revenge?"

"The other Guards." Meah's eyes were like granite. "I had to wait until they were far away from Misner."

"What would you have done if Kylara had turned me over to you?" Tigh asked.

Meah stared at her.

"I was bound and helpless within a few paces of you in Kylara's quarters in Lukria."

Meah's eyes widened in shock.

"You didn't need the Lukrians to capture me," Tigh said. "Misner must not be very clever to have believed the stories you fed her about how I kept slipping through your fingers."

Meah gazed at the dark camp for several heartbeats. "I would have let you escape. That would have been enough to break the Lukrians' trust in Misner when she didn't deliver Emoria to them for your capture. Misner doesn't understand warrior honor. She wouldn't have understood the Lukrians expected payment for your capture whether you were delivered to her or not."

Tigh raised an eyebrow. "Did you have something to do with the wording of that agreement?"

A sly grin touched Meah's lips. "She doesn't know about how Guards operate either."

Tigh returned the grin. "Not if she thought you were jealous of Jame."

"Hey, what's that supposed to mean?" Jame shot Tigh an indignant look.

"It means, little princess, that Misner learned from the Lukrians of our relationship during the last campaigns of the War and mistook my devotion to my commander as something more than an admiration for her skills as a master warrior. As I said, Misner has no understanding of Guards." Meah unsheathed her sword. "I told you back in Balderon that we'd lead this dance together." She whipped the blade into a salute. "It's an honor to be a part of another one of your brilliant campaigns, my commander."

Jame and Goodemer stared in shock at Meah.

"We need to get into that cave," Tigh said.

Meah, eyes level with Tigh's, held out an arm. Tigh grasped it. Not letting go of Meah's eyes, she stretched her other hand out to Jame. Keeping a wary eye on Meah, Jame took the hand. Goodemer quickly grabbed Jame's free hand. Meah pulled them into the wizard's stronghold.

"THAT'S THREE," TAS said as Grener slipped through the back slit of Yanajin's tent. "Any problems?"

Grener shook her head. "It was just as Tigh said. The Guard heard me cut the slit, and I was able to dose her as her hand reached out."

Kylara peeked out the front opening of the tent. "We don't have much time."

"Come on, Wolfie," Tas muttered to the amulet in her hand.

"We need to go." Kylara beckoned to one of her escorts outside the tent. They had to get out of the camp before the unconscious Guards were discovered. No alarm had been sounded yet but their discovery was just a matter of time. "Get the horses and bring them here."

"Come on, Wolfie," Tas said in frustration.

The soft footfalls of the horses sounded outside the tent. Kylara turned to her old friend. "Keep safe, Yanajin."

"I'll be satisfied with ending this day as your prisoner." Yanajin bowed. "It's not the fate of this old warrior to die in a dishonorable battle."

"It's done," Tas said as the amulet flared yellow. "Olet. Go."

Tas grasped Olet's shoulder. Olet nodded and slipped through the slit in the tent and sprinted through the dusty chaos of the awakening camp.

By the time the others were mounted, Wolfie, wild hair flying, barreled toward the horse that Tas held for her. She vaulted onto the animal's back and caught the reins Tas tossed to her.

"You decide to do a little sightseeing?" Tas asked.

Wolfie let out a wild laugh as the twelve riders galloped through the camp to the foothills.

Chapter 19

CLUTTERED WAS THE best word to describe Misner's world. Parts of just about everything imaginable filled corners of chambers and barely traversable corridors. Machines, weapons, kitchenware, furniture, toys . . . all broken and haphazardly thrown together.

Jame picked up a piece of a crystal tribute to Laur.

"According to Misner, everything has magic in it," Meah said. "She consumes it from this stuff like a drunk drinks ale. I think the Lukrians' rebellion really started when they were sent out to collect these things. Demeaning work for anyone, much less a people born to be warriors."

"Interesting," Goodemer said.

"This way." Meah paused at the opening of a narrow, twisting tunnel. An uneasy evil radiated out to them.

"I was afraid you were going to say that," Jame said.

Tigh put a hand on her shoulder and gave it a reassuring squeeze.

Goodemer pulled a wolf pup amulet sculpted from purple quartz out of her belt pouch and spoke a few soft words to it. "Put this around your neck."

Jame took the amulet and slipped it over her head. "That's much better. That's amazing. I can't feel anything but the good coming off all of you." She walked up to Meah, who watched them with an amused smirk. "Even you."

Meah mustered her most uncaring sneer.

"Save it for Misner, Meah." Tigh laughed. "You were always more show than action."

Meah flashed an evil grin. "We had you around for any action that needed doing."

"And I guess the time for action is now," Tigh said as she brushed past Meah and strode into the tunnel.

They went maybe fifty paces when a howl of frustration and an echoing crash sounded from further down the tunnel. The four exchanged glances and continued at a more deliberate pace until they rounded a tight bend. Six paces away, the tunnel spilled into a large, brightly lit cavern. Low muttering followed by a splintering commotion sounded near enough for them to be more cautious.

Tigh put a hand on Jame's tense shoulder.

Jame captured Tigh's eyes, reading a confidence in her abilities and an overwhelming concern for her. She squeezed Tigh's arm. Tigh raised her eyes to the waiting Meah and nodded. Meah and Jame, blinking away the bright illumination, strode into the cavern.

In the middle of the rough cave, a short, round woman rummaged through haphazard piles of unbroken objects, mumbling incoherent words. Tas had warned them that the evil Misner had the sweet face of a grandmother so Jame wasn't shocked as the wizard looked up and latched onto Meah with startled eyes.

"Meah." Her sugary voice filled the cavern. "What are you doing here? Why aren't you with your regiment?"

Meah shrugged. "My second in command is with them."

"And who is this?" Misner squinted at Jame. "An Emoran spy? You left your regiment to bring me an Emoran spy?" She straightened and faced Meah, her features hardening into anger. "I'm preparing to give the order to attack. You're supposed to be with your regiment to receive that order."

Meah leveled a cold gaze at Misner, crossed her arms, and sauntered closer to her. "This is no ordinary Emoran spy. She's the Emoran princess and companion to Tigh the Terrible."

Misner's eyes widened. "Tigh the Terrible. It's too late to draw her to me, even with such a perfect hostage. I'm ready to attack. Tigh can't stop me now."

"You see, that's my point." Meah picked up a ceramic mug from a pile of objects and pretended to study it. "She's not my hostage. I'm her hostage." She shrugged at Misner's incredulous stare.

"What game are you playing here?" Misner's sweet voice took on the quality of hard candy.

Meah appeared amused by this. "Game? Why, a Guard's game. It's the only kind I know how to play. But Tigh has always played it better than any of us."

Misner wrapped a hand around her vulture's head amulet. After several heartbeats, she struggled to keep panic from her expression. She concentrated a little harder, flashing suspicious glances at Meah and Jame.

"Looking for your Guards?" Jame asked.

"How do you know what I'm doing?" The hard sugar of Misner's voice crystallized.

"I know a lot of things, Misner," Jame said. "Like, for instance, how my people disabled your Guards."

"Disabled my Guards?" Misner chuckled as she gave her amulet a puzzled look. "You don't possess the means to do that, even if your people could sneak through my army undetected."

"Why do you think we can't disable Guards?" Jame lifted up the stone vial tied to her belt. "I have the means right here to disable Meah. I don't think she'd be so amiable a hostage if it were otherwise."

Misner stared at the vial and then at Jame. "Unfortunately for you, young princess, that won't stop me." She lifted her amulet in Jame's direction.

"Are you trying to do something?" Jame asked.

Misner frowned and thrust out the amulet again.

Jame pointed her chin at the amulet. "Maybe that thing is wearing out."

"Why are you here?" Misner rasped from the failed effort of casting a spell.

"To stop you, of course." Jame shrugged, putting on her best impression of Tigh's casual disinterest.

Misner picked up an octagonal object crafted from clear crystal and replaced her fearful expression with a confident smirk. "You may have been able to stop my Guards. But you won't be able to stop my army. The spell has already been cast into this crystal. All I have to do is smash it against the ground, and my army will be imbued with the belief that they are invincible. The seconds-in-command know to lead the army with or without the Guards."

Jame's training as an arbiter allowed her to keep her expression impassive as she prayed Goodemer could handle this unexpected twist in this deadly game. "We know. That's why we have your army surrounded."

"And you think your puny forces can beat my mighty, well-trained army?" The grandmotherly face lit with pride.

"We have the element of surprise and have had the time to prepare for the most efficient attack on your troops," Jame said. "We can defeat you."

"Not if my army's invincible." Misner's warm laughter filled the cavern as she raised her plump arms and flung the crystal hard against the ground. It bounced twice.

Misner stared startled at the crystal and didn't see Tigh's dagger until it protruded from her chest. She looked into Jame's eyes, and her face creased into an insane grin before she sank lifeless to the ground next to the crystal.

Goodemer let out a startled yelp.

Jame and Meah whipped around as Goodemer bolted into the cavern, face scrunched in concentration, and arms waving in angular movements. Finally, she slowed her arms and appeared to be tying off invisible strands in the air. She then stepped back and took a deep breath.

"Is there a problem?" Tigh asked.

"When Misner died, she released the spell of invincibility," Goodemer said.

"But you stopped it. Right?" Jame gave her a hopeful look.

"For a while, I think," Goodemer said. "It's struggling against my hold even now. I don't know how long I'll be able to restrain it."

Meah grinned.

Tigh rolled her eyes up to whatever demented deity oversaw her destiny.

ARGIS WATCHED OLET appear at the top of the hill and glance back. She knew the others were escaping the camp, the faint gallop of their horses echoed from the open flats to the foothills adjacent to her position. Olet sprinted down the hill.

Argis ran to her. "Success?"

"Yes," Olet said. "And the others are almost to the Lukrian camp."

Argis nodded, staring down the line of catapults. Goodemer had handled the rough balls and put spells over them. She hoped Goodemer's efforts gave them the power needed to clear the small mound between them and the enemy.

Tigh had told her to make their presence known as soon as the Guards were out of the way. Without their leaders, Misner's army was just a group of volunteers and mercenaries whose loyalties didn't go beyond the next payday, and this could be used in their favor.

Argis strolled up the small mound and stood—not even attempting to conceal herself—and stared at the sprawled camp as it churned to life in the weak dawn light. She pulled from her belt pouch a stone amulet in the shape of a wolf pup's head. She wrapped her hand around it and concentrated on the words that Goodemer had instructed her to repeat over and over again. Warmth emanated from the amulet, and it first turned blue from Kylara and then green from Mularke.

"This really works." She returned the amulet to her pouch.

She looked down the line of warriors—every eye was on her. Time to meet her destiny. Shocked by this unbidden thought, she blinked at her waiting force as if seeing them anew. If this was her destiny, then she wasn't going to settle for anything less than complete victory. She strolled down the hill and unsheathed her sword with a sibilant hiss that hung in the still pre-dawn air. She positioned herself at the end of the catapult line and held her sword up high. Every eye was focused on her blade.

"For Emoria!" Argis cried out as she slashed the sword toward the ground.

Yodels and battle cries rose up first from the warriors, then echoed by the horse troops, picked up by the Lukrians in the adjacent hills, and then spread to the archers on the opposite side of the enemy camp. At the same time, the first volleys sprang from the catapults, sailing easily over the hill.

"Fire at will!" Argis cried as she and Olet scrambled back up the hill and flattened themselves as they topped the crest.

The catapulted balls spewed thick, misty clouds upon impact, surrounding three sides of the wizard's camp and spreading to the Balderon side. Shouts of commands and chaotic efforts to get into defensive position were undermined by a growing sense of confusion within the camp.

Argis imagined the seconds-in-command, upon discovering their Commanders had been taken down, struggling with their own commitments to this mercenary army. She knew now it was no longer a matter of fighting Misner's war for them but one of simple survival.

The first finger of sunlight flowed between the distant mountain peaks and illuminated a strange tableau in the valley of the city of Balderon. Four thousand foot soldiers and five hundred mounted troops were lined up in tense formation in defense of their lives. Before them crept an impenetrable mist, no closer than a hundred paces from the edge of their camp.

"What's that?" Olet stammered as the sun penetrated the mist. "By the waterfalls of Laur . . ."

Argis and Olet rose to their feet, staring dumbfounded at the impossible vision before them. The warriors at the bottom of the hill, taking in the stunned expression of their leader, trod up the mound until they also stood staring, unbelieving.

Argis barked out a laugh. "That daughter of a Yitsian snow monster of a wizard told me to expect some small illusions."

Olet snorted. "I'd hate to see what she calls a large illusion."

They gazed in wonder at the scene before them, knowing they would never witness anything like it again. Thousands of Emoran warriors stood, swords drawn, where the thick mist had been, and faced Misner's slack-jawed, wide-eyed army.

"IS THERE ANY way you can break the spell?" Jame sank down on a rather opulent chair, watching Goodemer, who was concentrating on holding Misner's spell within a sphere of magic.

"I can't break it." Goodemer's voice was strained. "There's only one thing I can do."

"And that is?" Tigh paused from prowling around the chamber.

"Redirect it," Goodemer said through clenched teeth. "At least most of it."

"Redirect. Most," Tigh said.

"It's a complicated spell," Goodemer muttered as she struggled with her hold.

"The only thing you can do is come up with the best way of dealing with it and tell us what to expect," Jame said.

Goodemer nodded with jaw tensed in concentration. "I'm going to have to redirect the spell into something."

"Something," Tigh said.

"I don't know what will happen exactly, but I can redirect it into something large enough to absorb it," Goodemer said as she shifted her arms to strengthen her magic.

"All of it?" Tigh asked.

"Most." Goodemer sighed. "I've frozen it like an arrow in mid-flight. The moment it's released, it'll move at the same speed as when it was captured. Some of the magic will slip through."

"What will happen?" Jame asked.

"It'll have some effect on Misner's army, but not as strongly as if they were hit with the full spell."

"Something large," Tigh said. "Can you hold it long enough to get out of these caverns?"

Goodemer nodded. "I can try."

"Let's get out of here." Tigh held a hand out to Jame and pulled her from the chair.

"With pleasure." Meah, who had been lounging on a pile of broken rubble, stretched and hopped to her feet. "This place has lost its charm."

Tigh turned to Goodemer. "If you feel you can't hold it any longer, cast it into the walls."

They ran through the caverns without having to worry about traps and spells. Goodemer felt as if she was ready to explode but she was determined not to fail. She had to prove her mentor's faith in her. She stumbled and felt strong hands grasp her arms as Jame and Tigh pulled her along through the rubble-strewn tunnels.

The day had dawned by the time they emerged from the cavern, but they staggered ahead, not stopping to adjust their eyes to the blinding morning sun. Tigh pulled Goodemer through the Lukrian camp into the surrounding meadow where towering boulders sat like solitary giants casting long shadows on the foursome.

Tigh waved a hand. "Pick a boulder."

"I don't know what will happen." Goodemer eyed the looming granite rocks. "Misner could have anticipated something like this happening."

"We have no choice. Pick a rock." Tigh leveled steady eyes at her.

"Go on," Jame said. "We'll get through this."

Goodemer focused on the farthest boulder within their view. She pulled in all the stray magic she could, sliced her hands through the air, and the spell exploded from her hold. She flew backwards several paces and landed hard on the rocky ground. The funnel of stray magic held, guiding the spell to the boulder with only bits of magic sparking off and darting down the mountain slopes to Balderon valley. The ground shook and rumbled for several heartbeats as the boulder took the impact of the spell.

Silence hung in the air as they stared at the boulder. Tigh and Jame trotted over to a stunned Goodemer and helped her to her feet.

The Lukrians from the camp had gathered on the edge of the meadow, mystified by what looked like a strange pantomime followed by an earth-shake.

As Jame opened her mouth to speak, another small tremor captured their attention. They stared at the boulder. The tremors increased as the rock moved.

"Misner certainly knows how to keep things interesting." Meah sauntered up next to them.

Goodemer realized the rock was doing more than moving. It was reshaping.

"This doesn't look good," Tigh muttered, as the shape became more defined.

"Uh, Tigh," Jame said. "You're not planning on fighting that, are you?"

Tigh arched an eyebrow. "I don't think it's capable of reasonable discussion."

"I'd fight it, but Tigh was always so much better at this kind of thing," Meah said with a shrug.

The rock grew from being round and squat to tall with limbs. A human shape emerged as if manipulated by an inspired sculptor.

"It's invincible." Jame wrapped her hands around Tigh's arm, fully capturing her attention.

"It only thinks it's invincible. Right?" Tigh turned to Goodemer.

Goodemer nodded, staring at Misner's handiwork.

"It's a rock. It's not in the habit of thinking," Jame said.

"It's a spell." Tigh met Jame's eyes. "How long is the spell of invincibility supposed to last?" She looked over Jame's head at Meah.

"Until the battle is over," Meah said.

Tigh returned her attention to Jame. "I'm just going to whack at it and keep it out of trouble and hope that Argis has a good day fighting."

Jame nodded as their eyes met. "We'll help as best we can."

They all turned at an earth-rattling pair of thuds. Tigh sighed and unsheathed her sword. "I'll never complain about not having enough challenge in my life again."

KYLARA SHUT HER eyes and gave her head a shake. The incredible vision was still there as she re-opened them—thousands of Emoran warriors. She applauded Goodemer's attention to detail, right down to the casual arrogance that was trained into Emorans as intensely as any weapons skill.

She shaded her eyes and viewed the adjacent hill where Argis shouted commands to her warriors, who scrambled into formation. It wouldn't do to let Misner's troops know that this army of Emorans was not expected and not real.

Kylara signaled her warriors to the top of the hill, proud that they held their composure at their first glimpse of the unimaginable spectacle dominating the Balderon valley. She then turned to the hills opposite Argis and nodded with approval as Mularke commanded her archers into neat double lines following the contour of the hills.

Tindal, following her warriors up the hill, joined Kylara. "Wizards can be handy to have around."

"I'm glad we didn't have them during the Wars," Kylara said. "The Guards were unpredictable enough."

"So what now?" Tindal shaded her eyes as she scanned the rows of tense soldiers in Misner's camp.

"That depends on if Jame and Tigh can stop Misner," Kylara said. An unpleasant chill shot through her. "What was that?"

The answer was swift as the defeated posture of Misner's army snapped into alertness.

"Looks like Jame and Tigh have run into some problems." Tindal gestured to her group leaders, who in turn shouted directives to the lines of warriors.

Barked commands echoed through Misner's camp, and hundreds of arrows arced over the outer circle of foot soldiers into the illusionary army.

Kylara locked her eyes onto Argis, waiting for her to give the signal to attack. Too many heartbeats passed by, and Argis continued to study the scene before her. Puzzled, she returned her gaze to the valley and was surprised to see the illusion not only held but moved forward.

The shouts from Misner's camp were precise and confident as the foot soldiers drew their swords and advanced on the menace before them. Argis's sword flashed. Mularke's distinctive yodel penetrated the air, and hundreds of arrows sparked off the intense morning sun.

Kylara waved her sword and shouted, "For Lukria!" She charged down the hill followed by four hundred bellowing warriors with swords flaring and the sharp glint of joy in their eyes.

OLET AND ARGIS watched as the Lukrians raced through the outer edge of the counterfeit warriors. At first, Argis couldn't distinguish between the Lukrians and the illusions because of the sunlight on the mist surrounding them. Then she let loose a surprised whoop. Instead of dissipating the illusion, a whirling mixture of mist and Emoran warriors covered the Lukrians' wake.

"Remind me to kiss Goodemer." Argis grinned, now seeing the difference between the puny magic of Misner and the illusions of a skilled and imaginative wizard like Goodemer. "The confusion just may be enough to put this in our favor."

Kas wore a maniacal grin as she galloped down the line of her horse warriors. Yodels and shouts rose up as she passed. The ground rumbled as two hundred warriors on horses draped in leather and armor rounded the smaller mounds closer to Balderon and flew across the plain, swords flashing in unrestrained ecstasy.

"For Emoria!" Argis's voice rang out, and the Emoran warriors bolted down the hill, filling the air with high-pitched cries of "Emoria!" Her body was galvanized as she crashed through the misty illusion, the magic-soaked vapors penetrating her skin and heightening her sense of awareness.

Argis's army pressed through the illusions as Misner's troops charged into the vaporous warriors and discovered they had been deceived.

Argis almost stumbled in amazement when her sword rang against another. Her defensive blow had the inexplicable power to repel her opponent. With swift, agile movements she knew were beyond what she truly possessed, she downed her stunned opponent. A crazy laugh erupted from deep within her soul as she slashed through the line of Misner's so-called invincible warriors.

"We've been given the skill of the Guards." Her hoarse voice reached those closest to her. "Pass the word." Kiss Goodemer? By all the waterfalls of Laur, she'd take her as her life partner and beg for the honor on her knees.

Chapter 20

"OH LOOK, IT has a sword." Meah clasped her hands in mock delight. "A very sharp looking sword."

"Glad you didn't pick one of the largest boulders," Tigh said as the stone giant staggered to a halt, as if trying to remember what it was doing.

In a short time, the granite face had transformed into disquieting human-like features.

"Are you going to help with this or are you concentrating on what's happening in the valley?" Tigh flashed Goodemer a quick look before fixing her attention on the stone menace.

"I think they're going to be just fine," Goodemer said with an intriguing half-smile touching her lips.

Jame frowned. "But they're fighting soldiers who think they're invincible."

"But the Lukrians and the Emorans think they have the skills of the Guards." Goodemer sheepishly dropped her eyes.

Tigh half-turned to Goodemer. "That beats invincible any time."

"Wonder if that works for invincible rocks?" Meah watched the struggling stone creature.

Jame shot dagger looks at Meah as she worked to bring her own fears for Tigh's safety under control.

"She'll be fine," Goodemer said. "She's beaten Misner's magic before. It may look nasty, but it's still made from the same kind of magic."

Jame turned to Goodemer. "You know something we don't know."

"All I know is what I've seen and heard." Goodemer spread her hands and shrugged.

"You're going to help her, aren't you?"

"If I can," Goodemer said. "I have to keep watch over the spells in the valley. One slip, and it could be disastrous for your warriors. Tigh has the skill to beat Misner's magic without me. You must believe this."

Before Jame had a chance to probe further, the ground shook again. This time the rhythm of the tremors reflected a more confident movement from the stone creature. As she stared at the threat, terrifyingly close to Tigh, another transformation changed the stone giant's limbs from blocky and cumbersome to sleek and muscular.

"Be careful," Jame whispered, as Tigh whipped her sword above her head to stop a brutal blow from the stone warrior's blade. She winced as the clash echoed in the still morning air.

TIGH HELD ONTO her sword with little more than stubborn determination. She was thankful her blade didn't shatter and basic sword-handling skills weren't a part of the magic that filled the stone warrior. Instead of holding the blade against her sword, the rocky giant let it bounce off, giving Tigh the chance to hop out of striking distance.

This lack of skill could be good or bad, Tigh mused as she flipped away from another clumsy swipe of the large blade.

The stone face worked into a dozen planed expressions of frustration.

Tigh whacked a solid rocky knee with the flat of her blade, just to test the reaction.

The stony features labored to express annoyance at the clout.

Tigh cursed in three languages as the painful jolt from the blow reverberated through her body.

"Great." She sighed as she backed away. Why didn't she think to have Goodemer channel the spell into a tree? At least a sword had a chance against living wood.

The stone warrior straightened to twice Tigh's height as the spell rippled across the rocky surface, smoothing it, as if finely chiseled by a master sculptor. With this change came a more fluid movement as the giant whipped the sword over its head and tried to split Tigh in two with graceful downward swipe.

Tigh sidestepped the blade, then jumped on its upper edge. She balanced on the sword and mocked her foe with a grin. The frustrated stone warrior reacted with an upward swing, flicked Tigh over its head, and delivered a staggering blow to its own forehead.

As the rocky tormentor careened around in the grass, Tigh sheathed her sword, vaulted onto its back, and climbed until she had one arm wrapped around the huge neck. She carved into the top of the stone head with her hunting knife and narrowly avoided a cleft in her own head from the enormous blade before she shimmied down the stone body.

The ground trembled as the stone warrior crashed to the ground in a rocky daze.

"Amazing," Goodemer murmured.

"What?" Jame asked.

"Every time the stone giant injures itself, Misner's army falters," Goodemer said. "I wasn't sure if the redirected spell would work under the same rules as the original spell. It does. This means it doesn't matter if Argis or Tigh wins, either one can break the spell."

TAS FELT AS if her body was under the control of a manic warrior. Being agile and quick was already a given for someone of her size, but this was beyond anything she had ever dreamed. Her senses sailed to an exhilarating battle high as she slashed and spun and flipped past her victims. *Daughter of a shaggy mountain goat. This is what it's like to be Tigh.*

A wild, demented sound erupted from her throat as she faced a wide-eyed soldier, her sword finding its mark before the soldier had time to react. Then she swung but no one was in front of her to fight. She had battled all the way through the enemy line. The sight of the abandoned camp reminded her that the rogue Guards could give them trouble if they regained consciousness.

"Wolfie!" She could barely hear herself above the chaotic din. She squinted in the misty swirl of the battle before catching the unruly hair of the Council's guard.

Wolfie caught her eyes, then grinned as she removed the three soldiers in her path. She greeted Tas with a joyous laugh. "Can you believe this?" She flipped and swung her sword with graceful abandonment.

"I'd give anything to feel this every day," Tas said. "But I'll be happy if it lasts as long as this battle. It's been several sandmarks since we knocked out the Guards. Goodemer said she wasn't sure how long that potion would keep them under. Interested in checking them out with me?"

"Let's go." Wolfie bounced on the balls of her feet.

They jogged through the camp. Tas took in the litter of abandoned plates and cups and blankets and couldn't help but feel pleased the enemy had been caught off guard.

"Do you think this is Goodemer's doing?" Wolfie asked as they padded past a picket of nickering horses.

Tas grinned. "Who else do we know with the skill to turn us into Guards?"

"And she created that magical army." Wolfie sighed with a faraway look in her eyes. "I swear, I'm ready to join with her forever. I'll even plead for the honor on my knees."

Tas laughed. "And everyone calls me the impulsive one."

They approached the front opening of a large, light colored tent and paused. Tas took a deep breath and looked inside. She pulled her head back from the tent opening and blinked at Wolfie. Wolfie stuck her head through the opening and took a long look around.

"She's not here," Tas said. "Argis needs to know."

Wolfie nodded. "There're only four of them, and we already have the upper hand in this battle. How much trouble can they make?"

A blood-freezing chuckle floated to them. Tas realized their words had been picked up by the enhanced hearing of four black-clad warriors standing maybe fifty paces away. She emitted harsh blue jay cries and prayed Argis heard the incongruous sounds above the battle noise.

"Look, Patch," a black-haired Guard with dead gray eyes said. "It's a half warrior."

The four chuckled with an evil glee that touched every nerve in Tas's body.

"Emoria must be desperate to allow such tiny women to become warriors."

Tas labored to fight the paralyzing chill that wafted off the arrogant foursome. She wished she had more of the potion-covered darts. Wait. Her mind froze for a heartbeat on the most astonishing revelation. She possessed the same fighting skills as these menacing Guards.

She raised confident eyes and gazed at them as if they were equals. "This from a former peace-loving book pusher?"

The Guards' grating laugh almost undermined her confidence.

"There's a fine line between being courageous and being stupid," the one called Patch said. "Although in this case, it comes to much the same thing."

The crunch of grass caught their sensitive ears, and the four Guards twisted around. Tas and Wolfie held their breaths as they watched Argis and Kylara rush through the camp toward them. They stopped some distance from the Guards.

"Kylara." A tall light-haired Guard sounded the name with malicious delight. "What an interesting surprise."

"Let's just say I came to my senses about Misner," Kylara said.

"You think joining the losing side means coming to your senses?" The blonde Guard's laugh was like sleet against Tas's ears.

"No. I joined the winning side." Kylara grinned. "Look around. Our army has all but cut through your lines."

"You think a little illusion can stop us?" Patch said. "Have you forgotten about the spell of invincibility?"

"I haven't forgotten. But it doesn't seem to be very effective against the spell our wizard has cast over us." Kylara flipped her sword and laid the blade on her shoulder. "After all, the four of us fought through your invincible army without a scratch."

"Your wizard?" the blonde said, as the four Guards exchanged questioning glances.

"A wizard much more skilled and powerful than Misner," Argis said. She straightened to her full height and sauntered up to the Guards. "As I see it, as long as you four are around, your army will continue to labor under the illusion they can win this battle. I know only one solution to that problem."

She sent a quick prayer to Laur and swung her sword, only to have it stopped by four black blades. Her arms felt as though they'd been plunged into an ice packed river, but by some miracle, she pushed all four Guards back, giving the other three time to join in the battle.

Argis felt the snow-cold sting of the sword of a worthy opponent and thanked Goodemer a thousand times over for the ecstasy of negligent skill that wiped the arrogant smirks off these offspring of Yitsian snow monsters.

"YOU SURE YOU don't want to join in the fun?" Tigh shot a look at Meah, who lounged on a nearby boulder.

"Don't tell me that a rock-brained invincible stone giant is too much for you," Meah said.

Tigh flipped away from another clumsy swipe of the stone warrior's sword. "Nah. Just making sure you don't mind me having all the fun."

"Tigh." Jame's strained voice reached her.

Tigh turned sheepish eyes to her. "I'm being careful." She sideswiped what would have been a rather messy encounter with the insistent blade of her rocky opponent.

The rock sword penetrated the ground with the ease of a hand through water. Face contorted with anger and frustration, the stone warrior focused on pulling the stubborn blade from the hard-packed soil.

Tigh picked up a fist-sized stone and pitched it at the rocky body. The stone warrior flinched at the impact but continued to tug at the sword hilt.

"Start throwing stones at it," Tigh shouted to the others. "Try to get it away from the sword."

Goodemer and Jame picked up stones and lobbed them at the rocky creature. The impacts sounded like loose stones scuttling down steep cliffs.

Tigh scanned the boulder-strewn meadow for anything that could be used to their advantage. The hole to the underground tunnels was too small. Then her mind snagged on a fleeting memory from when they emerged from the hole.

Jame and Goodemer performed their task with enthusiasm, and the stone warrior's attention was now on avoiding the strength reducing chipping of stone against stone.

Tigh noted the rocky warrior's instinct to lunge in the direction of its attackers and ran behind it and whacked its leg with the flat of her blade. The stone giant snarled, twisted around, and glared at her.

"Stop throwing the stones," Tigh called out. She hopped out of the way of the blocky hand grabbing for her. "You want me, you have to catch me." She scooped up a rock with her boot and kicked it into the stone giant's forehead. The sculpted features grimaced in anger, and it chased after her with earth-shaking steps.

"WHAT'S SHE DOING?" Jame's voice was raspy with fear. "Why is she leading that thing away from us?"

Goodemer laid a hand on Jame's tense arm. "Have faith."

Meah stared at Tigh with rapt attention and slid off her boulder.

"Come on, you pebble." Tigh kicked up the occasional rock for emphasis. "You think you're invincible?"

The stone warrior flung lethal legs out and propelled the heavy body faster, arms wildly swiping the air, just missing Tigh.

Tigh flipped ten paces away, and landed on her feet but then grimaced and fell to the ground.

"Tigh!" Jame shouted and took off running.

The stone giant's planed features shifted into a hardened smile. It took a lunging step forward.

A thunderous avalanche of noise echoed through the meadow as a cloud of stone dust puffed into the air, obscuring the giant and Tigh. Jame skidded to a stop, just paces from the dust cloud, frantically trying to see through it.

"Tigh!" she cried in a raw voice.

Tigh flipped through the stone dust and landed a few paces away from Jame.

Jame rushed to Tigh and toppled her onto her back. She choked back a sob as she wrapped her arms around Tigh's neck.

Tigh laughed and rolled to her feet, bringing Jame with her. Hand-in-hand they walked to the edge of the pit.

Jame could barely make out the shattered remains of the stone warrior.

Meah sauntered around the pit. "You always had the best improvisational skills."

"The spell is broken," Goodemer whispered.

Jame tightened her hold on Tigh. "Clever. But if you scare me like that again, I'll stop speaking to you."

"Seeran wouldn't have been very happy if there wasn't some suspense and excitement," Tigh said.

Jame gave Tigh a mocking glare before giving up and grinning. "Something for the Chronicles, indeed. I wonder how Argis is doing."

Goodemer simply smiled.

FIGHTING AN ORDINARY soldier while possessing the skills of a Guard was one thing. Fighting someone who possessed the same skills was an entirely different matter. The arrogant Guards had the advantage in that they were comfortable with their enhancements. But their reaction time seemed to be ragged from the potion that had knocked them out, making the encounter deadly and exhilarating at the same time.

Kylara sidestepped a sword thrust from the blonde Guard. "You'll have to do better than that, Nark."

"Meah should have killed Tigh when she had the chance," Nark said as she swung her sword in angry swipes at Kylara. "Only Tigh could have worked out a plan to beat us."

"So you think you've been beaten?" Kylara took Nark through a series of wildly executed thrusts and parries.

"This puny army, perhaps. Misner, perhaps. But never the Guards."

Nark's guttural response was like ice against Kylara's spine. But she concentrated on warming her reaction with a skillful thrust that ended with the two blades scraping together down to the hilts.

"That reminds me." Kylara knocked Nark's sword away. "Where's Meah?"

"She disappeared before we got here." Nark shrugged before crashing her sword against Kylara's.

Kylara's arms ached from the bone deep frost flowing off Nark's body.

"We thought maybe Tigh got her."

Kylara hoped it was true.

ARGIS STARED INTO the cold gray eyes of Patch Llachlan. Patch was almost as legendary as Tigh for her skill and cruelty. Which meant . . . She got her blade up in time to stop Patch's sword. This sneering former Guard had been a gentle soul before the enhancements.

Reeking with cruelty, Patch lunged at Argis with a dizzying quickness.

Argis flipped, catching her boot on Patch's chin and snapping her head back.

Patch tumbled backward and hit the ground hard, shock overwriting her smirk. Argis fought the agonizing frostbite that tightened around her foot and stomped the same foot onto Patch's wrist, forcing the hand to open and the sword to clatter to the ground.

Argis kicked away the blade and whipped her own around until the tip was pressed against Patch's throat. She struggled not to kill her. She growled in her frustration but wouldn't give in to her desire for blood. She couldn't shake the knowledge that deep within this person, who would kill her without a thought, was a peaceful, gentle soul. Someone who had been used, first by the Southern Territories and then by an insane wizard. She replaced her blade with her boot and slammed the hilt of her sword against Patch's head.

Argis took the opportunity to check the progress of the battle. She was surprised to see the fighting was now scattered throughout the camp and the Emorans looked as though they had whittled down the enemy with little problem. "Good spell, Goodemer. Good spell."

Kylara held her own with Nark, but Argis was ready to put an end to this battle. She took a step and collapsed to the ground. She pounded her cold, numb foot, trying to work some warmth back into it. She spewed enough curses to curl every hair on the heads of Laur's acolytes until enough feeling returned to her foot that she could hobble on it.

She feinted a movement she expected Nark to detect through her enhanced senses.

Nark parried a thrust from Kylara, then spun to stop what she thought was a blow from behind, but Argis moved around to her blind side and slapped the side of her head with the flat of her blade. Nark, with a stunned expression on her face, slumped to the ground.

Kylara blinked at Argis in confusion.

"Don't kill them," Argis said. "I think Tigh should be the one to deal with them."

Kylara gazed at Argis for a heartbeat and nodded. "Let's help the others."

They knocked out the other two Guards with no problem, and Tas and Wolfie took a few heartbeats to rub the feeling back into their frozen hands.

"Now I know what it's like to fight a Yitsian snow monster." Tas pressed her sword hand beneath her other arm.

"Now what?" Kylara stared down at the Guards. "They're not going to stay out for long."

"Let's tie them up. Not that it'll do much good when they come to." Argis looked around for rope. She pulled out her knife and sliced one of the ropes holding up a nearby tent. "This'll do."

Tas and Wolfie divided the rope and tied the Guards' ankles and wrists. With the help of Argis and Kylara, they dragged the Guards to the nearest tent, out of the way of the fighting.

The air crackled. The hairs on their arms lifted and a whirlwind almost swept them off their feet. Just as swift, the flapping tents and the dust settled down. Shouts of dismay rose up around them. Emorans and Lukrians stopped blows in mid-strike and stared as the enemy dropped their weapons and fell, sobbing, to their knees. Terror-stricken cries for mercy replaced the grunts of battle.

Argis dashed to the picket of horses and untied a noble warhorse. She threw herself onto the beast and galloped through the camp, waving her sword. "Victory is ours! Secure the prisoners. Victory is ours!" Jubilant cheers rose up in her wake.

In the distance, shouts and drums erupted from the walls of Balderon. The city gates opened and people bolted onto the meadow as if it were the first day of spring. Argis pulled up on the horse and stared at the thousands of ordinary people rushing out to welcome them as their saviors. She had just led the army that saved Balderon from an invading army. The prediction on the statue of Hekolatis had come true.

"You did it." Olet jumped up and down.

Argis rested weary eyes on her. "We did it. All of us."

"But you led us." Olet stopped jumping and grabbed the horse's reins. "Let them honor you for that." She waved at the people of Balderon who filtered through the camp, helping with the prisoners and the wounded.

"They will remember us all," Argis said.

Chapter 21

JAME TOPPLED OVER from laughing so hard. Fortunately, she sat on the large cushions in Jyac's private eating chamber. Tigh pulled her back upright.

"Poor Argis." Jyac wiped a tear from her eye, her face flushed from laughing.

"If you think her expression when that sculptor asked her to pose for him was funny, you should have seen her actually trying to pose." Poylin could hardly squeeze the words out, she was laughing so hard. "He kept insisting she hold her sword in a heroic way, and she kept insisting you couldn't hit a full grown cow holding a sword like that. It went on and on until, in sheer frustration, she showed him the proper way to hold a sword by slicing his pile of wet clay into a thousand flying bits."

The small group around the table held their sides from their aching mirth. The tension had been so strong for the last several weeks that this release was as much from relief as from the amusing tales of the battle of Balderon.

"Here's to Argis. Hero of Balderon." Jyac raised her mug of spiced wine.

"Here's to Argis," the others intoned with raised mugs.

"Here's to Jame, Tigh, and Goodemer. Heroes of Emoria." Jyac looked at the trio with a sly grin. Jame shook her head, Tigh rolled her eyes, and Goodemer reddened as she found the remnants of her meal fascinating.

Quick footfalls sounded in the corridor, and a beaming Eiget stepped into the chamber.

"They're on their way?" Jyac asked.

"They've cleared the outer border." Eiget nodded with the silly grin.

"Let's go welcome our victorious army." Jyac rose and put a hand out to Ronalyn. They strolled out the doorway, followed by Sark and Goodemer.

Tigh stepped back to let Jame go ahead of her, but Jame put a halting hand on her arm. "What's wrong?"

"I just wanted a quiet moment before all the excitement," Jame said. "I'm missing just the two of us. Being on the road. Not having to share you with anyone else."

Tigh captured Jame's lips in a long, reaffirming kiss. "Anytime you want to leave, just say the word."

Jame sighed. "We can't leave until we're joined in an Emoran ceremony, but everyone's going to want to celebrate this victory first."

A pondering hum rumbled in Tigh's throat. "You can request to make our joining ceremony a part of the victory celebration. Two rabbits with one arrow."

"I like the way you think." Jame nuzzled Tigh's strong neck. "In fact I like everything about you."

Tigh laughed. "That's good to know, because we're about to be joined."

THE STILLNESS OF the valley was the only indication that something out there was threatening enough to silence the birds and put the grazing deer on alert. The women on the top of the gate wall and atop the bluff walls focused on the single entrance into the valley.

The endless echo of hooves, clattering against the rocky floor of the tunnel that led into the valley, broke the silence. Kas, atop her elegant white mare, both decked out in full battle gear, shot out onto the valley floor and galloped toward the opposite bluff before pulling up and turning to face the tunnel.

A sharp whistle cut through the fading echoes of the horse's hooves. A heartbeat later, horses and riders in full, shiny battle gear galloped single file from the tunnel, trampling out intricate coordinated patterns in a proud display of horsewomanship. The thousands of Emoran citizens who had been left behind in the city cheered louder and louder as each pattern built on the one before it.

Much too soon the patterns wound down as the horses, one by one, pulled into a line next to Kas that stretched from bluff to bluff beyond the farthest side of the tunnel.

"Do you think they spent the whole journey back planning this?" Jame bent her head to Jyac.

"Of course." Jyac grinned. "How many chances does one have to lead a victorious army home from battle?"

Kas sounded three shrill whistles, and a line of archers marched from the tunnel, their gear so polished that the afternoon sun glinted off the tips of the arrows bobbing in the quivers on their backs.

A double line of archers stood at attention in front of the horses, and Mularke ran from the tunnel. The archers, in formal age-old embellishment and enviable precision, pulled arrows from their quivers and cocked their short bows upward as Mularke rushed past them. A smooth ripple of movement flowed from one end of the double lines to the other.

The last two archers snapped into readiness with bows tightly drawn. A cutting whistle sounded, and the cavalry tossed banners from Emoria, Lukria, and Balderon, anchored with light stones, up and over the archers.

Mularke shouted a sharp command. The front line of archers raised their bows and let the shafts hurtle through the air, impale, and carry each banner almost as high as the bluffs before they fluttered to the ground. As soon as the first wave of arrows hissed through the air, the front line of archers dropped to one knee, and the second line sent their own shafts to capture the colorful cloth filling the sky.

The gate wall came alive with movement and deafening noise. This legendary salute had not been attempted since Hekolatis's victorious homecoming.

"I think the people of Balderon got to Argis," Tigh murmured in Jame's ear.

"I bet Kas and Mularke pestered her to do it until she had to give in or explain why she had caused her friends bodily harm," Jame said.

Tigh chuckled. "That I believe."

The horse warriors and archers stilled. The shouts from the wall faded into a tense silence of anticipation. The late afternoon wind brushed against the dry grass, a reminder that the cold season was upon them.

A pair of warriors on horseback, holding standards with images of Laur's waterfalls, emerged from the tunnel and took positions on either side of the opening.

Yodels and battle cries crashed around the cavern as if fighting to burst into the valley. Hundreds of warriors, waving flashing swords and making enough noise to reach Hekolatis's sleeping ears, sprinted from the cave and covered the field in front of the archers and horse warriors. Swords crashed in mock battles as the warriors flipped and capered in abandoned ecstasy.

The Emorans gathered on the wall gasped and twittered in wonderment.

Tigh sucked in a sharp breath and whipped her head around to Goodemer, who watched the spectacle with childlike delight.

"It's only the fighting skills," Goodemer said. "They haven't changed in any other way."

A haunting uncertainty flickered across Tigh's face but she nodded.

"I think it's a wonderful gift." Jame wrapped her hands around Tigh's arm and grinned at Goodemer.

"It's an incredible gift," Jyac said. "We have the greatest fighters in the world once again. Thank you."

"A wizard always leaves a little something behind for people to remember her by," Goodemer said.

Piercing whistles bounced off the bluff walls. The crashing of swords halted, and the warriors sprinted into rows of eight down the middle of the valley.

The rhythmic stomping of soft boots echoed from the tunnel. A puzzled murmur rose up from the women on the wall.

A column of Lukrians marched in rows of four into the sunlight. The stunned silence gave way to a thunderous cheer of greeting.

Jyac nodded and straightened—her pride for her people so strong she could barely contain it.

The column of Lukrians marched to the front of the Emoran warriors. They wove into the Emoran column and transformed it into a crosshatch of Lukrians and Emorans.

Something profound caught in Jyac's throat, and her eyes brimmed with tears. She glanced around and was relieved to see the others struggled with their own intense emotions. The vision of a united Emoria and Lukria was so appealing that she sent a prayer to Laur in hopes it was truly their destiny.

"Argis knows what she's doing," Tigh said.

A CLATTER OF hooves heralded Argis and Kylara entering the valley at a dignified pace atop horses trimmed in full commander dress. Tas and Tindal trotted behind them on equally resplendent horses—gifts from the grateful people of Balderon.

The standard bearers guided their mounts to positions in front of Argis and Kylara and led them at a rousing gallop to the head of the column.

Every bit of portable metal had been dragged from cupboards and chamber corners in anticipation of this moment. The clanging rang out from the wall and the city in a deafening clatter.

Argis halted at the head of the column, kicked her horse, and sprinted away from the others. She spun around and took in the thousands of solemn eyes riveted on her with an unshakable respect. This was an army that could hold its own against any army in the world, and at that moment, it was her army.

She fought a wave of lightheadedness as she allowed the reality of the last few days flood through her. She took a steadying breath and raised her sword. The clean sound of an army stepping forward in precise unison as she aimed the tip of her sword at the ground was the sweetest noise she had ever heard.

ARGIS LET OUT a healthy selection of curses as she paused at the threshold of a tiny meditation chamber in Laur's temple. Tigh was sprawled on a stone bench, clothed in formal Emoran leathers, dead asleep.

"You lost that bet," Tas said in her ear.

Argis shook her head. "I've never seen a warrior who wasn't as nervous as a mouse around a cat on her joining day."

"She's been through this before, you know," Tas said.

Argis fiddled with the unfamiliar addition to her dress uniform—a single purple sleeve draping down her right arm to the elbow. She had balked at it, but Jyac insisted she wear the sleeve of Hekolatis on formal occasions at least. "Why does it have to be so uncomfortable?"

"I don't think it's the sleeve that's uncomfortable," Tas said. "I think you're just uncomfortable wearing it."

"I don't think I'm the one who should be wearing it." Argis gazed at the slumbering Tigh.

"She may have drawn up the battle strategy, but you made the decisions on the field that led our army to victory," Tas said.

"It was Jame's plan, Tigh's strategy, and Goodemer's magic—"

"And your quick thinking." Tigh stretched and pulled her body around to sit on the bench. "Don't fight it. The opportunities to be a hero are too few. Treasure them when you can."

"It's time." Tas raised her chin at Tigh.

In a disgusting display of casual ease, Tigh got to her feet and took the time to make sure all the intricate parts of the unfamiliar Emoran uniform were in place. Argis was struck with how much she embodied the ideal Emoran warrior, wearing the crosspatch of armor and leather as if it were a part of her skin.

"Ready?" Tigh quirked an eyebrow at them.

"That's what we should be asking you." Argis cocked her head.

"There are worse things than being joined to Jame." Tigh grinned as she and Argis followed Tas into the main chamber of the Temple.

"You're very lucky." Argis looked across the chamber at a vision as shimmering as the waterfalls around them. Tigh's attention was already fixed on the center of her world.

Surrounded by a lavender cloud of flitting acolytes, Jame stood in her warrior uniform looking as natural as Tigh in the intricate armor and leather. Her calling may have been a peacetime judge and defender of justice, but there was no doubt she had the heart of a warrior. The easy way she carried herself under the weight of the armor and the ceremonial sword on her back showed she had the physical soundness to back up her mental strength.

"I could only dream of this day," Jame said, as Tigh approached and took her hand.

"I'm open to any opportunity to reaffirm my love for you," Tigh murmured in her ear.

"All right. Save it for after the ceremony," Argis said.

"Come on, my princess." Tas grinned as she took Jame's arm. "We go first."

Jame squeezed Tigh's hand as they shared a private smile before Tas tugged her out the Temple door. Thunderous cheering exploded, affirming that every Emoran was in the city that night.

Argis took a deep breath and shook out her arms. "Remember what you have to say?"

Tigh raised an eyebrow. "Say?"

"The words for the ceremony," Argis said.

"Not at the moment." Tigh shrugged. "But I'm sure they'll come to me when needed."

"Aren't you afraid of messing up?" Argis asked.

"It won't be the end of the world," Tigh said. "It's not a life-or-death situation if I don't get the words exactly right."

"I'll never understand you," Argis muttered, catching a signal from the door. "It's time. Try not to improvise too much."

Tigh grinned and stepped into place next to Argis.

TORCHLIGHT BURNISHED THE square as it seemed to pulse in rhythm to the drums thundering from different parts of the city. A path was cleared from the Temple door to the fountain in the middle of the square, and uniformed warriors lined the way to maintain the distance of the excited throng. The Council formed an arc in front of the fountain, creating a space for Jyac to stand.

Jyac beamed at Jame as she walked toward her on Tas's arm. Jame's heart swelled at the pride in Jyac's eyes.

Jame stood before Jyac as Tas stepped to the side. She exchanged wry grins with Jyac as a new wave of shouts and cheers caused the bells in the temple tower to juggle against each other from the vibrations.

Jame struggled to not turn around and stare at her approaching warrior. Her mind's eye captured the vivid spectacle as it was reflected in the faces of the Council. The approving expression in Jyac's eyes told her that Tigh's eyes were on only her.

After what felt like an eternity, Jame finally soaked up Tigh's warm presence next to her. Argis stepped back and winked at Tas, who couldn't keep from beaming.

Jyac reached over her shoulder and pulled her delicately etched ceremonial double-edged sword from its soft leather scabbard. She held the sword in both hands and lowered it, flat side up between Jame and Tigh until it pointed straight out.

"Jamelin Ketlas, princess of Emoria, and Paldar Tigis, adopted warrior of Emoria, have come before the citizens of Emoria to be joined," Jyac said.

"They are here to declare their lifelong pledge to each other. If anyone feels they are not meant to speak these words make your protest now."

The silence was so profound the only sound was the fluttering banners and the hissing torches.

Jyac raised her eyes to Tigh.

Tigh and Jame faced each other. The sword blade hovering between them kept back Jame's yearning to reach for Tigh's hand.

Tigh captured Jame's brimming eyes with her own. She pulled a wrist bracer of woven leather from her belt pouch and held it up. "I give my life to be with Jamelin Ketlas, princess of Emoria, for as long as I walk this earth and until Laur's waters stop flowing."

Jame, with trembling hands, pulled a matching wrist bracer from her belt pouch. She tried to clear the roiling emotion from her throat by narrowing her world to those wonderful familiar eyes gazing at her with raw adoration. With a clear voice, she repeated the vow that Tigh had intoned.

Tigh took Jame's free hand over the sword and slipped the bracer onto her wrist. The contact after even such a brief time of denial sent a warm jolt through Jame.

Jame took Tigh's hand and pushed the bracer onto her sword-strengthened wrist.

Tigh ran a finger over the sharp edge of the sword, then held up her hand. Jame slid her finger across the blade and held her hand in front of Tigh's. They pressed their hands together, the warm blood mingling.

"Let it be written that the citizens of Emoria have witnessed the joining of Jame and Tigh." Jyac dropped the sword out of the way.

Tigh gathered Jame in her arms for a gentle kiss.

The magic that crackled in the air needed no help from Goodemer. Noisemakers baffled Jame's hearing with wild metallic sounds, and the tops of the bluffs erupted in an astonishing fireworks display that could only be the work of the good wizard.

Tigh wiped away an errant tear from Jame's cheek. A gaping hole in Jame's psyche was finally healed, and she felt fully home, at last.

A BEMUSED GOODEMER strode into the palace hall trailed by a half dozen warriors. Warriors had been following her, doing little chores for her, helping her get around the city . . . basically making nuisances of themselves since they returned from Balderon. She understood they were grateful for the warrior skills she had given them, but this was going on much too long.

"I would be honored if you joined me at the table."

Goodemer spun around to find Argis standing next to her. Argis flicked her eyes at her entourage and lifted an eyebrow.

"The honor would be mine." Goodemer smiled, grateful for one levelheaded warrior in the bunch.

The cluster of warriors looked on, disgruntled, as Argis led Goodemer away.

Goodemer grinned. "Thank you for rescuing me."

"I'm the one who should be thanking you for rescuing all of us," Argis said.

A crash from the middle of the room followed by a stream of creative curses could only be Mularke and Tas giving an impromptu performance.

"Perhaps I can talk you into teaching a few of my warriors some social skills," Argis said.

"You crazy archer." Tas snorted as Mularke stared at what was left of her meal on the floor. "You either have to try that completely sober or drunk out of your mind before it can work." She tossed Mularke a wine skin. "Since you're halfway there, you can try it later when you're stinking drunk."

Mularke grabbed the skin out the air and nodded. "Good idea."

"If you don't rescue Tas soon, she'll be passed out in a doorway somewhere," Jame said from the long table on a rise at the end of the hall.

"Let her have her fun tonight." Seeran watched Tas with great affection. "I won't have any chance to speak to you or Tigh for a while, now that you're leaving."

"I'm glad you decided to stay here," Jame said. "Emoria needs a chronicler."

"Thank you for bringing me here. It's strange, but it feels like I've come home," Seeran said. "Tas and I are going to visit Artocia in the spring to get my things. I'll be able to show her a bit of my world."

"And you'll also have quite a story to add to the Archives there," Jame said.

"Now that's an understatement." Seeran laughed. "There's still one thing I don't understand. Why did Meah go against Misner?"

Jame glanced at Tigh, who was engaged in a discussion on battle strategy with Jyac. "Meah was never on Misner's side to begin with. You see, one of the Guards that Misner killed before Tigh disabled her was Meah's lover, Ocarla. She pretended to join Misner's army to get close enough to get her revenge. It turns out she never stopped being loyal to her old supreme commander, Tigh."

Seeran nodded. "Now she's on her way back to Ynit with the others to be cleansed again."

"Hopefully she'll finally be able to find some peace in her life," Jame said.

"So where are you going next?" Seeran broke off a piece of thick bread and sopped up the remains of her meal with it.

"We're continuing over the mountains. We haven't been that way yet." Jame wrapped an arm around Tigh, capturing her attention.

Jyac gave them an indulgent look and lifted her mug. "Thank you, Jame, for restoring my faith in the Mysteries and leading Emoria into a new age."

"Emoria has entered a new age because it was ready and willing to do so." Jame squeezed Tigh's arm. "Now I know how you feel about being called a hero."

The small party gathered around the table laughed.

Jame raised her mug. "Here's to Emoria."

The others grinned with mugs in hand. "To Emoria."

T.J. Mindancer may be a figment of someone's imagination or just someone who likes to imagine she's a figment while she creates worlds for her characters to inhabit. She has spent her life working with books as an academic librarian and as an editor for two publishing companies and has had some of her scribbled words published under a couple of pen names—at least one, not a figment. Her work includes the *Tales of Emoria* series of books and shorter tales set in the Emoria world. She also likes to make up places in the real world and write about them. She lives in her Tiny House of the Dragons in Northern California.